Where Gable Slept

Riveredge Books

Praise for the novels of Irene Bennett Brown

HAVEN
"Give yourself a treat…a keeper to be enjoyed again and again."
— Dorothy Garlock, *New York Times bestselling author*

THE BARGAIN
"…a compelling and beautiful novel."
—Richard S. Wheeler

THE PLAINSWOMAN
"…storytelling…this novel provides some of the best!"
—Doris Meredith, *Roundup Magazine*

The Women Of Paragon Springs Series:

LONG ROAD TURNING
"…vibrant and engaging tale of brave settlers."
—*Booklist*

BLUE HORIZONS
"…good read …I'm anxious for the third installment!"
–-Carol Anne Germain, *The Historical Novels Review*

NO OTHER PLACE
"… like going home to visit family."
—*Amarillo Globe*

REAP THE SOUTH WIND
"Superior historical fiction…heartfelt and briskly paced."
—*Statesman Journal*

Irene Bennett Brown

Where Gable Slept

Riveredge Books

Riveredge Books

Copyright © 2010 by Irene Bennett Brown

This book is a work of fiction. Names, characters, places and incidents are products of the author's imagination or are used fictitiously. Any resemblance to actual events or locales or persons, living or dead, is entirely coincidental.

ISBN: 978-0-9801558-7-7

All rights reserved, including the right to reproduce this book or portions thereof in any form whatsoever without written permission from the publisher.

For information address:
Riveredge Books
P.O. 75
Jefferson, Oregon 97352

To Bob

For his help
love and support

Chapter One

"If the house were mine I'd get rid of it, burn it down, replace the old relic and grounds with something—else."

"Excuse me?" The woman's remark was outrageous. Was she joking? Celia Landrey, walking-tour guide to Pass Creek's historic buildings, studied the speaker, a woman of a certain age, blonde, dressed in ivory silk shirt and slacks and exquisite diamond and gold jewelry.

Tierney Jones was her name and she stood a distance away, her bitter smile directed at historic Gable House. She said again, "Oh believe me, dear. I would see it come down."

The rest of Celia's group of five tourists waited on the sidewalk before the green Victorian house where actor Clark Gable once lived. They stared at the Jones woman with mouths dropped, as stunned as Celia. They'd come in answer to Celia's promotion about her quiet rural hometown located in one of Oregon's loveliest areas, the Willamette Valley. This nonsensical incident was decidedly not on her brochure!

It was a darned good thing Pass Creek's prize landmark didn't belong to this outsider, Celia decided in another moment, trying to shake off her anger. On the other hand, Gable House would go up for sale soon. Celia was perplexed. Moments ago Mrs. Jones had gazed at the lovely old Queen Anne mansion in awe, as entranced as the others—before her attitude suddenly changed. She had a right to her opinion, but any harm to Gable House would come over Celia's dead body!

Celia struggled for composure, not easy in a mothball-smelly 1920's peach chiffon shift and pointy toed shoes from Goodwill, her period costume for the day. She continued her presentation, convinced that Pass Creek's 2,100 citizens wouldn't stand for anyone destroying Gable House. Her smile warmed as she said, "Clark Gable was in his early twenties when he used a small inheritance from his grandfather to come west. He worked in the timber industry in more than one Oregon town. In fact, he worked in a lumber mill here in Pass Creek for two years, a mill that no longer exists. At the time, this home was operated as a small hotel by an elderly widow, Mrs. Hannah Blake."

Not that different from Celia's own situation. Following the death of Ethan, her beloved husband of twenty years, she'd remodeled their home—a simpler Queen Anne style than Gable House—and named it Landrey's Inn. One of the four upstairs rooms she rented out was presently occupied by Tierney Jones, who'd arrived in Pass Creek two days ago.

A barrel-chested man in the group who persisted in addressing Celia as *pretty lady* spoke up. "Say, pretty lady, when was the house built? Looks okay to the eye, but you never know what it's like underneath or in the joists. It'd be a shame if the old girl was rotting away." He removed his hand from his trouser pocket to point out a flapping roof shingle to another fellow in the group.

Celia answered in firm defense. "This house was built as a private residence in the 1880s with the finest materials. Few houses with such charm and stability are being built anymore." Her glance landed on Tierney Jones specifically. "This is just one of the reasons it should be preserved. The house is periodically inspected and repairs taken care of. We had a wind storm recently." She looked up, nodding with her chin. "The loose shingle and other repairs to the roof will be seen to soon." She saw no reason to mention that the late owner, Otis Peek, had died in an unfortunate tumble from the roof. It was believed he was trying to fix it himself, rather than part with the money to have a professional roofer do the job.

"May we have a look inside the house?" a rosy-cheeked little woman in a red hat and purple pantsuit asked.

The lady's friend, holding her own red hat to allow a warm breeze to riffle her gray hair, asked, "My goodness, can we see the bed where Clark Gable *slept*? When I was a lot younger, he was my favorite actor. I don't know how many times I saw *Gone With The Wind*, but my husband, bless his soul, claimed it was too many." She grinned. "Jealous, I guess, of that good-looking Clark Gable."

The smaller of the two women swatted at her fellow red-hatter. "My husband had a moustache like Gable's. I had high hopes, but that's as far as the resemblance went."

Celia laughed with the others. "I'm sorry we can't go inside today. Normally the tour would include tea and cookies provided by the owner." She sobered. "But he recently passed away." Otis Peek, the crotchety old miser, should never have been on the roof in the first place.

She told her group, "An out-of-state relative who inherited Gable House asked that it be sold, after a bit of cleaning and repair. But there's nothing seriously wrong with this sweet old house." And if Pass Creek's Heritage Club had their way, they would be buying Gable House as soon as enough funds could be raised.

"The house would be open soon to prospective buyers, would it not?"

Celia didn't want to answer, hated the shrewd expression on the Jones woman's face as she surveyed the mansion. Celia told her, "I believe Flagg Realty will be showing it." She hurried on to add a bald-faced lie. "However, the property is already spoken for and may be unavailable." Darn this Mrs. Jones woman, who appeared well-off enough to buy Gable House three times over if she wanted. If she did buy it, would she then fulfill her suggestion that it be destroyed? Or was that just an off-hand, meaningless remark and Celia needed to calm her overactive imagination?

Swallowing against a dry throat, Celia said, "Gable House is a superb example of this version of Queen Anne Victorian architecture. Note the steeply pitched roof lines, like different sized *cones*. The prominent front-facing gable adorned with textured shingles and the fancy wood trim on the columned porch and side porch."

Minutes later, she led the group along the stone paths that bounded and criss-crossed the spacious estate. Now, in late May, red azalea and pink rhododendron bushes bloomed profusely on the grounds. The sun was shining brightly again.

"There's a story told," Celia began as they circled to see a blooming orchard in back, "that after Clark Gable became famous, he slipped into Oregon with his wife, Carole Lombard, to show her this place. They were here for only a couple of days, but they slept in the master bedroom and breakfasted on the side porch behind the rose trellis you see there. He picked roses for her in the rose gardens that were planted by the original owner, Hannah Blake, decades ago."

A red-hatter knuckled at moisture in her eyes. "How romantic!"

"A fairy-tale place!" the other red-hatter exclaimed and hugged her friend.

"All of that." Celia nodded with conviction, taking a moment to wave at elderly Mrs. Kemp, who watched through a gap in tall shrubbery that separated her cottage from Gable House. She was a dear old soul, one of Pass Creek's many residents that Celia and Ethan had taken on like family when they'd returned to his hometown.

After a last look at Gable House, she told her group with a smile, "That concludes our tour." The herb-and-yeast fragrance of baking focaccia bread from the restaurant across the street wafted around them. "Feel free to wander about the town. Main Street's small shops offer souvenir gifts, nice antiques, books, as well as clothing. There is a bank and post office on the west side of Main if you have need of either. Since it is noon . . ." She checked her watch. ". . . you might want to have lunch first."

Everyone in the group nodded. She told them, "I need to see to some errands but for you all, I recommend the Mellow Mushroom Restaurant across the street." She gestured toward the cream and forest green trimmed restaurant where several cars were parked out front. "They serve delicious gourmet sandwiches, and their hazelnut fudge cake with ice cream is to die for. Or try the Pass Creek Bar and Grill at the other end of Main, if you like steaks or burgers."

One of the red-hatters turned to Tierney Jones. "Will you join us?"

The slim, pale-faced Mrs. Jones reminded Celia of an elegant white swan as she finally nodded, reluctant but polite, and floated after them across the street. Celia watched her closely. The woman looked so out of place in their simple country town. Was she up to something here or not?

Celia chewed her lip, watching the three women enter the Mellow Mushroom below the hanging baskets of pink and purple cascading petunias. The two fellows, talking animatedly, headed for the Pass Creek Grill. She could hardly wait to return home and get out of her ridiculous outfit, but that would have to wait.

She headed back toward the center of town, groaning with each step in the pointed-toe shoes. She prayed that that fiddle-foot rodeo cowboy, Jake Flagg, would be in his family's realty office. That this time he'd have the good sense and consideration to agree to what she asked for. If his brother, Caxton, until recently an older confirmed bachelor like Jake, were here, she knew he'd agree to her plan. But Caxton had retired to Hawaii with his bride, one of Celia's good friends, Ellie Winters.

In her private opinion, Jake would lose Flagg Realty to bankruptcy before and unless his brother Caxton returned to run the business. She minced on toward the realty office, remembering Ellie's prediction that she would like Jake a lot once she got to know him. Ellie had carried on about how good-looking he was and how his drawl was "pure music." To which Celia had grinned and mimed the word, "Barf."

Scolding her, Ellie had said, "You've only seen Cax's brother from afar, honey, when he was back in town for their parents' funerals."

Actually, Celia did remember seeing the tall, lanky brother of Caxton's a few times. It seemed he always kept himself apart, at the back of a room, as though he didn't care to mingle with ordinary Pass Creek folk—his booted feet itching to bolt from their presence and hit the road.

She'd mentioned Jake's standoffishness to her husband, but he'd chuckled, seeing nothing wrong with the outsider; Ethan was a man who liked everyone and rarely saw a flaw in another person.

"Rope the guy the way I roped his brother Caxton," Ellie had encouraged Celia concerning Jake. "Life is a lot more exciting when you have someone to share it with." She finished with a big hug. "My dear friend, it's time you thought of getting married again!"

Remembering her friend's words, Celia scoffed as she reached Flagg Realty. Why would she want to remarry? She was doing just fine running her life her way, thank you very much. So she was single. She was also content—well, most of the time. She had enough on her plate operating the inn, guiding walking tours of Pass Creek during tourist season, writing a history of Pass Creek for the county historical society, not to mention attempting to writing her novel during what little time was left.

Before entering the realty office, she tucked a strand of graying auburn hair behind her ear and smoothed at the wrinkles in her ancient peach dress. Ordinarily she probably fit the bill of *pretty lady,* but my goodness! The sash of her dress was slipping down, the pink satin slip underneath riding up. She tugged and pulled and geared up to face Jake Flagg. Darn his good-looking soul! Last time she came here to discuss the Pass Creek Heritage Club's hopes to buy Gable House, he barely listened, leaving her fuming and frustrated for days.

Today he sat at a large desk off to the left of the small room, picking up stacks of papers and photos of houses, then slapping them down and scowling.

"Help you?" he growled rudely without looking up.

Staring at the top of his head, his mop of thick brown hair threaded with silver, she had to admit he was one of those men who got handsomer with age. Not that it made a difference about anything.

"Yes, you can help me, Jake. I've come to remind you how much Pass Creek wants to keep Gable House for the community."

Otis Peek's only survivors, a cousin and his wife, retired professionals living in Palm Springs, had no interest in the house. They had asked that it be sold as a complete package, furniture and all, which made it perfect for her club's plans.

"You may remember our previous discussion?" she asked the top of his head. "The Heritage Club is doing everything it can to raise funds to buy Gable House. There are several resources we're looking into, including grants offered by trusts to preserve historically important buildings. Combined with Pass Creek efforts, I'm positive we can do this."

Other old Pass Creek houses had sat empty a long time before they sold, and she hoped the same would be true in this instance. But Tierney Jones' weird interest in Gable House made this a different kettle of fish, made it important for the Heritage

Club to move as quickly and firmly as possible.

He nodded, scratched his head and waved his hand. "Yeah, I know. I'll give your group time if I can, but remember, Celia," his deep silky voice droned, "business is business." He stared at the flier he held in his hand as though it was a rattlesnake about to rattle and bite, while ignoring her pacing.

"Jake. Mr. Flagg"—she wanted so much to hit him over the head to get his attention—"did you hear that I'm sure we can raise funds? Salliebeth Parker, a member of the Heritage Club and volunteer at the library, has located dozens of funding sources on the internet. We intend to review them to find the right one, or more than one, and we'll apply." Her silly slip was riding up around her hips, which meant there wasn't a lot left to imagination through the chiffon dress. If she could just get Jake Flagg's guarantee and get out of here…

"Heard you," he answered offhandedly as he continued to scan the sheaf of papers, a deep scowl riddling his thick brows. Finally, his deep blue eyes met hers, took in her costume and her discomfort. His amused smile irritated her intensely. He said, "To be honest, what I'd really like to do is chuck Flagg Realty and leave Pass Creek in my dust. If I had my brother in the same room, I'd for sure make him sorry for leaving me this mess!"

"I assume you're not a businessman?" The frosty insult was out of her mouth before she could stop it. He was terrible for Pass Creek, though. What this town needed was business folk ambitious for the community and its welfare, not an idiot dying to dust off down the road!

His slight frown at her vanished and after a hesitation he answered. "Sure I'm a businessman, Celia. I just care for some business ventures over others. Thanks to my old man, I got a degree in business from the U of O, although at that time it wasn't what I wanted to do. I even sold real estate with Pop for a couple years. Then we butted heads—over something I can't remember—and I took off for better parts. And with few regrets.

In my book, a man ought to be able to choose what he wants to do for his living and where he wants to do it."

"I agree." She tugged at her sash that was headed for her knees, wished she could do more about the slip. "But Flagg Realty has been around a long time, and I know Caxton and Ellie want the business to continue to thrive. Maybe the ins and outs of dealing with real estate will come back to you and you won't hate it so much." Ellie had been sure of it, claiming that Jake was an intelligent guy despite his wanderlust tendencies and desire to work as a common ranch hand over much of the West.

"I doubt it." He scratched his jaw. "I'd put money on this mess of paperwork killing me with boredom first. What was it you came here for? Something about that old house Clark Gable supposedly slept in, and the old guy, Otis Peek, fell off of? What was the old fool doing up there on the roof anyway? Damned old idiot." Shaking his head, Jake went back to perusing a letter he took from an envelope, mumbling a question mostly to himself: "Did anybody consider that the mean rascal was possibly *pushed* off the roof intentionally, to help your group get the place?"

"Jake Flagg, this is nothing to joke about." Celia disliked his taking the matter lightly. For one thing, Otis Peek had been a prominent member of the community, if not well-liked by everyone. His tragic passing deserved respect, as did the house for its history. Was this Flagg guy just trying to get under her skin? Annoy her?

With teeth gritted, she reached for his hand, holding onto her sash with the other. "I want to shake hands on the matter, Jake. Give us first chance, please. Gable House means everything to Pass Creek. *Do not* sell to anyone who isn't interested in preserving the place and keeping it available to tourists. I'm begging."

"That's a lot to ask, and anyhow, it's just a big old house," Jake protested, catching Celia's hand in his large one. "Nothing to get your feathers ruffled over."

"My feathers are ruffled," she said tightly, "because that property, the mansion, is so important to this town. Clark Gable *did* live in Pass Creek in the 1920s. You might not know"—she gave him a small dig for his obvious ignorance about the matter—"that last year we had visitors from as far away as Germany and France sign the Gable guest book. These tourists spend money eating in our restaurants. They buy antiques and books from the shops, and groceries at Thrifty Market, plus clothes from our clothing stores." She took a deep breath. Much of her livelihood came from tourists who rented her rooms, but pride kept her from imparting that tidbit to Jake Flagg.

She continued. "Travelers fill the gasoline tanks of their cars or R.V.s at Jolly Hoffman's service station out on the highway. We're a bedroom community with no large industries to sustain the town. We need every penny from outside that we can get." She tried to remove her hand from his, but he was still shaking it up and down and staring at her as though he'd just seen a funnel cloud touch ground, and it tickled his funny bone.

She yanked her hand away. "You get it, don't you?"

"I get it," he drawled. "But like I told you more than once, Celia, business is business. Flagg Realty has to find ways to stay afloat same as the rest of the town."

Of course he was right, but darn it, once again he left her feeling more frustrated and angry than before their conversation started. If only she personally had the money, she'd buy Gable House. But the only one around who appeared to have that kind of money was Tierney Jones, who had—God forbid—expressed interest in buying the place. Buy it to destroy? No way could that happen. If it did, the whole kit and caboodle of Pass Creek might as well pack up and move.

Chapter Two

Out on the sidewalk, Celia removed the sash and slung it around her neck. She yanked off the hateful shoes and, carrying them, started for home. Normally, she was known around town for her fine sense of fashion but today...well, today was just not her day.

Back at her inn, looking into the backyard from the kitchen window, she found that the neighbor had released his eleven dachshunds to run free on her property. *Again.* The fat brown little sausages were everywhere, doing their job in her flower beds, sending her cat Freebie fleeing for the house, running squirrels up into the trees bordering her creek.

She snatched up the shoes she'd dropped on the floor and ran screaming out the back door. She heaved her shoes one after the other at the dogs, her fury at the happenings of the day sending the shoes flying far—without touching a single animal. The dogs did, however, race for home.

"Watch out for the neighbor's stupid dogs, Freebie," Celia warned several mornings later as she opened the back door to allow her longhaired gray cat outside. At the same moment the doorbell jangled at the front of the house. Celia opened the front door with an apologetic frown at her friend Salliebeth Parker and said, "I'm so sorry to put you to this trouble."

"Shush, Celia, I don't mind at all. I have errands to run in Adkins, anyway."

Celia closed the door behind Salliebeth, a petite honey-blonde and "Jill-of-all trades" in Pass Creek.

"Mrs. Jones is pretty unhappy with us for not having a pharmacy in town, or a real taxi," Celia said, keeping her voice low. "I told her there was no need to call an out-of-town cab to come get her. In the end she seemed to like the idea of another woman driving her." Tierney Jones hadn't made further reference to Gable House, and Celia was holding her breath, praying the matter was of minor importance, just words, over and done with. For now the woman was a guest at the inn, no more, no less.

"We're a small town, we can't have everything," Salliebeth said.

"But we try. And we're lucky to be not that far off the I-5 freeway." With a sigh, Celia added, "I'd take her to Adkins, or Carrollton myself, but Lilly is visiting a sister in Idaho for a couple days. I've tons of sheets to launder, miles of dusting and vacuuming to do alone—well, it seems that much!" she said wryly. "This afternoon I have a tour group scheduled." Heading toward the stairs, she said, "I'll let Mrs. Jones know you're here."

A minute or two later, as they waited for Tierney Jones to come down, Celia told Salliebeth, "The lady hardly leaves her room or this house, except to go for a meal or to the library. She doesn't seem well, but when I tried asking after her health, she was a bit affronted and she changed the subject. Too personal, I guess. In any event, this outing may do her good. Hardly anyone could feel down or sick around your sunny personality, I'm thinking."

Salliebeth preened and laughed. "We'll see."

Minutes later, Celia sighed as she watched the women vanish down the drive in Salliebeth's silver Toyota sedan. She mentally wished her friend good luck with the strange Mrs. Jones.

It was nearly lunchtime when Celia finished cleaning her guest rooms, tired but chin lifted. There was little doubt she'd spent too much of the money Ethan had left her on redecorating, but her rental rooms were her pride and joy. She walked through them again, making sure each was as it should be, everything in its place and spotlessly clean.

Each of the four rooms was named and furnished in the period style of a favorite author. Johanna Spyri and Louisa May Alcott were Celia's childhood favorites, and Edna Ferber and Jessamyn West, her later faves. The Johanna room followed an alpine flower theme, with various editions of *Heidi* on the bookshelves. The Alcott room was furnished in ornate Victorian, with copies of *Little Women* for guests to read if they chose.

Entering Edna Ferber's room was walking into the 1940's. Her books, *So Big, Cimarron, Giant* and *Showboat* were grouped on the gracefully curved, triple dresser. A large framed movie poster of *Showboat*, starring Kathryn Grayson and Howard Keel, hung above the Federal style mahogany bed.

Tierney Jones was installed in the Jessamyn West room. Its sparse furnishings of Quaker mission oak furniture that Celia had had shipped from Indiana hardly seemed to fit Mrs. Jones elegant, worldly style, but was the only room available when she arrived. Celia resisted the urge to snoop; saw nothing lying out that offered a clue as to Tierney Jones' purpose, secretive or otherwise, for being in Pass Creek. An unusual tourist she seemed to be, though.

After a quick lunch, Celia bathed, donned a comfortable "pioneer mother" calico dress and bonnet, and for the next two hours told Pass Creek's history and showed the town's historic buildings to a tour group. She was back in her study, had been working for some time on research for her Pass Creek history—no time for her novel today—when Salliebeth and Tierney returned. They'd been gone for hours, much longer than she expected. "Have a good day?" she called into the hallway from the open door of her study.

"Thank you, yes," Tierney murmured, and without looking in Celia's direction went straight on up to her room, back like a ramrod but hand on the stair railing.

Salliebeth entered Celia's study frowning deeply.

"What's wrong? What happened? Is Mrs. Jones all right?" Celia got to her feet, her heart thumping. There was a chance that Tierney Jones had seen a doctor while in the larger town and was found to be seriously ill. Dying?

If so, she'd be no problem regarding Gable House. Shocked at the line of thinking that sprang unbidden to her mind, Celia's eyes widened and she clapped a hand over her mouth. How could she think that way? Awash with guilt, she reprimanded herself severely, if silently.

Salliebeth shrugged and threw herself into an overstuffed chair by the window. "She's all right, I suppose. I'm so sorry, Celia.'

"You're sorry about what, for heaven's sake?" She took the chair next to Salliebeth and with her own panic climbing, studied the many emotions playing in her friend's small heart-shaped face. "What on earth happened?"

"*Gable House.*"

"Gable House?" Celia straightened. "She didn't. Did she?"

"She did. After we returned from Adkins, where she bought her meds and did some banking tasks, she insisted we stop at Flagg Realty. I wasn't sure what it was about, could hardly poke my nose into her private affairs to ask. I hoped that she might be looking into investing in industrial land outside town. We could use that, a business that would employ hundreds of folks."

She waved her hand. "I thought perhaps she had decided to stay in Pass Creek and would want one of the new houses on Douglas Avenue. She apologized for keeping me waiting so long. Fortunately I had a mystery novel to read and nearly finished it. Celia, the Jones woman made a cash offer on Gable House! Jake Flagg made phone calls, and the seller liked the sound of the offer. It's the same as done, Celia."

For a minute or two, Celia couldn't speak. It was as though the floor had opened under her chair. Tears of shock and disappointment burned her eyes, and it was hard to catch her breath. "Did she say what she planned to do with the house? Does she plan to live there?" *Or level it, taking away a lot of Pass Creek's chances of survival?*

"She didn't say. Our chasing around in Adkins and her business doings here in Pass Creek wore her out. Otherwise we could've sat her down for a chat."

"Is Jake still at the office?"

"He locked up as we were leaving."

Running for his life, like as not! He had to know how upset she would be with him for breaking their agreement.

As soon as she could get away from the inn next morning, leaving a small *Be Back Soon* sign hanging on her front door and counting on residents to get in and out with their own keys, Celia headed for Flagg Realty. Tierney hadn't been up and about, yet, but said through her closed door that she was all right. Later, Celia meant to insist on knowing her intentions for Gable House, but first, Jake Flagg was getting a piece of her mind!

"Why in the world did you agree to sell Gable House to Tierney Jones?" she demanded as she stormed into his office. Today he couldn't leer at her for wearing an odd get-up. She had on ordinary white jeans and a gauzy navy blue shirt.

"Why wouldn't I?" He looked up from his computer and messy desk with a quizzical, half-guilty grin. "I'm here to buy and sell properties. Mrs. Jones has cash to buy right now. I know what you wanted, Celia, but it would have been stupid of me to reject her offer. I'm just getting the hang of things around here. I'm probably going to make mistakes, but this wasn't going to be one of them." He looked at her triumphantly. "I'm quite proud of the sale, to tell you the truth."

"Well you're not a good friend and not a good booster of

Pass Creek, I can tell you that."

Muscles in his cheek twitched and his eyes glinted. "*Booster*—of Pass Creek? I'll admit that's not high on my priority list." He snorted. "I've got enough to do to keep this business percolating. From stuff I've overheard, folks around town have been comparing me to my brother, and they're of the opinion that I'll fail. They could be right. As to being a friend, I'd like to be your friend, Celia, but when someone has full price in cash for one of our properties, I can hardly turn them down. That sure as hell wouldn't be fair to the seller."

She paced back and forth in the narrow confines in front of his desk, burning with anger, wishing with all her heart that the man had never come to Pass Creek.

"You're a good person, Celia, and normally I'd go a long way before disappointing a nice, pretty woman like you. I'd be knocking myself out to be in your good graces, actually."

Despite her dark mood, she was slightly taken aback at his sincere tone and sympathetic expression, which of course he could be faking in order to smooth the moment, charm her into dropping the matter. She glared at him.

He began again, "There might be something else we can do…"

"Tell Tierney Jones the deal is off, that the Heritage Club had their word in for the house, first? That you and I shook hands and you then violated our agreement?"

"Celia," he drawled softly, "there was no agreement. I told you from day one I couldn't promise to hold the house if another buyer stepped in first. I don't relish being responsible for your disappointment. But the Jones woman wanted the house enough to lay a large amount of money on the table. I would've been a fool to tell her no deal."

Celia barely nodded, even as her eyes scorched him to ashes and her foot tapped loudly.

He cleared his throat and looked at her hopefully, "What

about that gray, Italianate house over on the east side of Roulette Street? It's going up for sale again. Turns out the last interested party can't come up with a loan. The house has the kind of history you like, being built by a Pass Creek civic leader in the 1880s. It's in fair shape and comes on a large lot. I can probably talk the seller into lowering the price so these Heritage Club folks can afford it. Sell it quicker for him."

She looked at Jake in disgust. "That old Wyndham house is not on a par with Gable House. The main thing is Clark Gable didn't live there." She threw up her hands. "You're missing the point entirely, Jake."

"How about one of the other older houses…?"

She shook her head. "Gable House is, or was, our main draw. Clark Gable was a popular movie star, known all over the world, and his being here for a time gives Pass Creek its chief importance. Since the big mill closed, that's pretty much all we have." How many times did she have to explain it?

He shrugged and his lips tightened. Anger flared in his eyes. "Well, if it's not possible to interest you in one of the other historic houses, I guess there's nothing else I can do to make this up to you. Make it up to you and your group, I mean."

Celia, pacing, cut a glance at him as an idea occurred to her. "There is something you can do. If you want to make up this…grievous wrong, you can attend this evening's meeting of the Heritage Club. We'll want your input into the discussion of what the town's to do now that we've lost Gable House. I'm sure you'll have some fine suggestions."

He looked as if she had whopped him over the head with a frying pan. He groaned in protest, "Attend a meeting of clucking old hens and crowing old roosters about this town from nowhere? You got to be kidding."

"They're fine people, and this is a good town. You know that as well as I do, and no, I'm not kidding. We meet at the library at seven-thirty, sharp. I'll see you there."

Chapter Three

He followed her to the door. A quick look over her shoulder caught him checking her out, head to toe, with a look of appreciation—that she was a woman, a pretty woman? Or simply that she was ready to fight for the good of her town? Didn't really make a difference; he was still the enemy. A skunk in sheep's clothing, or was it a rat? She could never remember how that went for sure.

His smiled in temporary defeat, "Okay. See you there."

Celia headed toward home feeling better, murmuring aloud to herself that she was going to "involve Jake in Pass Creek's betterment, or else."

Despite his sister-in-law's prediction that Celia was going to like Jake a lot, truth was she hated the ground he walked on. "Well not literally," she told an ant crossing the sidewalk. "It's that I have little use for him." She stepped over the ant, looking down to say, "But darn his hide, he'd better get Pass Creek out of this hole he's got us in, right?"

Realizing she'd been talking to an ant, Celia's face heated. She looked around, noted a car moving slowly along the street, the driver facing ahead. Few people were out and about. No one was close enough to hear her. She laughed at herself and kept going.

She'd been teased over the years for talking to herself, although she saw it as thinking out loud, and a big help to solving problems. The habit had worsened since Ethan passed, and she was trying to break herself of it. She was making progress and never talked to herself in the presence of others.

That evening, Celia arranged plates of cookies and a tray of punch and coffee cups on a long table in the basement meeting room of the library. Soft chatter swirled the room. It appeared they were going to have a good turn-out. She looked toward the door at the latest arrival, and her heart flip-flopped. He didn't have to be so good-looking. Jake stood in the doorway, long legs encased in Levis, his blue shirt doing miraculous things to his eyes. He ran a finger around the inside of his collar, appearing as uncomfortable as a bull in a tea room. She smiled to herself. Too bad for him the library wasn't a dusty corral. He could just make the best of it. He appeared relieved to see her, approaching as though she were an island in an unknown sea.

"I'm glad you came, Jake."

"Didn't know I had a choice."

Darn right you didn't! "Well, now you're here," she said more mildly than she felt like, "let me introduce you to the others in case you haven't met some of them. Most are merchants and other citizens who have a strong interest in Pass Creek's survival and betterment." As Celia circled the room with Jake looming at her side, it turned out that he already knew most members of the Heritage Club. It impressed her how easily he conversed on any subject that came up; talk that had nothing to do with cattle, or horses or rodeo.

The elderly women at the meeting fussed over Jake, remembering him and his parents from times long gone. Ancient Mrs. Kemp tossed aside her cane in order to embrace him. "Jake Flagg, it is you! My blue-eyed baby boy! Everybody," she said loudly to get everyone's attention, "I used to change this fella's diapers when he was a baby, and I come over to the Flaggs' to help out his mama."

Jake turned scarlet under his tan, and Celia burst into

laughter before she could stop herself. "Sorry," she murmured, trying to keep her face straight.

Despite his embarrassment, he had the decency to hug old Mrs. Kemp, thank her, retrieve her cane and tell her how nice it was to see her. Jake's eyes flashed accusingly at Celia. She shrugged innocence and they moved on.

Salliebeth came over and whispered in Celia's ear, "You two sure look good together!"

"Oh, for heaven's sake!" It was Celia's turn to blush.

Salliebeth smiled. "What I came to ask is, did you get Mrs. Jones to talk about her intentions for buying Gable House?"

"She clams up when I press, and I don't want to make her so mad I have no chance getting her to talk at all. Hardly ever comes out of her room. She orders her dinner in from the Mellow Mushroom. Earlier today, she took a short walk down to the creek, but when I went out to corner her and talk, she'd already gone back upstairs. I asked later if she'd like to come with me to tonight's meeting, but she said she was going to read and go to bed early." She sighed. "I won't give up, but the woman is like a ghost in my house, doing her best to avoid me."

"That sounds almost spooky."

"Yes, well, that's how it feels."

"I don't see Locke Vinson here tonight," Salliebeth mused, looking around.

"He sees himself as too big for our little town, I'm afraid," Celia commented as she watched others enter the meeting room. "I heard he's opened his seventh print shop, this one up near Portland. With others looking after business for him here in Pass Creek, Locke comes to town a lot less often."

"Been like that since you dumped him, Cele."

"I didn't dump him. It was mutual."

"That's not what I heard. He was nuts about you, girlfriend."

"Listen, Salliebeth, if the man's available, and you know

he's got a different young thing on his arm much of the time, why don't you go after him?"

Salliebeth grinned and shrugged. "No way. He's not my type either. Oops, speak of the devil." She nodded toward the door where Locke Vinson had just entered.

"Shoot!" Celia muttered under her breath as she forced a smile and gave a small wave back at him. "He's the last one I'd want at tonight's meeting. He doesn't have much use for Pass Creek and cares even less about the people who live here." Fortunately, if he followed his usual pattern, he wouldn't be at the meeting long. He'd state his case and be up and out, much too important in his own mind to have time for the locals.

"I miss Otis Peek, obstinate and ornery as that old man could be sometimes," Salliebeth said. "He hardly ever failed to show up at our meetings and for all his faults he was behind the town, wanted the best for Pass Creek."

"No argument there," Celia agreed. From the back of her mind she remembered Jake's comment that maybe one of her group had killed Otis to help them gain Gable House. He was teasing, of course, although such things did happen in other places. She raised her voice. "Will everyone take a seat and we'll start our meeting."

The question most on her mind was the first asked. Service station owner, Jolly Hoffman, spoke around a mouthful of sugar cookie. "Does anyone know what this Jones lady plans to do with Gable House?" He licked the crumbs from his lips. "She gonna live there and maybe let us continue showing it to tourists?" Jolly had lived most of his adult life in Pass Creek, but his Oklahoma accent was still strong.

Celia shrugged, "I honestly don't know. She's not saying. I can't tell if she's angry at the place for some reason, or sad, or just arbitrarily wants it gone."

A loud voice blotted out the murmurs of concern up and down the meeting table when Locke Vinson, wearing his usual overbearing smile and expensive clothes, said, "I think this Jones person, whoever she is, has the right idea. Downright excites me. It's time for a change. Tear down a lot of these old houses, upgrade this poor little burg, that's what's needed."

"I doubt that many agree with you, Locke." Celia spoke tightly. This was old ground the community had voted on dozens of times. The man didn't care a fig for town history, or the beauty of the older buildings. He was all about money and a playboy style of life, which was fine, as long as it didn't infringe on others' lives and their wishes. The majority never voted with him, but he wouldn't give up.

At the moment, dissent to his statement was soft thunder rolling from every corner of the room, making Celia smile in satisfaction.

"Hell, no!" Jolly slapped the table in front of him hard. "Locke, you got the wrong idea about our town and what us folks intend for Pass Creek."

"Give it time and you folks will agree with me, I guarantee." Locke's expression challenged them all as he drained his coffee cup. After a few more moments of argument, he moved away from the table. "Sorry. I don't have more time tonight but at least you have *my* opinion regarding this woman who sees things how I do. Gotta run. You all have a good evening." He stepped close to where Celia waited to regain control of the meeting, and he whispered, his hot minty breath brushing her cheek, "You especially think about what I said, Celia. When you're ready, I have a business proposition to discuss with you personally."

For several reasons, Locke Vinson was the last person on earth she wanted to do business with. Taking a deep breath in relief, she watched him go.

Within a few minutes she had the meeting back on track.

Myrna Hall, a husky-voiced older waitress from the Mellow Mushroom, who came to these meetings as a social outing, spoke up. "I know what you mean, Celia, when you talked about the Jones woman's attitude. The woman's got real strong feelings about the house, and I'm afraid they ain't all good. Place upsets me, too, you know," she said as an aside. "I found Otis's body and I still ain't over that awful picture of him dead on the ground." She shuddered. "Crumpled up and his head—so bloody. Poor old fella." She blinked at the sudden tears in her eyes, looked at all of them like they couldn't possibly understand that she'd really cared about him.

Mrs. Kemp stood up and leaned halfway across the table past two others to pat Myrna's arm. "I saw the old coot on the roof when I went to let my cat, Junie, out the back door that afternoon. I yelled at him to get his darned fool carcass down from there, but he just waved me off." She sat back down, fingers rubbing the back of her other purple-veined hand. "Complained that the roofing company he planned to hire for the job wanted to be paid an arm and a leg for the work. You know how Otis was about turning loose of a dime extra. Sorry you had to find him like that, Myrna."

Myrna sniffled, "I went over after I got off work to ask him if he wanted to go with me to a movie in Salem." Her hands went up to hold her head, squashing the red curls. "Darn it all! If I'd got there sooner maybe I could've sent for the doctor, saved his life."

"I feel bad 'cause I might've done that, myself." Mrs. Kemp nodded. "But after I let Junie out, I went back in the house to watch Oprah and forgot the whole thing."

"I guess he'd lain there a couple hours before I found him," Myrna said with a muffled sob. She shook her head with regret, "If only I'd been there. The poor man. He had to've suffered bad." She accepted a tissue Celia offered and wiped her eyes.

It was commonly known that Myrna had been a friend to Otis Peek, doing him small favors, checking on him when he was sick, sitting with him at community suppers. Some conjectured the two might get married one day, but when so much time passed without it happening, the idea was abandoned. Old Peek was just too tight-fisted to share his life with someone else, it was decided.

Myrna had long since reached the age of retirement, but as she often jokingly remarked, if she quit working, "I'd have to live on dog food, and my social security check would only pay for the cheap brands." She continued to dye her gray hair strawberry pink, paint her nails, and keep on as the Mellow Mushroom's oldest, friendliest, and most efficient waitress.

Now, she dabbed at her eyes again, wiped her nose, and struggled to regain composure, "That Mrs. Jones was in the restaurant a day or so after she came to Pass Creek, and she was drawing something on a napkin."

"Drawing something?" Vivian Tyler, owner of Viv's Antiques And Collectibles asked, a frown meeting the widow's peak of her raven hair. A good friend of Celia's, Viv was a single mom of three grown children. Her personal history went deep in the old hotel that housed her antique business, the place a highlight on Celia's tours of Pass Creek.

"I sneaked a look as I was serving her Caesar salad," Myrna answered with a nod. "She was drawing a house! And you could tell well enough it was Gable House, those cone roofs and all."

Myrna waited for the group to digest her information. "So I complemented her that she's a pretty good artist. 'That's Gable House, right?' She said it was. I went on about my business. Later, I looked over and saw her scratching at the picture so hard with her pen; it tore the napkin to pieces. Looked about to cry, too, she did."

The others in the room were now hanging on to Myrna's every word. "I thought maybe she was a close friend of Otis's, maybe a relative even, and was torn up over him, something to do with his house. When I asked, she didn't seem to know what I was talking about. I tried to calm her down, get her to stay and finish her chicken soup and salad, but she tossed a twenty on the table and left."

"Real strange." Viv wore a perplexed frown and raised her palms in the air. "She's sad about the house or hates it for some reason, and buys it anyway out from under us. And nobody has the foggiest idea what she plans to do with it, other than her remark she'd like to see Gable House demolished. Celia's right. This whole thing is just crazy and makes no sense."

"For sure," Celia agreed. "But in any event, right now she's in the driver's seat." She took a deep breath. "If it turns out that we've lost Gable House, or I should say the opportunity to show it to tourists, does anyone have other suggestions for bringing travelers to town?"

The only response was a chorus of mumbling that dragged on for nearly half an hour and threatened to erupt into serious yelling. Celia told them, firmly interrupting the racket, "Mr. Flagg." Her glance sailed his way across the table. "Mr. Flagg has made a suggestion that we buy the Wyndham place. He'd arrange as low a price as possible. As you all know, the house is a beautiful example of 1880's Italianate. The grounds could be made lovely with a lot of work. The Wyndham place could house our proposed museum, such as we hoped for with Gable House if we bought it."

"It'd be sorta nice, I reckon." Jolly Hoffman put his coffee cup down and shook his head. "But Clark Gable when he was young didn't live on the old Wyndham property. Big difference, you ask me." He brushed a cascade of cookie crumbs from the front of his service station jacket and looked around. His chest puffed when he saw agreement on most faces in the room.

Salliebeth nodded. "A museum in the Wyndham house would be okay, but it wouldn't be much different from a museum in any other small town. And certainly not the draw that Gable

House has been. Gable House is exceptional."

Celia looked at Jake, the tilt of her chin saying, "I told you so."

He got to his feet slowly. He spoke to the group, although his eyes were on Celia's face. "I want to apologize that I wasn't able to hold Gable House for you all. I know how much it meant to you, to the town. I don't agree with that guy who just left here, and if there's anything else I can do to support your efforts, just let me know."

Celia nodded and led the quiet applause. He'd agreed to help. How serious he was in his pledge remained to be seen. She gave a report on her progress with the county history she was working on, and a few minutes later the meeting ended.

Jake stayed after, collapsing folding chairs and helping to put them away in the storage closet while Celia cleared the long table of cookie crumbs and washed coffee cups. "I'd like to walk you home," he said in a tone of gruff doubt after everything was back in place, "if you don't hate me too much."

She considered his invitation without getting into whether she actually hated him or actually liked him a little bit. "You don't need to see me home, and I'm not sure I'm going there directly anyway. But thanks." She needed a walk by Gable House, have a chance to be alone and think. If he were along, they'd probably get into another argument.

He touched her arm. "See you later then."

Though normally not afraid to walk at night, and it wasn't terribly late, at nine-thirty or so, after a couple of blocks, Celia had a creepy feeling she was being followed. Twice she turned to look, only to find the darkish street and sidewalk empty. *Foolishness, thinking someone is back there,* she reproached herself and continued with a light step.

Who would be following her, anyway? Locke Vinson, trying to scare her into what he wanted? If there was someone back there—she faced straight ahead—it'd more likely be someone innocently heading home from the meeting, as she was.

Within a short while she stood on the front sidewalk before Gable House. Even in the pale moonlight it was a beautiful, impressive mansion.

When giving tours, she loved to tell how Clark Gable as a young man had worked in the local mill owned by the Peek family. He dated a farm girl who lived outside town on Finney Road. Of course that was long before his career as an actor and his marriage to the beautiful actress, Carole Lombard.

Moving from the streetlight's soft glow, Celia made her way across the dark grounds toward the side porch and rose gardens. She stood for a minute, breathing in a lungful of lovely fragrance.

Hearing a sound, and not sure in the gloom what direction it came from, she walked stealthily around the back of the house—tiptoeing across the lawn, as if anyone could hear her approach! If someone was trying to break in, she would quietly spot them and then call the police chief on her cell. She was just taking another step when suddenly she was shoved from behind. Her breath whooshed out as she went down, and the ground met her full force. She lay there a few seconds, hurting, face in the grass, disoriented and wondering what had just happened. Fighting to breathe, she tried to rise, but the dark yard tip-tilted, made crazy circles. Whimpering from confusion and fright, she managed to locate her cell in the grass. She got to her feet, brushing grass from her mouth and off her face.

When hands touched her, her scream tore the night.

Chapter Four

"Hold still," Jake demanded, pulling her back when she tried to get away.

"In the name of God, why did you knock me down?" She shook violently.

"Celia, I didn't. It wasn't me. As I was circling the house from out front, I saw a bulky shadow come at you from behind. I couldn't get to you in time. I tried!"

"Who was it?" She was clinging to him now. "Why did they knock me down like that?"

"All I could see was a dark figure. Could have been a man, or maybe a woman gave you a shove. Whoever it was disappeared like they were never there. I'm so sorry. Sorry they hurt you and sorry they got away."

Gradually, her composure returned, but her voice came unsteadily. "I'm n-not really hurt, I don't th-think. N-no stab wounds or broken bones," she joked thinly. "If you're not the one sh-shoved me down—wh-what are you doing here, Jake?"

"Let's get out of here where it might not be real safe, and I'll tell you." He put his arm around her waist, heading them back around the house to the front sidewalk.

"Someone else besides you must have been following me. But why attack me, knock me flat?" She shivered and he held her tighter.

"Whoever pushed you down was already here and they

didn't want to be seen, is my best guess. Maybe it was just a transient or a kid fooling around."

"Nothing against me personally you don't think?"

"I strongly doubt it, not that we shouldn't report what happened."

She nodded in the dark. "I suppose, though the more I think about it, the less serious the incident seems." She'd decide later if she should report what happened to Pass Creek's likable chief of police, Pete Erdman. She hadn't been injured, so that was of no consequence, but if someone was trying to break in and rob Gable House, that did need looking into.

As they continued on Jake said, "I've made a mess of things, selling Gable House out from under your Heritage Club. If it means anything, I'm feeling sorrier by the minute, although I don't know what else I could've done. Mrs. Jones wanted it badly and had the money."

Celia sighed. "Like you said, business is business. Unfortunately, sometimes what is good business for one can hurt others. It happens. I suppose we'll find a way to keep Pass Creek going and growing, which is always the plan."

"If I can help, I will."

"Thanks." They approached her inn, a pale yellow, wood-laced beacon in the distance. There were lights on in the four windows of her guests' upstairs rooms. On the ground floor, she'd left a light on for her return, and it spilled softly from a bay window onto the porch that circled the front. Urns overflowing with geraniums, verbena and alyssum filled the night with fragrance as she and Jake took the steps moments later.

"Will you be all right?" he asked, clasping her arm gently.

"Yes, I'm fine. I think I was just startled, being knocked down like that, but I'm okay." Freebie sauntered out of the shadows. He curled around Celia's ankles before flopping to the porch floor to give his paws a good washing with his tongue.

"I appreciate your coming to the meeting, Jake."

He opened the door for her and stepped back. "I was glad to be there, except"—he grimaced—"for the diaper remark. I could've done without that."

She laughed with him and stooped to pet Freebie.

Above her, Jake spoke. "I decided tonight as I was walking home that there's something I should mention. That's why I switched direction and was behind you."

"What?" She stood up quickly at the tone of his voice.

"When Mrs. Jones was in the office yesterday and we spent a long time over the house deal, I got the feeling I'd known her from somewhere before."

Celia gripped the door and peered at him in the soft porch light. "Really, Jake, you think you might know her?"

"I asked, but she blew me off. I got the feeling she really dislikes personal questions."

"Well, yes, most of us have come to that conclusion about Mrs. Jones. And of course, few of us would welcome probing questions from strangers, any more than she does. But if you do know her—!"

"I was probably wrong. I'm positive I've never known anyone whose first name is *Tierney*. Anybody'd remember that."

"She could've changed her name. People do. If she's someone you might've known sometime in the past, you'll have to figure it out if she won't tell us! It would help a lot to know why she's here and what's behind her odd, almost malevolent interest in Gable House."

For a few seconds he was silent. Then he boasted, with a smile in his voice, taking steps backward off the porch, "Mrs. Jones could resemble an easy dozen of the many women I've known. Attractive, rich women."

"Really?" Not that she was interested in his romantic prowess.

"That was a male boast, a joke, with little truth behind it," he admitted with a rueful grin from the bottom of the steps.

"Tierney Jones seems vaguely familiar. That's all I can say. But I can't place her."

"You'll try, won't you? It's very important."

Minutes later they said goodbye and she watched him turn to go, his tall figure loping along the lighted street in the direction of the Flagg home on Benedict Street. Joker that he was, it was still possible that he might know Tierney Jones from somewhere in his past and might possibly help puzzle out the woman's strangeness, her real reason for being there.

Then maybe they could convince her to allow them to advertise and continue the tours. The shock surrounding Peek's recent death there was fading.

A new thought brought Celia up short as she went inside, her cat trotting alongside. Earlier in the evening, she'd dismissed as idle chatter Myrna's wondering if Peek and Tierney were connected. What if that were somehow true? "He's dead," she told Freebie, picking him up into her arms, "and can't give me an answer. But Mrs. Jones has no such excuse. She has to talk to us."

When Lilly arrived for work at the inn next morning, Celia was glad to see the strapping young woman. But in seconds she realized that Lilly was more subdued than usual and tied up with worry. "Did things go all right at your sister's in Idaho? Did you have a good time?"

Dressed in blue cropped jeans and pink t-shirt, sandy hair pulled back tight in a ponytail, Lilly didn't answer right away as she hauled the vacuum cleaner from the hall closet. "It was okay." She sighed. "But I was hoping she'd float me and Mac a loan and shoot, turns out she and her husband are worse off than we are!" She appeared embarrassed at having said more than she really wanted and she muttered, "No big deal."

In Celia's experience, when someone used those words it usually was a big deal. She touched Lilly's slender shoulder, "If you need help with finances, Lilly, maybe there is something I can do."

She shook her head, giving the ponytail wings. "No, Mrs. Landrey. It's enough you give me work and pay me more than minimum. Mac will be out of school for the summer in another month, and he'll be able to work more hours." She moved away, anxious to have the conversation over with.

"College debt can be enormous, can't it?" Celia said gently to Lilly's back.

"Sure is." She turned, her expression changing to a soft, proud smile as she spoke of her husband. "But Mac is determined to get his degree in engineering. When he's out of school, and the debt all paid, none of this hard work and struggle will seem so bad. But thanks anyway, Mrs. Landrey." She plugged in the vacuum and it started with a roar. Talk was over.

Celia shook her head and went on into the kitchen for a cup of coffee. Lilly and Mac were good kids. Neither had had the best start, but both were hard-working and determined to make themselves a good life. Lilly had been a child when her mother died. A stepmother had decided the family was too many by two and forced Lilly and her sister out on their own. The girls were fifteen and sixteen at the time. The parents then took off for parts unknown.

Lilly was eighteen when she married her high school sweetheart, Mac, who'd been raised fatherless by his mother, Louise Strand. For years, Mrs. Strand was Otis Peek's housekeeper. Mac and his mother just barely got by on the small salary Peek paid, and Mac had been taking odd jobs from the time he was ten. Since starting college, he worked night-times as janitor at the Mellow Mushroom and for other businesses about town. Two years ago, Louise Strand died of cancer. Mac had been devastated and it was just lucky he had Lilly.

Celia, finished with her coffee, washed the cup in the sink and promised herself to give Lilly as much work as she could afford to pay for, and maybe a small raise.

After working for a while in the study on her county history, Celia found Lilly dusting furniture in the dining room and told her, "I have an errand to run, Lilly. If you don't mind keeping an eye on the place, I'd appreciate it. The Humphreys may plan to leave today. If I'm not back, just check them out. They've already paid by credit card. Remember to give them a receipt and get their opinion about their stay. We want to keep folks happy."

"Sure, Mrs. Landrey. I'll take care of them. I'll wait till they're gone before I leave the house to pick some bouquets for the dining room and front desk."

"Oh, yes, I almost forgot to tell you. We have a new lodger: Mrs. Jones in the Jessica West room. She's been a little under the weather, so if she needs anything, would you help her out?"

Lilly frowned. "Mac says he heard that Mrs. Jones is buying Gable House, and then after she has it, she plans to get rid of it. She can't do that, can she?"

"I hope we can talk her out of it. I sure mean to try."

"Well, I hope you can. I could hardly believe it when I heard about it. Gable House is beautiful. It's been here so long. Pass Creek just wouldn't be the same without it."

"We agree on that." Celia smiled and gave Lilly a quick hug. Moments later, she set off for Gable House, her mind on last night's trespasser.

She took some time wandering the grounds and examining the building closely. She found no windows broken, and all the doors were locked solid. She was around back, staring up at the lower section of roof Peek was trying to repair at the time he fell, when a strong male voice broke the silence.

"'Morning, Celia. Where's your people?"

"My peop—? Oh, you mean my tour folks," she answered, turning. "I don't have a walking tour scheduled today. I'm here on my own. How are you, Chief?" she returned the law officer's friendly smile. "How are Thea and the kids?" She liked Pete and Thea; had from the very first time they met. Which was right after Pass Creek citizens voted to have their own law officer and her Ethan was instrumental in Pete's being hired. Sometimes Pete had had a deputy or two working with him, but the city budget the last few years hadn't allowed for it.

"My family is fine. Thea's probably washing the corn flakes off half of 'em about now and changing diapers on the rest."

Celia laughed softly. His passel of cute kids sometimes distracted him from his job, no matter how he and his wife struggled to see that they didn't. Celia had a lot of admiration for the couple, in any event. She grew serious as she told him about last night's incident, downplaying her being shoved to the ground.

He frowned and held up a hand to keep her from speaking further. He took out a notepad and pen. "You were here last night after dark and someone assaulted you?"

"I wouldn't say assaulted, exactly. More like someone gave me a rough shove from behind. You know, pushed me off my feet." She smoothed her hair that was being tossed by a soft, peony-scented breeze. "Nice day, isn't it chief?"

"Yeah, nice," he said. "Is there anything you can remember about the person who shoved you? Did you see them run away? Tell me whatever you can about the incident."

"I didn't see them. The wind had been knocked out of me and my face was buried in the lawn for a minute. I wish I had seen the culprit."

"Did you hear anything? Sounds of something they might have carried, like tools?" She shook her head. He continued, "How about smells—sweat, grease, a man's cologne, or a woman's fragrance—anything?" His pencil was poised.

"Sorry, no, Pete. I can see I'm a lousy help. No particular smells or sounds, nothing I can remember. It all happened so fast.

Jake showed up right after, but not in time to see who it was in the dark, or stop them. We both think the person who struck me was taking a shortcut, in a hurry and not wanting to be caught trespassing, that's all. I don't see any sign of a break in or anything like that."

The chief shook his head and muttered something under his breath.

She continued, admitting, "You could consider me a trespasser, too. Gable House is being sold to a woman staying at my inn. Tierney Jones. She's made remarks about wanting the house to come down. "

"So I've heard. What do you know about this lady?"

Celia shook her head. "Next to nothing, but I'm working on it. I intend to find out why she's come to our town out of the blue, evidently with intentions that could ruin us."

He nodded, seemed to consider a number of things. "It's interesting that she turns up just now. I expect to question Mrs. Jones concerning Otis Peek's death."

"Some of us have wondered if she has a connection to Otis, since the house most recently belonged to him." She gave second thought to his words. "How do you mean *concerning his death?* It was an accident, wasn't it? Mrs. Kemp saw him working up on the roof, and Myrna found him where he fell. What else is there to know? And how could Tierney Jones be involved in how he died? It happened before she got here." She watched Pete's face, saw his hesitation to talk further.

"All I'll say now is that there are questions needing answers. I'll be talking to several folks. Did you see anything suspicious the day he was killed? Were you by here with your tour group?" When she didn't answer right away, he finally told her, "I had a phone call early this morning from the coroner. He's leaning pretty heavily toward the conclusion that Otis Peek's death was no accident."

What Jake had said might not turn out to be a joke, then?

Celia couldn't believe it. "Are you talking about—murder? You and the coroner think someone deliberately killed Otis?" She took a step back, looked up at the roof again and at the low brick wall near where Otis was found. "Murder," she repeated, trying to accept the possibility.

Pete's expression didn't change. "We'll see. Otis's head wound was consistent with a hard fall on the brick wall there. But it could've as easily been caused by somebody striking him with a blunt instrument. Either would be enough to kill him, the way he bled."

"But he was on the roof. Mrs. Kemp saw him up there around four o'clock that day, just before Oprah."

"That's what she told me, too. So far I haven't found a witness to what actually happened. The backyard here is pretty secluded, what with the trees and shrubbery all around." His eyes squinted as he looked at the roof. "A couple of neighbors said Peek talked of hiring out the repair of his roof, but tight-fisted as he is—was, he probably decided to do the work himself. I'm asking you again, Celia. Did you happen to have a tour the day he died? Did you see anything unusual? Someone coming or going who looked suspicious?"

She was so surprised to hear that Peek's death could be *murder,* Celia had forgotten she hadn't answered the chief's earlier question. She thought back to the day it happened and shook her head. "I was at the inn all that day, working in my study on some writing. What do *you* think, Chief? I just can't believe there's a cold-blooded murderer lurking around Pass Creek."

"I don't want to believe it, either, Celia. All I'm saying is that the coroner sees homicide as a strong possibility. We'll get it settled one way or the other." He looked around with a shadow of guilt in his expression. "I wish I hadn't been so accepting that his death was accidental. But at the time there was no reason to believe otherwise."

"His death may yet prove to be an accident."

He looked doubtful as he said with regret, "On the other hand, if he was murdered, what clues were possibly here have since been compromised by folks coming and going." He looked around with a deep frown at the landscaped yard, shrubbery and fruit trees in bloom. "I'm putting up a police tape and hope it's not too late."

"I won't be able to show tourists the place then?" It was a statement more than a question. Of course she couldn't.

"Not for a while, Celia. Keep the story of the place as part of your tour if you like, but otherwise no one is allowed anywhere near it. If this is homicide," he finished grimly, "I'll get him or her for committing the crime. And Celia, be careful. You could get badly hurt the next time you're in the way. Not just knocked off your feet. Watch yourself."

"All right, I will." She bit the inside of her lip and considered that it would require new thinking to feel there was anything truly sinister or dangerous about last night. "I'll leave you here to your investigation, Pete." She patted his arm, feeling sorry that he felt he'd failed in any way at his job. "You'll get to the bottom of this soon, I know." They waved at one another and Celia was again on her way downtown. *Murdered? Peek murdered?*

Unbelievable as it seemed, had the killer returned to Gable House last night for some reason, and accosted her?

The whole matter churned in her brain as she picked up laundry at the cleaner's, dropped off a letter at the post office, and then headed home. Over and over she asked herself: if Peek's death was murder, not an accident, who could have done it? Why would they? Was there a connection between his death and Tierney Jones' attitude concerning Gable House? The whole matter was like musty fog filling her mind.

What would it hurt if she did some investigating on her own—going about it safely, of course? A question here and there, like that. She'd not bother Pete, who'd be attending to the more official side of police business, but maybe she could find out things he couldn't. Move things along faster as it were.

Chapter Five

When Celia arrived home, the inn smelled sweetly of the bouquets of lilacs and roses Lilly had brought in, but even those lovely scents were not enough to lift the cloud of dread Celia felt. After letting Lilly go for the day, she went to her study and called Jake to tell him what she'd learned from her talk with Chief Erdman. Jake had been there, too, last night, and would want to know.

"Be careful, Celia. Pete can be right about this being murder. And the killer could have been the same one who shoved you down and ran. If whoever that was thinks you know something, you could be in grave danger."

She'd already come to that conclusion herself. "I intend to be careful, Jake. I have no desire to be anybody's next victim. But I can't help but hope it will turn out that Peek's death was an accident, and that the shove I took was a very minor happenstance."

"Just don't count on it. Until the truth comes out as a known fact, you've got to watch where you are, who you're with—be on constant guard for your own good."

"I will, I will, Jake! I'll be fine." Lordy, he made her feel like they were in the middle of a *Lifetime Movie of the Week*. He wasn't her keeper, after all.

As soon as they said their goodbyes and she'd hung up the phone, Celia booted up her computer to do research.

There it was: falls were second only to traffic accidents as cause of accidental death. Close to 15,000 such accidents ending in death occurred every year. Mrs. Kemp saw Otis Peek up there. Otis took a tumble after she went inside, hit his head on the brick wall and bled to death. Clear as day. Once it was proven nobody else was involved, the case would be cleared. Gable House didn't need a shadow of murder spoiling its appeal.

~~~

Her intention wasn't without motive, means to an end. "It's such a lovely day! I'm glad I was able to entice you to this picnic for two." Celia poured iced tea and passed Tierney the plate of cream cheese and cucumber sandwiches. She spoke over the sound of the small waterfall and Eden creek chortling through her property. "I trust that you continue to enjoy your stay at the inn? Let me know any time there's more I can do for you."

The refrain was one she used with all her paying guests, but in this case she believed that if she had the woman's friendship and confidence, Tierney would surely reveal her plans for Gable House. Open up about her reason for being in Pass Creek, whatever it was. And in the process, like picking nutmeats, she might discover if Tierney had anything at all to do with Otis Peek's demise.

Tierney, impeccably dressed but wan under her attractive sun hat, sipped her tea. She looked up at Celia, then around at the park-like setting. "You've been very kind, a wonderful hostess and I find your inn peaceful and comfortable. It must be a lot of work, though, for a woman alone."

"It is, but I have Lilly's help doing up the rooms, and she stands in for me occasionally at the desk. Lilly's husband, Mac, comes each week to mow the lawn, care for the flower beds, and keep the creek and waterfall clean of debris. When time allows, I love getting my hand in with the flowers. Those in planters are my doing." She nodded to where Freebie lay curled up asleep in the sun near her pots of fragrant petunias. Celia prayed her neighbor's dachshunds stayed away, for all their sakes.

"Have you lived here long?" Tierney asked.

Celia smiled to herself, *Yay, we're talking!* She explained as they ate, "We'd only been married a few months when my husband Ethan inherited this six-acre property from his aunt. He took over the *Pass Creek Chronicle* as editor and publisher. I fell in love with the house and town the minute I arrived. Except for when he died, I've been happy here."

"Pass Creek is—such a small town." Tierney's manicured fingers tamed the white tablecloth when a warm breeze riffled it. "Peaceful, as I mentioned, and picturesque. But is that—enough?"

"Well, yes!" Celia answered, wondering why Tierney was here if a small town wasn't to her liking. She explained her own feelings. "Ethan and I weren't fortunate enough to have children, and Pass Creek residents became our family over the years." She laughed softly, "I've gotten to know most folks in town and from farms around really well. I know how and where they live, I've heard their family histories. Maybe I know them too well, as I've also been exposed to their problems, heartaches, downfalls and foolish mistakes. But no, luckily I get in on their good days, their accomplishments, too. Do you have family, Tierney?" She tinkled the ice in her glass and took a bite of sandwich as she waited.

The woman sighed, as though reluctant to answer, but finally said, "No family, no, not anymore. I lost my husband, Joe, last year. He died peacefully in his sleep. He was seven years older than I, the love of my life and I miss him."

"That's how it was with my Ethan and me," Celia declared, her glance meeting Tierney's eyes in understanding. "I loved him so much. I really came undone when he died. Only in the last year have I felt restored to the living, realizing that I'm going to make it after all."

"Do you think you'll marry again then?"

She shook her head. "It doesn't look that way. I've had opportunities since Ethan died, going out a few times with men who were likable enough and nice guys." She nibbled a slice of cucumber that had fallen to her plate from her sandwich. Locke Vinson, long-time business acquaintance of hers and Ethan's, had asked her to marry him. From the get-go she'd known Locke wasn't her type. He'd been pretty persistent. As much as she regretted having to hurt him, she was more than relieved to be shed of his attentions.

Her women friends here in Pass Creek were constantly trying to set her up with a visiting relative or friend. "No spark with any of them," she told Tierney, "and compared to what I had with Ethan, I doubt they'd measure up in the long run. It wouldn't be fair to get involved in a relationship, be disappointed, and hurt the guy when I wanted out."

"Maybe you weren't ready when you dated these fellows?"

"That, too, but I doubt I ever will be."

Ellie's urging her to go after Jake came to mind, making Celia fidget and she repeated, "No, I just can't imagine it." She and Jake would never work. They had little in common, were as different as day from night. She liked small town life, he preferred the open road. She was steady as a grounded rock, he was a rolling stone. Even if they were interested in one another, the gap was too wide to ever bridge. "How about you, Tierney, will you remarry?"

"No. That's all done." There was a long silence before she continued. "No man would want a wreck like me. But you, Celia, you're still healthy, very attractive and vital. You could have years of a second wonderful marriage. In your shoes, I'd give love another whirl."

Like a ghost, Jake's image appeared at the table, grinning down at her. Celia closed her eyes and begged the handsome apparition to vanish. This was ridiculous! And how did the focus get changed to her and men, anyway? Her mind scurried to the subject this meeting was intended for, then she carefully asked, "Where did you and Joe live? Was it somewhere here in Oregon, in the Willamette Valley?" *Where are you from? Why are you here? Who are you? Could you possibly have some connection to old Peek's death? Are you the one who knocked me flat?*

Celia held her breath and silently prayed Tierney would open up.

"Joe and I didn't live in Oregon. We lived in California for a long time, and other places."

"How did you meet? Were you schoolmates? Did you grow up together?" Celia prodded.

"No, we met much later. My passion as a young woman was dancing..." For an instant she might not have been in Celia's backyard. Her eyes had a faraway look. "I was fairly good at it, and was a member of a troupe in Seattle in my younger years. On vacation in California, I met Joe Jones. He ran a talent agency. He encouraged my dancing and helped me get roles as an extra in several movie musicals."

"You knew Clark Gable!" Celia nearly spewed tea, and she snatched up a napkin to blot her lips. If Tierney had known him personally her attitude about Gable House might start to make sense.

"No, I never met him. Did he make musicals? I don't remember. But I was never in any of his pictures."

Celia had difficulty hiding her disappointment. She'd been certain she was about to make a connection between Gable House and Tierney—finally have some answers. Something to build on so she could dissuade Tierney from getting rid of Gable House, if that's what she really planned. Still, Tierney was talking, and she wanted that to continue. There might be a clue yet. If not this time, she'd still enjoy Tierney's story. "Did you travel a lot, you and Joe? I'm always fascinated by the lives of my guests, their work, things they've done and seen."

Tierney brushed at a strand of golden hair that blew onto her cheek. "Yes, we traveled the world. My Joe was very smart." She clearly liked talking about the love of her life. "And he invested wisely in real estate. We were lucky enough to own homes in Seattle and Hawaii. Life was a ball with Joe. We were hands-on owners of a rancho in Mexico for a few years and spent a lot of time on horseback. I loved being his partner." Her eyes were shiny with tears and she shook her head. "Two lifetimes weren't enough for all we wanted to do in places we wanted to experience." She laughed softly. "Of all things, we owned a gold mine in Colorado, besides several properties in California."

"My goodness, I'm impressed!"

"Well, we were lucky as I said, and it wasn't all glamour. Many years we worked hard renovating houses and apartment buildings."

"Oh." Celia sat back, her hand to her mouth. *This was it.* "You're going to renovate Gable House, make changes, then sell?"

Tierney frowned and shook her head, "Not at all!"

"What then, Tierney?" Celia sat forward with a frown, unable to dally another second. "Are you going to stay in Pass Creek and live in the house?" she demanded to know.

Tierney hesitated, resenting the pressure Celia was putting on her. Finally she relented. "I considered it briefly. I've been looking for a quiet place to spend my final years. I—I knew about Pass Creek and your 'Gable House'. My original plan was to buy the house and preserve it in memory of someone special to me."

"*And?*" Celia was about to come to pieces. She refrained from throwing a plate on the ground and stomping it, and instead said as calmly as possible, "Please go on, Tierney."

"I've seen the house, the town and—I've changed my mind. As I see it, the acre and a half the house stands on could be put to better use. I intend to demolish the house, burn it down."

Celia stood up, mouth gaping, her lawn chair tumbling over on the ground. She couldn't have been more shocked at the blunt announcement, despite the fact that Tierney had said something to this effect from the start. No use to hope it had been just talk. Today, the woman's manner and words showed she was dead serious in her intentions.

Chapter Six

"You can't mean it, Tierney. Surely you wouldn't destroy that lovely old house and its history. Please, tell me you don't really mean this."

"But I do."

"Why? Does it have something to do with old Mr. Peek? The fact he was maybe murdered?"

Tierney dropped her iced tea spoon, her eyes wide in surprise. Celia reminded herself that at one time, however, Tierney Jones was a professional actress.

"You suspect my wanting to do away with the house has something to do with Mr. Peek, the previous owner? And you're telling me there's a possibility he was murdered? That's horrible, but it has nothing to do with me or my plans." Her hand shook as she reached for her glass.

"But the house—why would you want it destroyed?"

"Sorry, dear. My reasons are private. The property belongs to me now, to do with as I wish." She rose from the table, gripping the edge to steady herself. "I need to retire to my room. The lunch was delicious, Celia, and I thank you. I enjoyed our conversation." Her smile was bittersweet. "Even though I was aware that you were trying to pump me for information." She caught Celia's hand. "There are things in my life I prefer *not* to talk about. Painful matters, Celia, which have been difficult enough to work through and try to forget. So forgive me if I can't give you what you want."

"I'm sorry. I didn't mean to pry." Of course she had intended to pry, with all her being. She'd just hoped not to create a fuss or give herself away, she thought guiltily. In any event, she should have been more cautious and considerate, should have remembered what Myrna said about the drawing on the napkin and Tierney's tears. Whatever Tierney Jones was hiding, Celia believed it was honestly painful to her. Best to back off for now, although that, unfortunately, left everything up in the air, unresolved.

Unless Jake remembered who this woman was from his past, if he'd actually known her. By the minute, Celia was growing convinced that Tierney had a closer connection to Pass Creek than she was revealing. A connection buried in yesterday. A connection that might or might not have something to do with Peek's unfortunate passing, which might prove to be murder.

Celia dialed Jake's office from her kitchen phone a short while later, but there was no answer. Evidently he hadn't yet found someone to take over for him in the office. Maybe he had a cell phone with him, but she still didn't have his number. Her fingers tapped the kitchen counter in a rapid *rat-a-tat-tat*. At the Heritage meeting she'd heard him talking about two or three farms outside town that were up for sale, besides a few houses in town. She had half a notion to go looking for him, but she'd probably not find him, and besides she had a tour to lead.

She left a message: "Jake, I need to talk to you. It's urgent."

It was hard to keep her mind on the job and fulfill her promise to the dozen tourists she'd grouped in front of the library a short while later. Today she wore an emerald green formal, probably made for a high school prom, but the closest she could come to Scarlet O'Hara in *Gone With The Wind*. Her "people," as Pete referred to them, were watching her expectantly, waiting, and she plunged in with a few words about Pass Creek's history, her usual opening for a tour:

"Welcome to Pass Creek, which, as you already know, is located in the lushly beautiful mid-Willamette Valley. Our town got its name when an early homesteader instructed another land-seeker to 'pass creek, thence on west three miles to the Santiam River where a ferry will carry team, wagon, and passengers to the other side.' He'd misunderstood the homesteader's directions and before he reached the river, he found three other families camped by the creek he was supposed to pass on by. He believed Pass Creek was the name of the spot. Some of the families were ill and didn't want to go any farther. They homesteaded where they were and a small community they named Pass Creek sprang up."

Her audience was delighted, and one of the men commented, "You'd have thought somebody would have wised up and changed the name of the town after they realized the mistake."

"You would think so," Celia agreed, "and early on some residents did want to name our town 'Douglas,' for the Scottish botanist, David Douglas. He discovered many plants in our area, including native tobacco. There is a story that in November 1826, he swam the cold, swollen Santiam River just west of Pass Creek. He thought little of the danger, but was very upset that his precious collection of plants got soaked in the crossing."

Celia faced the library, nodding toward the simple cottage-style building.

"Let me tell you now the story of our library." Her words came automatically, while her mind roved over everything going wrong in Pass Creek at the moment: *Gable House sold. Otis Peek possibly murdered, and the murderer could be a neighbor. And where the heck was Jake Flagg today, when she needed to talk to him?* "Our beloved library began as the home of a woman named Mary Wallace who, at age fourteen in 1860, rode a mule bareback to Oregon. She settled here in this spot. At the time this was open land and became her farm. She was a saving person, hard-working and a successful farmer. She lived modestly in her home, which had no indoor plumbing or furnace. Although well-off, you could not have picked her out in a crowd. She was thrifty because she did not want to outlive her fortune as had some of her family and close friends. When she died in 1941, she had willed her house and personal library of hundreds of rare books to the community of Pass Creek. Now follow me inside the library, where you'll see a painting of a small, timid-looking woman, the one and only Mary Wallace."

As they later continued the tour along main-street, Celia kept an eye out to see if Jake had returned to the Flagg Realty office. There was no sign of his Dodge pickup out front. For all she knew, he could've taken off for the open road, leaving a *For Sale* sign on the realty itself!

With effort, she stayed focused on the rest of her tour and flew home when it was finished. There were messages on the answering machine, none from Jake. Just as she decided to jump in her car and go looking for him, the phone rang.

"What's up?" he barked.

"Goodness, what's wrong with you? Why so cranky?"

"Lost a sale. Sorry, Celia, go ahead. What's on your mind?"

She got to the point. "I'm the one should be snarly, Jake. Just listen—Tierney Jones is going to burn down Gable House, probably as soon as the chief finishes his investigation into Peek's death. It wasn't just an empty remark she made when I was showing the house to her and the tour group that day. Truthfully, I could wring your neck for selling her the house!"

"Whoa, wait a minute. First off, I thought we were getting to be friends. You don't throttle a friend—you accept that he had to do what he did. Second, what's that about *burning* the house? The Jones woman said that's what she wants to do? You're sure?"

"She said it right to my face, Jake, and she meant it. I

can't get her to say any more than that, so the rest is up to you."

"Really? I'll be damned. Up to *me*?" There were several seconds of silence, and then he said, "Can we meet for dinner so you can bawl me out some more? It's been a couple days and I really miss you raking me over the coals."

She fought a smile even as she snapped, "This is not funny, but we do need to talk. The Mellow Mushroom in about twenty minutes?'

"I'll be there with armor on."

"Smart aleck!" She put the phone down and went to change her dress, fix her hair—and try some of her new "Cashmere Mist" Donna Karan perfume.

Under other circumstances, the soft lighting and romantic background music in the Mellow Mushroom might have convinced Celia she was on a date with Jake. But this wasn't a date, and it was best to keep that in mind. The matter of Gable House and Tierney Jones demanded attention—and that was only the beginning. As they settled in to talk, sipping wine, they went over again the chief's conversation with Celia and the possibility that Otis Peek's death might have been intentional, a homicide.

"If so," Jake said, "Peek's relatives are going to be shocked. I've kind of got to know them, discussing sale of the house. They've been nice folks to deal with—long distance."

"Back to the subject of *the house* and *the new owner*." Celia spoke dryly as she tore a piece of roll, buttered and ate it. "More and more I think Tierney has a specific, past connection to Gable House. If we could get to the bottom of that, I think we could solve a lot of things—saving Gable House in the process." She forked a bite of salmon and waited for his response.

He shrugged. "Maybe her saying early on that the property could be put to better use was nothing more than a simple opinion. But now the stink of crime is her reason to level the house."

"I'm afraid you're wrong. She mentioned burning the

house *before* I told her about Peek. Plus, she seemed genuinely surprised when she heard he might have been murdered." She was thoughtful for a moment. "I wonder if there's something about the house she doesn't want anyone to know, and she wants to be rid of the place before they find out?"

"Or," Jake said, taking a sip of coffee, "it's possible she has no connection to Peek at all, and there's nothing sinister involved." His eyebrows rose, emphasizing as he looked at her that he considered Celia's concern a hullabaloo over nothing. "It could be that she simply doesn't see the house the same way you and others do, Celia. Doesn't see it as a 'historic wonder.' Clark Gable and his fame may mean zip to her, and I doubt she'd be alone in that." He ignored Celia's sharp glare and continued, "Maybe she wants to build another mansion twice as big, or a business of some sort. Pass Creek could use a new industry." His voice rose and he circled the air with his empty fork. "Maybe she just wants the acreage to stake out a cow or two. Who knows? It's her property now."

"Darn you, Jake Flagg! She's too emotional over it to just want a place to stake out a cow!" Celia shook her head, furious. "Or establish an industry—badly as we need it."

"Sorry. Don't get upset. You're serious, and I have no right to be flippant." After a moment of silence, his hand reached over and smothered hers, the gesture calculated to be calming. It was.

In fact it felt—wonderful. In Jake's face she saw a reflection of how she was all at once feeling—goofy, dizzy, warm inside. Her throat went dry when she tried to say something. Her face felt hot. What was this? An attraction blooming between them right out of left field? *The last thing she needed or wanted.* She withdrew her hand from under his and put in her lap, safe. "This is business," she reminded him in a thin voice.

It was as if he looked inside her, and he *knew*. This

moment between them was anything but business. Still, he said with a twisted grin, "Right. We need to talk about the Gable thing and the Jones woman." He cleared his throat and sat back, gazing at her. "I've tried remembering who Tierney Jones might be, if I really did know her from somewhere sometime. There could be a lot changed about her besides her name. I can't figure out our mystery woman any more than you can, Celia, and I've tried."

"You have to keep trying, and remember in time to stop her from doing such a heinous thing as burning down Gable House—or committing another murder, if she was the one who did away with Mr. Peek. No." She shook her head at the questioning expression on his face. "I've wracked my brain for a motive, something about the house that gave her reason to kill him, but I've come up empty. Chief Erdman is determined to get to the bottom of this mess. No matter what, I intend to save Gable House and do what I must to stop her from burning it to the ground."

"This is her right if that's what she wants to do, as long as it's managed safely by the fire department so that the fire doesn't get out of hand and damage other buildings."

How could he say such a thing? "Burn down that treasure, Jake?" Tears stung Celia's eyes and she didn't wait for an answer. "Besides their fine architecture, the likes of which will never be again, Pass Creek's old houses have heart and soul. That's why I enjoy telling their stories. I speak for the houses, and I'd like to see them stand into infinity."

"Sorry." His hand reached for hers again.

She pulled it away and told him, "Even if Clark Gable hadn't lived there, even if there's been a killing on the premises, it doesn't make sense to get rid of that wonderful old house. I wish I could have bought it, or the Heritage Club could have raised the funds in time."

There was a softening in his expression, mixed with guilt,

and he pulled a clean handkerchief from his pocket for her tears. "You're blaming me again, ever the rotten skunk for selling the place to Tierney Jones."

"Sorry, but that's how it plays." She wiped her eyes, blew her nose and returned his handkerchief. She motioned him to continue with his meal. "I hate all this wrangling. So—I'll drop the subject for now."

He looked relieved and with renewed relish, he tucked into his steak and mushrooms. Celia almost felt sorry for him. She forced herself to think of something else. "We don't have to talk at all, but it you want to, I'd like to hear about your day."

He nodded, ate for a while, and a few minutes later told her about a large mint farm south of town that the owner had listed with him and that he'd been showing all day to prospective buyers.

She told him, "I love the smell of mint when it's crushed and steaming, truck loads of it on the way to being mint oil for toothpaste and candies."

"I like it, too. But mint is being phased out as a crop in these parts in favor of other row crops—strawberries, raspberries, marionberries, and the like."

Talk of farming led to discussion of the beautiful weather they were having. They talked about Jake's desperate need for office help, with Celia saying she might be able to find the right person for the job. She told him in detail about her picnic lunch with Tierney Jones. "She's a fascinating woman, a talented dancer in her time. A world traveler who, with her husband, was very successful in a variety of business ventures."

"Like me, huh?" he wisecracked. "Ranch hand, surveyor for a while, game warden, bull rider—I won a silver belt buckle in that last venture."

"Wow," she said with a teasing smile.

"Listen, with any job, I was hardly ever out of beans and coffee! Most of the time I had a few coins to jingle in my pockets, buy dinner for the ladies."

"You sound like a *great* success." Celia chuckled.

For a long time, she looked at him, studying him, her hand propping her chin while Jake dug into his berry pie ala mode.

It was really odd, but she was beginning to realize that Jake's sense of humor was a whole lot like Ethan's had been—quirky, cute, boyish, never hurtful. Honest. She liked it—liked him, truth be told.

When he walked her home, she said, "I hope I didn't spoil your evening, Jake, but this thing with Tierney Jones isn't over. We have to keep working on it and come up with answers, soon."

"I felt like a beast, making you cry." He gave her a lopsided grin. "But you're pretty cute with your eyes all shiny with tears and your nose drippy."

She had to laugh and shook her head.

He continued, "And I'll stay in this thing about Gable House as long as it keeps me in your company. You're a special woman, Celia, but you must already know that."

"Hearing it from you is—nice," she admitted as they touched hands in parting. For a long moment they looked at one another. He gave her mouth a quick brush of a kiss, waved and walked off down the street. Celia willed her heart to be still, or heaven knew she was going to suffocate.

For the next several days, she used time she really couldn't spare and pored over her historical notes, old newspapers and high school yearbooks, searching for mention of someone named Tierney. She had no luck, which didn't mean a lot. Jones was Tierney's married name, to a Californian, and she could have changed her first name. Possibly it was the name she took when she had dancing parts in movies? She could ask, but she had the feeling that would delve too close to whatever it was Tierney was hiding and refused to discuss. There had to be other means to learn what she needed to know.

Chapter Seven

Giving up her own Tierney Jones search for the moment, Celia went to Jake's office, and finding him in, plopped a stack of school yearbooks on his desk.

"What're those?" He looked aghast at the books piled on the mess on his desk next to his computer. He waved her to a chair.

"It's just a hunch," she said, sitting down, "but I think Tierney Jones might've lived here at one time and was in the school system. She's about our age, I think, although poor health makes her seem older. Maybe you went to school with Tierney, and that's why she looks familiar."

"She hasn't said she's from here."

"She hasn't said a lot of things!" Celia smacked the edge of his desk. "But Jake, we have to get to the bottom of this, quick as we can. Look at these and maybe a familiar face will pop out, a younger version of Tierney. Please."

"We're talking a whole lot younger! A lifetime has passed since I was in high school in this little burg. And besides, I don't have time to go through this stuff. Is it right, anyhow, to poke our noses into the woman's private business? Dig out who she might be, or was, in the past, when she might not want it known?"

Celia remained firm. "You may be right. But Pass Creek is *my* business, and the business of our other citizens. We're trying to save what is vital to our town, as we should." She was thoughtful a second, then told him, "On top of that, I think there's opportunity to help Tierney heal from whatever is bothering her. She's going to need a friend if it turns out Peek was murdered and she's a suspect but didn't do it."

"Okay, you *Rebel With a Cause*." He clapped a hand on the stack of books. "Why don't you look through them and see if you can find a photo of someone that could be Mrs. Jones? You're a woman. You can do that better than I can."

"I did look through them, until my eyes nearly fell out. I wouldn't ask you to do it without trying myself first. I didn't find her, but that doesn't mean you couldn't." A smile hovered at the corners of her mouth. "I found your picture, Jake. Class of 1979. You looked kind of geeky back then." He was so much handsomer now.

"It was a geeky time, Celia. Most of us have changed a lot." He studied the papers on his desk a moment, his head in his hands. "Look at this mess. What'm I supposed to do? I've gotta find someone to handle the office, but so far no one has jumped at the job. Not anyone capable of handling the work, anyhow. I've had some grannies apply and even Mrs. Kemp, who claims she changed my diapers. A sweetheart, she is, but a hundred and ten if she's a day." He scowled. "A couple high school girls who chain smoke and can barely spell their names came in to apply. *Phew!*"

Celia was sympathetic. "The girl who was Ellie's assistant was supposed to be your office help. But she ran off and got married the minute your brother Caxton and Ellie were out of sight. I'll find someone for you, Jake, if you'll just look at the yearbooks. Please?" She pushed the books toward him. "If this doesn't work, we'll try something else."

"If this doesn't work, I'll have wasted my valuable time," he growled. "Now, Celia, as much as I enjoy your lovely presence, I really have a lot to do."

The kiss she jokingly blew him from outside his window

was meant to aggravate him. But she saw him jump up from his desk and hurry to the door. He called after her loud enough for everyone on the street to hear, "You want kissin'? Come on back!"

Her step speeded up and her face turned hot. Male laughter rang out from the direction of the hardware store across the street where a trio of men stood talking. She paid them no further attention and faced straight ahead. "What nonsense did I start, anyway?" she whispered into the warm afternoon.

~~~

"The little sweetheart is a wonder! I can't thank you enough for sending Salliebeth to me," Jake's baritone drummed over the phone into Celia's ear.

At her study desk, Celia nodded, smiled, opened her mouth to speak and again gave up trying to get a word in edgewise. She rubbed the tip of her nose, listened and waited. She was glad he liked Salliebeth. After all, who wouldn't? But there were more serious matters to discuss, blame it!

His voice had a "rodeo action note" as he announced, "She's updated and cleaned out files! Created a snappier website for the company! Hey, make sure you check the website out, and tell everybody! She's given me some ideas for generating real estate leads at social and business functions. Oh, my," he rumbled, "I tell you, she's just great."

Out of chute number nine, a strawberry roan…!

Celia had heard something like that on television one time.

"Yes, Jake. Salliebeth is very smart and capable," she said, grabbing an opening. "I knew you'd like her and that she'd be a big help." Her friend was one of the nicest people in Pass Creek: pretty, sweet, giving, and in her late thirties still single. For years she was her invalid mother's caretaker. Following Mrs. Parker's death a year and a half ago, Salliebeth had picked up numerous skills as a volunteer at the library and working one odd job after another around town. But what Salliebeth wanted most, Celia knew, was to fall in love, marry, and have children.

For a second, Celia had a vision of Jake and Salliebeth walking down the aisle in their wedding best, a fairy-cloud of white around them. She slapped her temple, chasing the picture into nothingness.

"In just a couple weeks, Salliebeth has turned this office around," Jake was saying. "And her being here to take care of everything allows me more time in the field with clients. For the moment she's out to lunch, so I'm hanging here for a few more minutes." He chuckled. "The busy little honey bee even suggested I trade my old pickup for a nicer car to escort buyers when showing homes. Don't know if I'm ready to do that, but she's probably right."

Dear heaven! The way Jake carried on. *Little sweetheart. Honey bee.* He could be falling arse over teakettle in love with Salliebeth and not even know it. A stab of jealousy caused Celia to groan with shame. She thumped a book on her desk too hard, jerked her forefinger back in pain and put it in her mouth.

Sensing a second of silence at the other end of the line, she plunged in. "Jake, have you looked at the school yearbooks I left with you?"

"The what?"

Her lips pursed and she shook her head. Clearly, it was hard for him to take his mind off the wonders of Salliebeth.

"The high school yearbooks, remember? You were going to search the photos to see if Tierney Jones might be someone you went to school with."

"Oh, yeah, I'll get to it."

At the other end of the line, Celia could hear him greeting Salliebeth warmly as she returned to the office from lunch.

With one hand holding the phone to her ear and her chin resting on the knuckles of the other, Celia was considering hanging up without saying goodbye when an odd sound made her look toward the open door of her study. Tierney Jones, in nightgown and robe, pale and mumbling strangely, clutched the doorjamb.

"Oh, dear God!" Celia cried out as Tierney crumpled to the floor.

At the stricken note in her voice, Jake demanded from the phone, "Celia, what's wrong? Celia!"

She clutched the phone and shoved back from the desk, "It's Tierney Jones. She's just collapsed here in my study. I have to help her, I'm calling nine-one-one."

"I'll be right there!"

Celia was on the floor beside Tierney, taking her pulse and prepared to do CPR when Tierney's eyes fluttered open and she tried to get up. "Don't move," Celia cautioned. "Just breathe and relax. Emergency medical technicians are on the way. How do you feel? You had your hand to your chest. Are you having pain, Tierney?" She held Tierney's hand, and stroked her cheek, her own heart crowding into her throat.

"Only—a little. Must be-be the flu," she said, her voice thin. "Haven't been able to keep my food down. I came downstairs for a pot of tea. G-got dizzy. Sorry I caused this fuss." She struggled again to raise her shoulders from the floor.

Celia gently pushed her back. "There's nothing to be sorry about. Please lie still until the EMTs check you over."

The next several minutes passed in a blur of efficient action. The EMTs arrived and after taking Tierney's vitals and asking questions about her heart and her meds, they administered oxygen and prepared to take her to the hospital in Adkins. Tierney tried to protest, but the medical technicians insisted. "As a precaution, Mrs. Jones," the blue-uniformed young man told her with gentle authority. "You were light-headed, and that needs to be seen to." Taking great care, he and a female technician lifted Tierney onto a gurney.

"You think she had a heart attack?" Celia questioned

them.

"That's for the doctor to determine," the female technician answered, covering Tierney with a blanket and motioning for them to move out.

Jake had arrived and stood close to Celia, his arm circling her. A distant part of her brain sensed his strength and without thinking, she leaned into the crook of his arm while the EMTs wheeled the gurney to the emergency vehicle parked at the curb outside the inn.

Celia's voice shook, "I-I have to get my car. I want to g-go to the hospital, make sure she's all—all right." Now that professionals had taken over, she was quivery as jelly inside.

"I'll drive you." Jake gave her a squeeze.

"That's not necessary." She suddenly realized she was cuddled against him, and she stumbled away in surprise. "I'll be fine in a second or two, really." Even as she protested, she knew she'd feel better with him along. "But if you want to go," she said, giving in, "let me get some of her personal things from her room she might need at the hospital, and I'll meet you at the car. Lilly is in the laundry room. I'll tell her to watch the inn."

They spent hours, a seeming eternity, in the hospital waiting room before a doctor came to tell them results of tests and Tierney's condition. It surprised Celia to hear that it wasn't Tierney's heart at fault for today's collapse, but weakening from food poisoning.

"Food poisoning? But from where? How?"

"We're not sure but we hope to find out. Right now it appears it's from something she ate, possibly mushrooms in an omelet she had yesterday for breakfast, or from seafood at dinner at a restaurant. Because Mrs. Jones' overall health is somewhat fragile, we'd like to keep her here a few days for observation and treatment."

"May I see her?" Celia stood up. Besides the concern she would feel for any resident of her inn, there was a blossoming friendship between her and Tierney. A friendship with scary baggage, but right now Celia wanted to put that aside.

The doctor nodded. "A few minutes, then she needs rest. We've moved her from ICU to a room."

Celia nodded and followed him, bracing to face the ill woman.

"They won't let me stay long," she said, holding Tierney's pale hand in both of hers as they talked about what had happened. "The doctor wants to take good care of you."

"I really don't feel that bad. Just a little sick at my stomach and tired."

"I'm sorry if it's anything you had to eat or drink at the inn that's the cause, Tierney. I intend to check out everything in the refrigerator and cupboards. I can't have my guests falling ill on my account."

"It's not your fault, dear. These hospital people are just overly cautious. I'm sure this is just a touch of flu that's got me down, and not even food poisoning."

"Maybe, maybe not. Regardless, let the doctors and nurses take care of you and make you better." Preparing to leave, Celia told her, "I'll be back to see you. Have a nurse call if there's anything at all you need." She squeezed Tierney's fingers. "You have a home back at Landrey's Inn as soon as you're able."

"Thank you, Celia. I think I'll sleep a bit. Go home now with your fellow."

"Do get some sleep." *Her fellow?*

In the car returning to Pass Creek, long moments of silence were finally broken when Jake said, "I know who she is."

"Who who is?" Then it dawned on Celia that he meant Tierney. She sat up straighter and turned to him, grabbing his arm. "You know who Tierney really is? You remember her?"

"I think so." He noted her hand on his arm with a grin, his expression changing when she placed her hand back in her lap. Eyes on the traffic and his tone serious, he said, "Seeing the lady with her hair down and not wearing makeup, vulnerable, scared, made her seem all the more familiar. She's changed about a hundred percent from a plain, chubby high school girl into a beautiful older woman. Brunette to blonde, and maybe some face work done, but I'm fairly certain she is Willeen."

"Willeen?" A name as odd as Tierney, Celia reflected.

"Willeen Monro. She was in a class a couple years ahead of me, a quiet girl who didn't stand out, didn't run with the *in* crowd. If I remember correctly, there was some kind of accident to her family, and she was left alone. After high school graduation that year, she disappeared and I never saw her again."

Chapter Eight

Celia was stunned into silence for several seconds then said, "I want to find her in the yearbooks. I want to be sure before I talk to her about any of this. And of course I have to give her time to get better."

Jake and Celia sat at her kitchen table that evening with the yearbooks spread in front of them. It didn't take long to find a girl's photo and the name Willeen Monro below it, in the yearbook when Jake would have been a high school sophomore. Celia stared at it long and hard. The shape of the face was the same. She silently catalogued the features: forehead and hairline, shape of the eyes, the nose, mouth, and chin, the same! "I don't think she's had cosmetic surgery at all. I believe this poor mousy little girl is our Tierney Jones! Time, a good life, knowledge of cosmetics, and money to spend has made the difference."

"I'll be darned."

Jake's further words disappeared as Celia stretched from her chair to abruptly catch his face in her hands and lightly kiss his mouth. "Thank you, Jake. Thank you, thank you."

What she'd done automatically and without thinking startled Celia. To the same degree it seemed to delight Jake, considering his expression. Her face heated with embarrassment. Kissing a man since Ethan's death was rare behavior for her and although it felt awfully good, it was a foolish thing to have done. She was just so happy to finally know Tierney's real identity.

This could mean everything to saving Gable House. Saving Tierney, maybe, to boot.

"May I say 'you're welcome' with a kiss back?" Jake was grinning devilishly, eager as a pup at the dinner plate, his hands on her shoulders.

"I'll take your word for it." She removed his hands, held one of them a moment. "I'm sorry, but we can't do this." *There was Salliebeth to remember, for one thing. If anyone had dibs on Jake, it should be Salliebeth.* "We need to keep our minds on the mystery of Willeen Monro, alias Tierney. Did you know her family, Jake? What do you remember? Try hard."

He grudgingly agreed. "I didn't know her family directly, but I believe besides her mother and father, she had a younger brother. I think the three of them were killed in an accident, a car accident." He studied the photo. "It's hard to believe she could change so much, but I'm sure the lady we know as Tierney is Willeen. From what you've told me, she lived a pretty good life after leaving Pass Creek. I'm glad for her."

"I am, too. I just wish she wasn't so bent on destroying Gable House, providing she still feels the same about the place."

A few days later, Celia prepared a tray with a lavender napkin, her best silverware and violet-patterned china. Tierney's doctors wanted Tierney to keep to her bed for a few days longer once she was back at the inn, to assure full recovery.

Celia poured steaming tea in the small cup, placed buttered toast on the plate, and added a small dish of blackberry jam and hurried upstairs to Tierney's reclaimed room. Tierney was sitting up in bed, a pillow across her lap to hold the tray. She cleared her throat. "You're so good to me, Celia. I can't tell you how glad I am to be back here and not in the hospital, although the doctors tell me you were right to call the EMTs."

"You'd have done the same for me, and it was no trouble," Celia smiled. "You're looking better today. There's a nice color to your cheeks, Tierney." *Willeen.* "Now, is there anything else I can get you, maybe some fresh water to take your meds?" Moments later she was back in the room with the water. It pleased her to see that Tierney was eating with a show of appetite, and she commented on the fact.

Tierney looked up, a smear of jam on her attractive lips, "Celia, dear, your homemade wheat bread with blackberry jam is manna for the gods. For years I've watched my diet like a hawk, and I still take care not to be a glutton for wrong foods, but I believe it is okay to splurge a bit once in a while. Don't you?"

"Emphatically. What would life be without a nice thick slice of toast with jam now and then?"

"Exactly. And I want to get strong and back on my feet. I don't care to feel so weak and . . . out of it. Besides, if I can't enjoy food in my autumn years, then when?" She laughed softly.

"You have a beautiful figure, Tierney. And right now getting your strength back is the important thing." Celia meant her words sincerely. But she also thought that if Tierney were stronger, she might better handle her hostility—if that's what it was—against Gable House. And if the heavens were rightly aligned, she might also have a change of heart about its existence.

"I used to be the chubbiest, plainest child you'd ever see," Tierney spoke up. She hesitated, and Celia thought that was the end of it until she continued. "But that didn't stop me from fantasizing about becoming a *world-renowned* dancer." She sipped her tea and gave Celia a half-smile. "Back then, you see, I idolized my high school drama coach. He was easily the most important person in my universe." She shrugged, straightened the front of her satin bed jacket and winked. "I even had a bit of a crush on him."

Celia, smiling, took the bedside chair, prepared to remain a few moments longer.

"One day I told my coach my dream of being a great dancer. I'd follow in the footsteps of Martha Graham, the mother of modern dance—a secret I would never have shared with anyone but him. I was positive he'd be supportive." A flare of anger and pain touched her eyes. "He laughed. It was impossible for him to hide his amusement, and I was hurt to the core."

Celia leaned forward in her chair to lay her hand on Tierney's arm in sympathy.

"The more I tried to convince him that I was truly serious about dancing and believed I was destined for 'great things,'" Tierney continued, "the more he urged me to 'be myself' and not set myself up for certain disappointment. He assured me I had a bit of talent for acting. There was no reason why I couldn't take roles in community plays and the like to satisfy my desire for performing. But surely I was aware that I was too clumsy, too awkward, to be a successful dancer. Not to mention that my weight was against my chances."

"He was a rat," Celia said with certainty. "Being a teen is difficult enough without a trusted idol stepping all over our dreams."

Tierney nodded agreement and took on a deep, masculine-sounding voice, "No, no, Willeen, dear, you'd be better off in secretarial work, or as a bank clerk, with performing kept as a hobby."

Celia's breath caught, and she tried not to show her excitement at Tierney's slip. "He really was blind and unkind, wasn't he?" She added cautiously, "You said, 'Willeen.' Your drama coach called you 'Willeen?'" *And did any of what she was hearing about a drama coach, about dance, chubbiness, and a person's dream, have anything to do with Gable House? Or Peek's undoing there, for that matter?*

"Terrible name, isn't it? I took my grandmother's maiden name, *Tierney*, when I went out on my own. One of the first things I fell in love with about my husband was his simple name, *Joe Jones*." She heaved a deep sigh and looked Celia straight in the eye. "I can tell by your suddenly careful manner and the look on your face, Celia, the jig is up. You've figured out who I am. My fault for spouting my real name, and yours, my dear, for making me so comfortable in your company that I wasn't more careful. I suppose you know more about me than my name?"

"Jake Flagg thought he might have known you in the past. We found your picture in an old yearbook. He told me a little bit about your family, what happened to them. I'm terribly sorry, Tierney. It must have been a terrible thing for you to lose them in the accident, to be left alone when you were so young."

Tierney's expression turned solemn. "What happened hurts me still, although I do my best not to dwell on it." Her eyes sparkled with tears. She reached for a tissue from the box on her nightstand. "I can't think about their deaths, about that time, without going to pieces. I enjoy talking with you, Celia, but let's not go there, please."

"Of course. You needn't talk about anything that's painful or stressful for you. The doctors want you to take it easy."

Celia started to her feet, her hands outstretched to take the tray, thinking the poor woman wanted to be alone, but Tierney motioned her back into her chair. "Stay another minute or two, please."

She had a million tasks needing her attention, but she sat back down.

With Celia's encouragement, Tierney continued with the more pleasant details of her life: how she applied herself to prove her drama coach wrong as she studied ballet and tap, paying for lessons and later college by work as a bank clerk in Seattle. "I'd made myself over," she told Celia, "into a completely new person by the time I met Joe. I was no longer the plain chubby girl. Dance and swimming competitively had made me slim and trim."

"You should be very proud of your accomplishments. It's not easy to rise above pain such as your drama coach caused you." *Or, even more so, the loss of your family.* Celia added, "Thank goodness that with time the sharp edges of pain are softened, even if we never forget."

That's how it was for her since losing Ethan and making a new life for herself. Slowly but surely, things got better and were improving still, with only a hurdle or two cropping up now and then. Like Gable House and Tierney's plans to get rid of it—she still meant to prevent that happening. Like the attraction she was feeling toward Jake Flagg. Emotions that felt like a disease needing a cure—and soon, before she made a fool of herself over him.

Tierney had again relaxed as she talked, smiling at her memories. Celia wanted to bring up serious matters like Gable House and probable murder, but didn't have the heart at the moment. But she was going to, soon. For one thing, Tierney's living here years ago meant that she also knew Otis Peek back then, or at least knew of him. Like the chief said, it was odd that Otis took his fall about the same time Tierney came to visit the town. When Tierney's eyelids began to flutter and her voice turned drowsy, Celia gave her a pat and suggested a catnap.

She was back downstairs only a short time when the inn's doorbell chimed. Her heart gave a start, thinking it might be Jake. Then she remembered that it was more likely the couple who had called late last evening to ask if she had a vacancy and were here to see the Alcott room.

Her *welcome to Landrey's Inn* speech stilled on her lips when she opened the door. *Jake.* Her foolish heart went bonkers, and a flush of joy warmed every inch of her body. He stood there with his Stetson held against his chest, a frown furrowing his forehead. "How is the patient?" he asked. "And how are you?"

"T-Tierney"—her tongue tripped—"is much better. She ate well this morning and is taking a nap." *As for me, I've not been right from the moment you showed up in town, Jake Flagg. To the point I hardly know myself anymore.*

She gathered strength to behave like a normal person, motioned for him to come in with a presence as cool as a cucumber—she hoped.

"I have a fresh pot of coffee on," she murmured, "and I have things to tell you. I believe we've started to crack the wall of mystery around here as far as Tierney's concerned. She has admitted she is Willeen Monroe, so that's settled. She lived here in Pass Creek as a young girl and although we haven't got to that yet, she would have known Otis Peek, surely. Not that that's proof she had anything with his death, but still..."

Chapter Nine

Celia pushed her grocery cart through Thrifty Market, stopping at the produce counter to sniff a cantaloupe for ripeness. She drew in the fruity fragrance, placed the melon with her other groceries and gave the cart a furthering push. Hearing the *tap, tap, tap,* of a cane coming up quickly behind her, and a quaking voice telling her to slow down, she turned with a smile. Mrs. Kemp, Jake's one-time babysitter, was out early this morning. Below a pink bow landed like a butterfly in her snowcap hair, her face was a sea of wrinkles clamped in a frown.

"What's the hurry, Celia Landrey? This ain't no Indy Five Hundred, I been racing after you since the bread aisle."

"Good morning, Mrs. Kemp. Sorry I didn't see you. I was trying to finish my shopping before my walking tour at ten this morning. Is there something I can do for you?"

"I been wanting to talk to you, Celia. Lots of strange goings on, like that yellow band the chief put up around Otis's place. Chief says he's investigating if Peek fell off the roof or was pushed or something. I don't know what."

"Yes, he's investigating, but I'm sure whatever happened it was an accident." *She was less sure with each day that passed but hated to admit the fact even to herself.*

"You'd think so, but there's plenty of people would like to've wrung Otis's neck more than once, you know. Oh, well, the truth of the matter will come out soon." She waved her hand, setting aside that subject. "Another thing. One of the church ladies saw an ambulance at your inn a while back. Word got around that your strange lady guest, Mrs. Jones with the funny first name, got took to the hospital. I never heard any more. Did she die?"

"No, Mrs. Kemp, she's very much alive. She had a touch of food poisoning, but she's coming along fine, resting a lot and getting her strength back."

The snowcap bobbed. "I thought she might've lived since I haven't heard nothing about a funeral. Well, that's good that she didn't die. Was it something you fed her that made her sick?"

Celia shook off a defensive feeling, although she was certain nothing she'd done had caused Tierney's sickness. "It isn't always easy to track down what causes a temporary stomach ailment. Could've been almost anything, although doctors concluded it wasn't a virus. Mrs. Jones takes most of her meals from the restaurant, but a thorough check hasn't found the source of the problem."

The elderly woman's brow furrowed. "You gotta be careful with raw meat, you know. That cola disease. Never know when poisons will jump out of food and take you just like that!" She waved her claw-like hands, launching into a long-winded story about a relative, who, years back, barely escaped death's door after eating bad pickles.

Celia only half listened. Mrs. Kemp had lived in Pass Creek a long, long time. When Celia had a chance to break in, she asked, "Mrs. Kemp, do you remember a family by the name of Monro living here in Pass Creek at one time? It would've been maybe thirty or so years ago, before I married Ethan and we came here to live."

"Did they eat something bad? Kill 'em, or did they live?"

"Nothing like that, I simply wondered…"

"Land, but you were the prettiest little new bride this town ever saw." Mrs. Kemp beamed. After a few seconds her mind seemed to snag a thought out of the air and she frowned. "But that ain't what you was asking about, is it?" She leaned on her cane, her faded blue eyes focused on a table of bagged potatoes as though the answer would be found there. Her head began to nod, and her mouth pursed with satisfaction.

"Sure do, now I think about it. Len Monro come here to work in the mill. His wife, Suzanne, was a quiet, sweet thing. They had a couple of young ones, but I don't remember their names right off. I sort of recall that an accident took most of the family 'cept a girl, and she didn't stay in Pass Creek. They'd lived here maybe ten or twelve years."

"Just where in town did they live while they were here? Do you remember?"

"Certain do. They lived in a little house south of town other side of Douglas Avenue." She motioned with her head. "Been painted so many times I can't recall what color it is, and new houses been cropping up around it for so long I don't know if you could find it. Well, I could, but I can't walk out that far. Anything else you need to know, Celia, for that history you been writing about Pass Creek, you let me know." She grasped Celia's arm.

"Thanks, Mrs. Kemp. I will." She wasn't thinking about her book when she'd asked about the Monro family, but who knew? When she found out more about them, it was possible they would be an interesting piece of Pass Creek history. She'd want Tierney's okay to use the information, of course. At the moment that appeared unlikely to be given.

"Hold up," Mrs. Kemp barked and held Celia's arm tighter when it appeared she was about to move on. "One more thing I been pondering. Do you think that good-looking Jake Flagg is going to stay on in Pass Creek permanent? He's got the itchy-foot, you know. Been a rover most of his life. I hope he stays here."

Celia flushed. "I hope he will, too, Mrs. Kemp. But I just

don't know."

"It'll take something pretty important to turn him steady. Get him to put down roots permanent in Pass Creek."

"Likely."

"Well, Celia, I can't stand here talking to you all day. I'm meeting some church ladies over to the Mushroom for lunch. Think I'll go early and have me a fuzzy drink of some kind until they get there. You want to come?"

Fizzy drink? A soda? Celia wondered. "I wish I could, but I have a tour to do, then some work to do at the library and possibly at the newspaper office. Not to mention some chores back at the Inn."

"We'll miss you."

"Thank you. Have a nice day, Mrs. Kemp, and tell the ladies hello for me." The elderly woman was already *tap tapping* away, no doubt looking forward to sharing what she'd heard about Celia's strange lady guest who'd survived bad food. With a wry smile, Celia hoped she'd not be incriminated in the telling. It'd been ages since she'd cooked red meat. Cola disease, indeed! Actually, lab work at the hospital had ruled out E. coli infection, among others, as Tierney's problem.

As Celia left the market, she glanced across the street at Flagg Realty. Jake's pickup was missing from its usual parking space. He was likely out showing a property. If she had more time, she'd stop in and ask Salliebeth how she liked her new job, but she needed to get these groceries home and get into costume for her tour. She made a mental note to try and locate the house where the Monros once lived. Even small and nondescript as Mrs. Kemp described, the place could still have historic significance for one reason or another.

"Any problems while I was gone?" she asked Lilly, who was in the kitchen filling a glass with water from the refrigerator door.

"No problems." Lilly shook her head and then took a

drink. "All the rooms are cleaned except the Ferber room. The couple in there told me to skip it. They were staying in and will do the room up themselves later." She removed the rubber band from her ponytail, finger-combed her light-brown hair, then smoothed it and replaced the rubber band. "You want me to stay and take care of the desk the rest of the day?" Her blue eyes were hopeful.

"Yes, please." Knowing of young Lilly and Mac's need for whatever extra money they could earn, she was happy to have her stay the afternoon. "We don't have a vacancy at the moment, but someone might drop in for future reference." Lilly knew not to show an occupied room, but she could answer questions.

Celia arrived at the library following an unsatisfactory tour without Gable House as part of it. She hadn't bothered to change from her tour dress, a red polka-dot 1940's number that had probably went jitterbugging with a soldier boy a few times.

There was little about Pass Creek on the internet so far. But this room behind the reference desk had several shelves of old newspapers, handwritten memoirs in spiral notebooks, diaries and badly typed "recollections" about the community by old timers. She had gone through most of the material before, but she wasn't looking for mentions of the Monro family then. Even today, she wasn't sure what she hoped to find other than answers, resolutions, and help for Pass Creek's problems.

Mrs. Kemp had said the Monros had lived in Pass Creek ten to twelve years, and Jake had indicated Tierney had graduated high school a few years before him, leaving town right after. Using that time frame, Celia perused copies of the weekly *Pass Creek Chronicle* printed in the years before her Ethan took it over. Thankfully it wasn't a daily back then, or she'd be searching forever.

A clock ticked quietly a few feet away as she scanned page after page of local news. There were numerous stories about Jake Flagg or his family—not what she was looking for.

Guarding against being distracted from her chief mission, she flagged them with post-it notes to read later. Finally, she found the story of the tragic automobile accident that took the lives of Tierney's family. Struggling against an enveloping sadness, her hand covering her mouth, she read:

TRAGIC ACCIDENT TAKES LIVES OF THREE PASS CREEK CITIZENS. Mr. Len Monro was at the wheel of the family's 1968 Ford automobile yesterday at 6:00 p.m. when the car missed a curve and struck a huge oak tree in the grove off Douglas Avenue. He and passengers, wife Suzanne, and fifteen-year-old son, Quentin, were killed instantly. The family was on their way to Pass Creek high school for the graduation ceremony of the Monros' daughter, Willeen, who survives. Burial services are pending.

Celia pushed the newspaper aside and stared into space, blinking tears as she thought about Willeen, aka Tierney. A tragedy of this magnitude would affect a young woman for a long, long, time. Through her dancing and her marriage to Joe, Tierney had known a measure of peace and happiness. But not enough to stop her from harboring old wounds that somehow had to do with Gable House. It was a pain so deep Tierney wouldn't speak of it. Celia looked at the story again. The address given in the article for the Monro home was the location Mrs. Kemp indicated, not Gable House. She sagged back in her chair, wishing all of this was resolved and behind her.

"Are you all right, Mrs. Landrey?"

She looked up into the concerned face of the town's head librarian, Jeanne Smith, an attractive, ramrod straight woman with salt and pepper hair. "Thanks for asking, Jeanne." She patted the hand on her shoulder, and dredged a smile. "I'm fine. What I was reading upset me a bit."

"The accident there in the paper?" Jeanne spoke solemnly and pointed at the photo of the car smashed like an accordion into a large oak tree.

"Yes," Celia answered in a thin voice. "Three members of a family named Monro were killed. Another family member, a high school girl named Willeen, wasn't with them and later moved away." She took a chance. "By the way, Jeanne, did you know the Monro family? They lived here in Pass Creek about thirty years ago."

"Sorry, Celia. I wasn't living here then, and don't believe I've heard of them. You'd think I would have, a terrible happening like that, but no, I know nothing of them. This is the first time I've seen that story and that photo. If there's nothing else I can do to help, I'll get back to work."

The librarian moved away, her footsteps whispering across the thin carpet, and Celia returned to her own task. She hoped that Tierney's *accomplishments* would be written up in later newspapers, but in the next thirty or so minutes, she searched in vain and her frustration climbed. Of course, by the time these papers saw print, Willeen Monro had become someone else entirely, someone who wanted Pass Creek left in her past.

Considering that she might find information about the Monro family in earlier sources, Celia hurried back to the burgeoning shelves. There had to be something helpful here, *something.* She thumbed through a stack of file folders containing reminiscences written by long-time residents. Finding no help there, she turned to a scrapbook collection of yellowed newspaper clippings dating back to the turn of the twentieth century. Could it be possible the Monro family came here to join relatives who'd been residents since an earlier time? She read until her eyes ached. *Nothing.*

She did uncover tidbits of information she'd somehow missed in previous research of Pass Creek's past she might use in her book and for her talks. One item concerned the old hotel building that housed Vivian Tyler's antique business. The tale of the Central Hotel was one of the most popular stories on Celia's tour, but now she read a small, surprising, addition to the story.

In 1918, Pass Creek was struck, along with the rest of the country, by the influenza epidemic. Vivian's great-grandparents and an infant they'd taken in were stricken with the deadly flu. Remarkably, their son, Viv's grandfather, a twelve-year-old boy at the time, escaped the disease and for days was in total charge of the hotel. His only help was a transient from China who cooked for hotel guests.

All of that, Celia had known. But now, in disbelief, she read and reread a tiny story from a later 1918 issue, something she was sure Viv hadn't been aware of, either. Once the epidemic was over and folks were back on their feet, the transient cook was driven from town. Stoned—for being *Chinese!* She shook her head in disbelief. *The poor soul, and after being such a help in the crisis!* Surely people had come a long way in regard for their fellow human in the years since. Not that there wasn't room for improvement still.

With the unkindness of the act toward the poor man still heavy on her mind, not to mention what she'd read about Tierney—Willeen's family, she read on. She was pleased to uncover a happier story, which she took to the scanner and copied. The write-up was about a woman who lived through the San Francisco earthquake in 1906.

According to the newspaper story, Lady Edwina spoke vividly and entertainingly of the San Francisco earthquake to Pass Creek civic and social groups, providing two hours of free entertainment, *"and giving fine ladies of the town the opportunity to dress to their nines in the latest fashions,"* she finished reading aloud.

Celia loved the high drama of the story and descriptions of the women's gowns. She was surprised she'd missed this fun addition for her walking tour.

She continued to take notes on this item and that, but began to tire of the whole thing. She missed Salliebeth's help in the library. Last year they had had such good times, seeking material for Celia's walks and for her community history book. Jake was fortunate to have Salliebeth working for him. *Salliebeth was fortunate to spend eight hours a day in the same room with Jake.*

And why should that bother me, anyway? Celia thought. Her own feelings for Jake were nothing more than growing infatuation, and it was time she got over it. The problem was he seemed to share the attraction.

The way he looked at her sometimes, the funny, endearing things he said to her, his support during Tierney's food poisoning episode—was he being just a good friend? Was she only a brief passing fancy to the rambling cowboy? Those occasions of his tender touch on her hair, her arm, had seeped into her bones and made her heart beat faster at the memories.

Ignoring the argument in her mind not to do this, Celia reached for the old notebook of clippings and the many mentions of Jake Flagg she'd tagged. *Twenty children attended the birthday party for ten-year-old Jacob Flagg at the Flagg home on Saturday afternoon. Jimmy Fitzgerald batted Lorna Stuart in the head during a piñata game. Young Lorna required four stitches to repair the wound. Parents were called to pick up their children an hour earlier than planned.*

A story when he was in middle school reported that he was home from the hospital after having his appendix removed. *On behalf of her son, Mrs. Moira Flagg wishes to thank everyone who sent cards and flowers and particularly the three eighth-grade girls for their offers to help young Jake with his missed school work.*

Celia had no explanation for her fascination with the mundane stories from the small-town newspaper other than she felt like a sixteen-year-old in the throes of first love, obsessed with the object of her affection. She couldn't stop reading.

Jake Flagg, home from a summer spent on his uncle's

Eastern Oregon ranch and entering his sophomore year of high school on crutches, the result of being thrown from a horse.

Jake Flagg, repeatedly winning saddle bronc riding, team roping, and steer wrestling contests in high school rodeo. Celia pored over the numerous photos of a youthful Jake Flagg on horseback carrying a flag to open a ceremony, another of him being tossed from a steer, and yet again one of him on a horse racing after a runaway steer with his rope twirling over his head.

Jake Flagg, salutatorian of his high school graduating class.

Jake Flagg, on the University of Oregon Freshman honor roll.

Much about his parents was already part of Celia's collection of notes for her book, but she reread their obituaries. Jake's father, Caxton Flagg, Senior, orphaned at fifteen, was a self-made, very successful businessman, a city councilman for ten terms, and Pass Creek's mayor for six. Jake's mother, Moira, home economics teacher at the high school, was a devoted wife and mother. She gave many hours to her community as a member of the library board, as a Sunday School teacher, and 4H leader.

Celia carefully replaced all the items she'd been reading on their shelves, closed her notebook and returned her ballpoint pen to her purse. She left the library intoxicated with Jake Flagg facts. Or was she feeling weak and wobbly because she'd missed lunch, and heavens—dinner too? She checked her watch, shocked that it was well after 6:00 p.m. The library would close at 7:00.

She hurried along the street. She needed to send Lilly home to her husband. Hopefully, Lilly had been able to handle whatever Tierney and the other guests' needs were this afternoon. For her personally, it had been a long and emotionally draining day. She would have a bite to eat, take a long soak in the tub and go to bed early.

Celia was passing the old stone building that housed the

fire department, police station, and city hall when she decided to drop in at Pete's office for a minute. Surely the chief could now verify that Otis Peek's death was one or the other, an accident or homicide.

"Celia!" he said, standing up from a battered desk that was covered with papers. From the back area of jail cells came a ripping sound of snoring, which both of them ignored. "How can I help you?" He studied her face. "Everything all right? You haven't run into trouble again, have you? I've been trying to learn who shoved you down that night. Maybe you've remembered something? Do you now have an idea who it might have been?"

"I wish I knew. I'm sure it would be helpful, but sorry, I have no idea. I'm okay, rather than feeling a bit down." She told him what she'd read about Tierney Jones at the library and about their earlier discussion. "She changed her name from Willeen to Tierney when she was in Hollywood." They mulled that for a few moments and then she asked, "Do you know any more about Otis's death?" She held her breath. "It was an accident, right?"

His expression was serious, yet official, as he returned to his chair behind the desk. "We have new facts about what happened to Otis, Celia. It wasn't an accidental fall. He was murdered."

"*Murdered?* All her hopes crumbled. The room seemed suddenly cold. "There's definite evidence then? Do you know who—?"

He hesitated, rubbing his nose, and told her, "To begin with, we were suspicious when his body showed no serious bruises or broken bones from the fall. Then I found a brick with bloodstains on it in deep in some shrubbery behind his house and hard to find. Because the coroner had some questions about the depth of Otis's head wound, we took DNA samples from Otis's bloodstained clothes. Luckily, we still had them. It's his blood and hair on the brick."

Celia grabbed a chair and sat down. Murder changed everything. She waved for Pete to continue. "Don't you hold anything back, Pete. I need to know what's going on." At his reserved expression, she added, "or do you want to find me next, in an alley with *my* head bashed in? If a killer is running loose, he or she has to be stopped. The more people know to watch out for, the safer they'll be until the criminal is caught. Go ahead."

Chapter Ten

"We believe whoever killed Otis heaved the brick into the bushes to be rid of it and left in a big hurry," the chief told Celia. "It's possible they were back to find the brick that night you were on the grounds. Your being there no doubt surprised them. When they became aware of your approach, they got rid of whatever light they were using and knocked you down before getting out of there."

"Wouldn't they have come back for the brick right after his body was taken away, not waited days to look for it?"

"Maybe they tried at some point but couldn't find it. In any event, we are convinced that particular brick was the murder weapon."

His words chilled her spine. *Good grief, was the murderer someone she knew well? A Pass Creek citizen she saw on a regular basis but wouldn't figure to be a killer?* "There are people who didn't care for Otis much, but to kill him—? Who would have gone so far as that?"

He admitted, tapping a pencil against the desk, "I don't know yet. Mac Strand had no use for Otis. Locke Vinson is another one who disagreed with Otis on a lot of things. There aren't any strong suspects, though. Just a few persons of interest." The chief tossed the pencil aside. "Matter of fact, I was over at your inn today, questioning Tierney Jones. She's an interesting lady." He leaned back in his chair, hands behind his head.

"She is, but she couldn't have murdered Otis Peek. He was killed before she came to town. I will admit something is troubling her deeply, and whatever it is brought her here to Pass Creek. But I doubt she is responsible for his death. The more I get to know her, the nicer she seems."

"Even 'nice people' commit crimes, Celia. They snap in a moment of rage. Or over time they stew themselves into a fit of resentment—until they're blinded to anything but the desire to get even. There are hundreds of motives for an ordinarily decent soul to lose it and kill the person they're convinced wronged them. Truth of the matter is Tierney Jones was in Pass Creek the day Otis Peek was killed."

She looked at him, puzzled. "Here in Pass Creek? But it was a couple of weeks after that when she took a room at my inn. That's the first I knew of her being here. You're sure?"

"Yes, she was in town the day he met his demise. A couple of folks saw her and provided information. A cab driver had picked her up at the train station in Adkins to bring her here. Also, a reliable Pass Creek witness saw her go inside the house with Peek."

"Go inside—?" Celia couldn't have been more surprised. "Tierney Jones was *at* Gable House some time before she joined my walking tour? She hasn't mentioned a whisper of that, and I thought we were beginning to *talk,* that we were becoming friends."

Pete shook his head. "She could be your friend and still have secrets."

"You're right about that. She holds back—on a lot of things."

Celia left the police station with her thoughts jumping back and forth and her stomach feeling queasy. Tierney Jones, a killer? Surely it was someone else who took Otis Peek's life. Maybe it was a stranger from out of town, someone trying to rob him. Peek, with his money and his beautiful residence, would be a tempting target. It simply couldn't be someone she knew personally and cared about who was responsible for killing Peek. *One step at a time*, she reminded herself irritably as she hurried on, intending to confront Tierney about her failure to tell Celia she knew Otis Peek, not to mention the fact she was in his house the day of his murder!

Nearing downtown, she caught sight of Salliebeth coming out of the Flagg Realty office. Jake was locking up. He circled his pickup and opened the passenger door for Salliebeth, took her arm, helped her in. They were smiling at one another. Celia's steps slowed. Her heart dipped. The pair looked so cozy. Was a romance in progress? And so what if it was?

Hardly thinking about what she was doing or why, Celia moved into the recessed entry of the city hall. She peeked around the corner and nibbled at her bottom lip. Jake and Salliebeth were talking a mile a minute and laughing as they drove off. Celia fought disappointment, but how could she help it? *She'd* never got to ride in his pickup! Were they going to Salliebeth's house or—to his? Out on a dinner date? Her feelings ran hot and cold. She didn't want Jake to fall for Salliebeth. The next second she was thinking, *Yes, absolutely. Salliebeth should be the one. It's okay. It's really okay.*

"What will be, will be," she mumbled aloud as she continued on her way home. "But any more revelations and surprises today and I don't think I could handle it."

Thank goodness she hadn't said anything to her friends or given any indication of special feelings for Jake. That nonsense could remain private and no one need know—Jake in particular.

Otis Peek's murder would get her full attention from this minute on!

Checking on Tierney when she got back to the Inn, she took a chair, making it clear she meant to stay a while. She had more than a few questions and with pleasantries out of the way, she got to the point. "I was talking to our police chief today. There's no longer any doubt. Otis Peek was murdered."

Tierney frowned, and her voice was thin with shock. "My goodness, that's terrible. It wasn't an accident he died from then?" She was sitting in a chair by the window, dressed in blue silk lounging pajamas. Her hand shook a little in her lap.

"Chief Erdman has evidence that someone killed him. He also told me that you were here in Pass Creek the day it happened." She studied Tierney's face for her reaction. "I was under the impression you'd never been here until the day you came to rent a room from me."

"I was here before," Tierney answered. With a shrug, she added, "But I can't see why that is important or a problem the way you're making it sound, Celia."

"You were *inside* Gable House, and yet the day of the tour, a body would have thought it was the first time you'd laid eyes on the place!"

"What are you accusing me of, dear? It's not a crime to have seen the house early-on. Pass Creek had been on my mind for some time and I thought I'd see the town. The first person I met when the Adkins cab driver dropped me off in Pass Creek was Otis Peek."

"And?" Celia sat forward, arms folded across her chest.

"We just ran into each other. I recognized him from when I lived here with my family. Peek was one of my father's bosses at the mill where Dad worked. Mr. Peek invited me to his house for a cup of coffee. But it was upsetting, remembering things about when I lived here before." She emphasized, "Matters that are really my own private affair. I called an Adkins cab to pick me up and take me back to Adkins, where I had a room at a motel. Otis Peek was fine when I saw him last, beyond his sour mood over something about a roof repairman. A worker who didn't show up for work? I really don't know."

Celia persisted. "That same late afternoon or early

evening, someone bashed in Otis's brains with a brick. What time did the cab pick you up?" Whatever Tierney answered, the taxi service would have record and she could check.

"Enough of this, Celia! I'm not sure what time I returned to my Adkins motel. I was upset, not myself." Her voice rose, "Do you really think I'm strong enough to do something like that or have reason to do it?"

You might've, if you were full of fury over some matter between the two of you, or feeling revengeful as Chief suggested. Maybe Peek didn't see it coming and you struck him just right. It could've happened. You might be among those who hated Peek.

"Good heavens, Celia, be sensible," Tierney might as well have read her mind.

Feeling guilty that she was practically accusing someone of murder who could be innocent, Celia back-tracked a little. "I'm trying to keep a clear head, but to be honest I don't know what to think. I'm sorry, Tierney, if you feel I've judged you unfairly. But there's a great deal going on here that needs sorting out. I hope you had nothing to do with Otis Peek's murder. But someone did, and the town's going to be in upheaval because of it until the killer is caught."

She didn't bring up Gable House, but somehow she must disentangle that matter from the mess, even if it was in no way connected to Otis Peek's death.

At the cemetery next day, on her knees by her husband's grave, Celia sprayed the headstone with Windex and vigorously wiped it clean with paper towels. She mentally apologized for not coming more often of late. "You can't imagine what's going on in our town that's always meant so much to us, Ethan," she said out loud. "I wish you were here to help me deal with it."

The year after he died, she'd come to the cemetery every day. Now she came once or twice a month or on occasions when she needed to talk, like today. She felt better telling him her concerns, just as she had when he was alive. In urgent whispers as she continued to polish the stone, she told him about Tierney Jones, her determination to demolish Gable House, and a murder taking place there. "Can you believe such a horrible thing could happen in Pass Creek, Ethan?"

A few moments later she said, "There's something else I need to tell you, husband-mine, though it's not nearly so major. There is a guy. Remember Jake Flagg? He's somebody I'd normally not give second thought to, but these days I can't get him off my mind, and—and I'm sorry."

Why should you be sorry?

Alone in the peaceful cemetery, Celia's head came up and the polishing stopped for a second. The voice in her mind, her husband's voice, was so real it was startling, and the question was exactly what her thoughtful Ethan would ask: what his spirit was asking, perhaps. Celia was thoughtful. Why was she sorry?

"Because I love you, only you, always," she answered. "That can't change." Sitting back in the grass, she sorted several stems of blue delphiniums and fragrant pink peonies and stripped them of extra leaves. She placed them in the headstone's vase and poured in water from the bucket that had held the flowers.

Doesn't need to change. Love can happen more than once.

She hesitated with a long stem of delphinium poised in the air. "But how and why should it? You were my soul mate, my only love for all time."

True, and you mine. But remember our discussion? Our pact?

"What pact? For goodness sake, Ethan, we had several. We'd always kiss goodnight, we'd never lie to each other. You preferred that I not smoke or forget to release the brake when I was about to drive off, but I don't think those were pacts. I never cared to smoke, and leaving the brake on only happened once or twice. What pact or discussion do you mean?" She began snipping thorns from the stems of red roses, Ethan's favorite flower. All of the perennials she'd brought today they had planted together, but he loved red roses best.

Where we agreed that if one of us passed on and the other was happy being alone, fine. By the same token, if the one still living craved companionship or fell in love again, that was okay, too.

Her heart stilled for a second, and then tears welled in her eyes. She whispered to him and to herself, "I agreed because I thought I would go first. I didn't want *you* to be alone and lonely. I thought you knew that."

It works both ways, sweetheart.

"Oh, Ethan!" Celia sobbed into her dirtied, thorn-pricked fingers. As she cried and the minutes passed, she felt the tension inside her slipping away. "I miss you so much."

It would be like Ethan, looking down on her and her struggles with life these days, to understand. He'd want her to be happy, exactly as she'd want him to be. She sat by his grave for a long time, arms clasped around her knees, remembering the tall, serious fellow with the little boy sense of humor who was the love of her life.

She soaked in the peacefulness surrounding her. A slight breeze whispered in the tall oak trees sheltering the cemetery. The sweet aroma of wild strawberries ripening by the fence floated on the late spring air. Finally, feeling renewed, and with at least some of her concerns resolved, she returned to the task of forming the bouquet. She kissed each red rose bud before adding it to the vase.

She gathered refuse from the flowers into her bucket and emptied it in a waste can at the back of the cemetery, picked up her clippers, Windex bottle and paper towels. She stood for a moment smiling down at the tidied grave, but her heart in turmoil still. "The guy and I—it may come to nothing, Ethan. He may be more interested in Salliebeth. He's not a stayer, either. He could be gone tomorrow." She heaved a sigh. "For now, my love, this is just between us. Whatever happens, you'll always be in my heart, and I'm glad I've squared the matter with you just in case." She headed for her car, wondering if she'd totally lost her mind.

~~~

A couple mornings later, Celia took a call from Salliebeth asking Celia to join her in the deli department in Thrifty Market for an early coffee before work, saying it had been too long since they'd shared girl talk and that she had exciting news. "Sure," Celia agreed cheerfully, guessing her friend's news was that she and Jake were dating.

Salliebeth carried their cups of coffee to the small table in the corner while Celia followed with their pastries on paper plates. Salliebeth said over her shoulder, "I thought I saw you after work one day last week in front of the city hall. I was about to wave, and then you just disappeared. I gathered you'd gone inside. Were you there on a mission?" She placed their coffees on the table, hooked a chair with her foot and sat down.

"I'd been to the library to do research." Celia licked a bit of frosting from her finger, drew the other chair up, sat down, and explained she was looking for information about Tierney but came up with nothing she didn't already know. "I stopped to see the chief."

"I couldn't believe it when I read the latest in the paper about Otis Peek," Salliebeth said. "According to the newspaper account, Chief Erdman wants folks to come forward with information, but those I've talked to don't know a blessed thing about it."

Celia wagged her head. "Hit with a brick by somebody is about all they know. He didn't fall from the roof."

"Although with the ladder there and everything," Salliebeth mused, "the murderer no doubt believed Otis's death would be ruled an accident."

"It appears whoever killed him didn't plan well or was in a frightful hurry to get away when they tossed the brick into the bushes." Celia took a sip of coffee, then continued, "Pete is questioning several people, among them Tierney Jones, alias Willeen Monro." She told Salliebeth that Tierney had been in town sooner than anyone believed and was inside Gable House the day Otis Peek was killed.

"This is all so hard to believe." Salliebeth shivered and rubbed her bare arms. "Do you think Tierney had anything to do with…what happened to Mr. Peek?"

Celia tried to soften her exasperation as she answered. "Who knows? I just hope the guilty party is found out and locked behind bars pretty darned quick."

"Everyone in town is getting nervous, just knowing Peek was murdered, but hey, can we change the subject for a minute?"

"Sure. That's why we're here. I haven't had a chance to ask how you like working for Jake." Celia braced herself. Drawing a deep breath, she began to choke and cough from the bit of sugary glaze she'd inhaled. She missed most of Salliebeth's reply except for a word that sounded like *love*.

Celia patted her throat. "Sorry. I was making so much racket coughing; I didn't hear what you said."

"I love my job! Jake is easy-going and fun. He gets excited over every improvement I make. He pays well, too."

"He's happier in the business then?" Celia took a sip of coffee to clear her throat. "Jake was like a porcupine in a constant snit when he first came back to Pass Creek."

Salliebeth laughed. "I think he's getting more comfortable in this different role for him and liking it better all the time. I doubt you could call real estate his passion, however. That would be the open road and rodeo. What it is, he likes my help with the work load, all the mundane stuff of running the office, no doubt of that."

Celia waited in silence, wiping frosting from her fingers on a napkin, hoping to hear more about Salliebeth's work. Put off as long as possible the news that Jake was asking Salliebeth out. Of course it was okay if he was, but listening to details was going to be like a toothache in her heart.

"Jake is teaching me the real estate business—you know—beyond office chores," Salliebeth was saying. "Using where I live as an example, he showed me the good selling points." She ticked them off on her fingers. "The house's period charm, solid construction, Daddy's large shop out back. We discussed what would have to be fixed before placing it on the market. How one would arrive at a selling price, and then match a buyer to seller."

Celia sat back in her chair in surprise. "Salliebeth, your father isn't going to sell your house is he? Where would you move? Wouldn't it break your heart?"

The Parker home on the east side of town was a 1940's craftsman style bungalow Salliebeth's father had built for her mother when he returned from the Second World War. The house was loaded with special charm and memories. Salliebeth had often said how much she'd like to create similar memories in the house for a family of her own.

"No, no. Nothing like that. Jake was just using it as a lesson. I'd never sell Mom and Daddy's house. But that's what I wanted to tell you. Daddy is getting married again! To a sweet little lady from Tennessee he met on a cruise. He's giving the house to me!"

"Your father is getting married and giving you the house? That's great news, hon." This was what Salliebeth had been dying to tell her? Celia felt her spirits begin to lift. She took a large bite of doughnut to hide her goofy smile. "I'm happy for you. Really happy, Sal!"

Salliebeth was looking at her intuitively. "Celia, did you think my news would be—Jake and me? Did you think we might be dating?"

"Maybe. He wouldn't be a bad catch for someone."

Salliebeth shook her head. "I don't have the time or the will to break down the resistance of a confirmed bachelor, Cele.

I'm looking for the marrying kind. Big time marrying kind." She laughed softly, but her eyes declared her seriousness. Then she caught on. "You're falling for him, aren't you, honey? Oh, Cele, good luck. Jake Flagg is already married to his old pickup and the wild, wild West, you know."

They were still laughing when they parted later, Celia feeling especially giddy over Salliebeth's news. At the same time, she was trying her best to be sensible. Her efforts weren't working well.

Within a day or two, Pete Erdman had completed his investigation at Gable House and the crime scene tape was removed. To Celia's relief—and feeling a bit guilty for being hard on her—Tierney approved keeping Gable House in Celia's walking tour for the time being. She could show the house from the outside and the gardens, but the indoor tea parties would remain on hold.

Celia had asked Pete what he'd found besides the blood-crusted brick, but he wouldn't say. He did tell her to keep her expectations in check. Crimes were rarely solved without painstaking investigation, and that took time. She understood, but it didn't mean she couldn't hope, didn't mean she wouldn't do her part to find a solution sooner. Knowing what his reaction would be, she kept this plan to herself. She wished him good luck. In the meantime, life had to go on as normally as possible.

Wearing her cool flowered print dress and low-heeled white shoes, straw hat and handbag from the 1930s, Celia led her flock of tourists on a slow walk around the estate, telling them that when Clark Gable was twenty-one and used his inheritance to follow his dream to be an actor—a dream that led him to perform with the Astoria Stock Company in Oregon—his father was very angry.

"He was so angry and disappointed that he didn't speak to his son for nearly ten years," she told them. "Poor Dad, how could he guess that Clark would eventually win three Academy

Awards for Best Actor?" When one of her tourists asked, she happily told them, "He won for the films *It Happened One Night* in 1934, *Mutiny On The Bounty* in 1935, and *Gone With The Wind* in 1939."

She was showing her group the rose garden where Clark Gable reportedly picked roses for the love of his life, Carole Lombard, when she noticed a familiar figure, Stetson shading his eyes, joining her group. *Jake.* She fell silent, her heart thumped wildly, giving him an opening to tell her what he was doing there. When he said nothing, just waited with the others, she continued her presentation, her words stumbling a bit before she regained control. He appeared to follow her every word, one of the bunch, totally engrossed in the history of Gable House and its famous occupant who had roomed there before he became famous.

As Celia and her followers were coming back past the rose garden, Jake took a small Swiss Army knife from his jeans pocket and cut a perfect pink rose from one of the bushes. Celia stood with mouth open as he held it out to her. "A beauty for a beauty."

"What on earth are you doing?" she asked him in a low voice, waving off the flower. "You can't just cut a rose here. This is private property."

He grinned. "I intend to ask the owner's permission. I just won't tell her the deed is already done."

Exasperated, she asked in a whisper, "Why are you here, anyway?" Heavens but he was appealing, this tall rugged cowboy holding a pink rose and turning her heart topsy-turvy with his grin. He made resisting him so blasted difficult.

"I saw you—pretty as a picture, I might add—and your group headed this way down the street past the office. I wanted to ask you something. When I caught up, I didn't want to interrupt so I stood around and hell, I got interested. What am I supposed to do with this rose if you won't take it?"

"Give it here." She grabbed for it. "And what is it you wanted to know?"

"There's a Western Days Festival going on, a rodeo, over at Shady Hill. I wondered if you'd like to take it in with me."

The invitation took her by surprise. She hesitated, realizing she was going to be in deeper emotional trouble if she said yes. She also wished her ten or so sun-hatted, floral-shirted tourists, grinning like a bunch of apes, weren't watching them. She looked away as her mind wavered in indecision. Another thing: it would feel like she was turning her back on Pass Creek's serious crises to leave town for even a few hours. "I don't know...I really shouldn't."

He said quickly, "This won't be a real date if you don't want it to be. Let's say I'm showing you my appreciation for sending Salliebeth to work for me, okay? That's all."

Not a date. "Okay," she answered quietly. A few hours pleasant diversion was not without appeal. It would only be a few hours.

Chapter Eleven

The morning sun shone bright over a long parade of marching bands, horseback riders, floats, and vehicles. At Jake's side, Celia felt almost as excited as a kid, clapping and cheering and pocketing the tossed candy he caught for her.

Bringing up the end, finally, was a gray-haired old man dressed as an early day miner riding in a donkey cart hung with rattling miner's tools. "Good show, fella!" Jake shouted. He was rewarded with a toothy grin, and a salute from the old man's tattered hat brim.

"He's darling. The whole parade was wonderful," Celia said, clapping hard. The day was warming up, but she was comfortable in blue jeans, white shirt and sandals.

"That was just the beginning! Are you ready for the rodeo?" Jake cupped her elbow in his palm and shouldered a path for them through the throngs leaving the parade for the main festival grounds. He pulled her safely out of the way when a horde of laughing, shouting teenagers would have run right over her.

Celia smiled up at him and he winked and smiled back. Her heart soared. She hadn't felt this cared-for in ages, nor had she had as much fun. She slanted a second glance up at him and felt a fresh wave of attraction. Today at Shady Hill, he was drop dead handsome in total cowboy garb, but she was drawn to him for more than his tall good looks. He was a sincere, straightforward guy. Plus, this morning she was learning how much fun he was to be with.

"Hup, hold on!" he said suddenly as they made their way past rows of vendor booths selling everything from belt buckles to candy apples. He steered her toward a booth with counters stacked high with cowboy hats. "You gotta have one." He grabbed a black hat and placed it on her head, then stood back and surveyed the effect with a wide grin and a sparkle in his eyes. She fingered a hat that was bright purple with a silver hat band and he shook his head. "Nope, no way. You're going to be a real bona fide cowgirl."

She protested, "I don't even know how to ride a horse!"

"I'm gonna teach you sometime."

He removed the black hat, studied others carefully, then clapped a dove gray hat on her head, tilted the brim a bit, and beamed. "This is the one!" He grew suddenly quiet as he looked at her, his eyes shining with an emotion she couldn't quite decipher. He whistled softly. "You're one beautiful lady, Cele. Look in the mirror they've hung there on the post."

She looked, obedient, and drew a breath. She wasn't beautiful, and it wasn't even the hat she was seeing, although somewhere in her mind she knew she looked different and somewhat attractive dressed western. What caught her attention was how natural she looked next to Jake as he stood looking in the same mirror over her shoulder.

He asked, "Do you like it?"

It was hard to breathe. "Yes."

When she reached to her fanny pack for money, his hand stopped her. "I'm buying. This day is on me, remember?"

"Do you remember this is not supposed to be a date?" *Never mind that it felt like one.* "I like the hat a lot, and I'm going to buy it to wear on my historic home tours."

He cocked an eyebrow at her, and a grin twitched at his mouth.

"I'm serious. I hadn't thought of dressing up western for my walking tours, but if I showed your family's house, for example, I could not only tell about your parents as prominent citizens of Pass Creek and the house's Dutch Colonial architecture, but I could also talk about you." He shook his head firmly *no,* but she continued, "Folks would love to hear about a small-town guy who made a name for himself in national rodeo."

"How do you know about that?"

"Well, besides hearing it from practically everyone in town, I was reading about you in newspapers at the library. I found it fascinating." She paid for the hat.

"I'm not sure I want to be on your tour," he said as they wandered on among the rows of craft and food booths. In the background on someone's CD player, Alan Jackson was singing that it was five o'clock somewhere although it was about twelve-thirty at Shady Hill. "I'd have to think about it," Jake said.

"All right, think about it." She tipped her new hat to him. He laughed and shook his head in response, then took her hand in his own, and they meandered on.

In a quieter area of the grounds, away from the crowds, he showed her the corralled horses. "I owned a sorrel gelding once," he told her, "God, but he was beautiful. I called him *Ketchup*. He was the best cow horse I ever saw. As they say, he could cut on a dime and give back change."

"Where is Ketchup now?"

He shrugged, sadly. "Sold him, and have regretted it every day since."

"You miss it, don't you? Ranching, rodeo, that life?"

"I'd be lying if I said I didn't miss it a little. It was a lot of fun, but I'm over it. Following the rodeo circuit isn't an easy life by any means. I got thrown, or *throwed,* as most cowboys say. I got stomped and horned. Saw my share of hospital rooms to take care of concussions and broken bones. I made some prize money, but it seemed to disappear fast. The next thing I'd know I'd be down to barely keeping myself in coffee, beans and cheap motels between rodeos, or ranch work. I wasn't getting any younger, and riding and contesting was getting harder and more painful every time up. It was a better living, announcing and organizing rodeo, but I was just beginning to get somewhere with that when my brother Caxton said to get my butt home and take over the business."

"But you came," she reminded him. "Couldn't you have said no?"

"Sure, I could've." His spoke thoughtfully, admitting, "Caxton was right, figuring that if I kept on rodeoing I'd be crippled. It was time I settled into a more stable life than seasonal rodeo."

"Do you feel you've found it?" she asked with a tremor in her voice. If he left Pass Creek again, there would be a large hole left in her life. She was coming to realize that more every day. Of course, if he did go, she wouldn't be fighting his constant charm. But could she forget him? Get over him? Right now that felt like the world's biggest impossibility. She tore her mind back to the moment.

"I like Pass Creek and the realty business okay," he was saying, "but I'm not sure it's what I want for the rest of my life. I may eventually go back to the dream I've had for a long time, to have my own ranch, raise cattle and horses. Some of the best times of my life were the summers spent on my uncle's ranch in eastern Oregon. 'Course, I was a kid then."

"I read about your summers on the ranch in the papers."

"I'd like to show you that country sometime."

Celia nodded, but still felt uncertain. If he wasn't sure what he wanted to do, which possibly meant he wouldn't be staying on in Pass Creek, then what did it mean that he wanted to "teach her to ride a horse" and wanted to "show her a part of the state" he loved? Did they have a future? Or were they just making friendly conversation? She decided she was getting ahead of herself, and she changed the subject to the delicious meaty aroma in the air. "What is that smell?"

He drew in a long draught and announced happily, "That is the sweet smell of rodeo! Fresh hay, dung, saddle leather, candy apples and barbecue."

"The sweet...?" she looked at him and he seemed so serious, she broke up laughing. Giggles turned into hysterical laughter. She clutched his arm and snickered. "I—I think I was speaking—about the barbecue." Though his comment had tickled her funny bone, it really wasn't *that* funny, she knew, but she couldn't stop laughing. Her jaws ached and her sides hurt from laughing. She doubled over, gasping for breath, vainly trying to stop the ridiculousness of what she was doing.

"Hey," he said. "Hey, are you all right?" He caught her arms and brought her up close to him. She was doing her best to breathe and not laugh when she saw how he was looking at her, and it was easy to guess what was coming. He tipped his hat back, then hers, and brought his mouth to hers in a soft kiss. "Okay?"

Gentle as his kiss was, it sent an electric shock through her body. "Okay," she said, pulling away and taking a few steps. She removed her hat and ran her hand through her hair. "I'm okay." Her head was spinning; her cheeks and her mouth burned.

"You're not mad that I kissed you?"

"Not mad." She shook her head but couldn't look at him.

"Are you hungry?"

"I am hungry. That's what I was thinking when I smelled the barbecue." She began laughing again, but this time more quietly. Maybe it was release from tension over the murder at home that caused her to let go so totally. With the back of her hands, she wiped tears of laughter from her cheeks. "I'm not sure why what you said struck me so funny, but it did. I suppose because you mentioned dung and barbecue in the same breath, and it didn't spoil my appetite a whit. Guess I'm turning into a real westerner. Yes, I'm hungry."

They drank iced tea and ate huge plates of barbecued beef, pinto beans, cole slaw, and buttered yeast rolls while sitting at a table in the shade. Celia wiped her mouth with a napkin, "Thank you. This is delicious."

"My pleasure." He smiled at her, his expression satisfied. Later he took their plates, napkins, and plastic utensils and disposed of them in a tall green trash can. After a stop at a restroom building with one door marked *Heifers* and the other *Bulls*, they headed for the rodeo arena.

For the rest of the afternoon they sat in the bleachers filled with whooping, hollering, beer-drinking spectators and watched cowboys and cowgirls ride bareback, rope calves and milk wild cows. There was barrel racing for the cowgirls, which Celia saw was no sissified event.

Fascinated, she observed a rider enter the arena on her brisk-stepping mount and wave to the crowd before she turned her horse loose. In less than twenty seconds horse and rider dashed a clover pattern around the barrels and then headed hard for home through an electronic eye to stop the clock. The beautiful and elegant event, done at breath stopping speed, left Celia totally awed. It wasn't surprising, she supposed, that Jake got excited watching cowboys try to stay on an ornery bull for eight seconds.

"This is quite the enthusiastic crowd," she said to Jake as she looked around at spectators of both genders and all ages.

"You bet. Some people look forward to the rodeo season the same as others look forward to their baseball or football. You've never been to a rodeo before, Celia?"

"I'm sorry to say that I haven't." Ethan and she had season tickets to the Oregon Symphony and to Pentacle Theatre in Salem. They loved outings at ocean beaches, and had attended small town festivals like the Brownsville Pioneer Picnic and Lebanon's Strawberry Festival. She wasn't sure why they'd never gone to a rodeo. It was just an accident that they hadn't, probably. "I'm having fun, though, Jake. I'm glad you invited me."

As he looked down at her, a smile hovered at the corner of his mouth. He said, "I'm glad you came. It's more fun than I would have guessed, sharing a day like this with a greenhorn. You probably don't know what a greenhorn is?"

"Of course I do. I've seen a western movie or two. A greenhorn is—*me*. Someone not used to riding horses, or…isn't acquainted with the 'sweet smell of rodeo.'" She burst into laughter again and leaned into him, trying to stop. "I-I'm s-sorry," she shook her head. "I don't think I'll ever forget that."

His lips brushed against her hair as he whispered into her ear, "I hope you don't, Miss Laughing Greenhorn."

She relaxed, sitting close to him. Being with Jake was turning her into a dozen different people, and she didn't recognize any of them. All she knew was that she liked being where she was very much.

Then, as she looked around, a man across the way, deeply tanned and with silver blond hair glinting in the sunshine, caught her attention and the day suddenly changed. "Why does he have to be here?" she said to no one in particular, annoyed.

"Who? What are you talking about?"

She nodded toward bleachers at the end of the arena, "The guy in the lime-green shirt, grinning and waving at us. Locke Vinson." Frowning, she returned his wave half-heartedly.

"Yeah, I see him now. He was at that meeting. Got everybody upset."

"Typical Locke," she said. "But I'm surprised he's here since his leisure tastes run a lot fancier as a rule. Maybe it's the pretty young woman with him who likes rodeo."

"Pretty young woman or not, now he's spotted you he can't take his eyes off you," Jake commented dryly.

"Nonsense. He's staring because of this hat I've got on,

and he's probably laughing about it. Anyone who knows me wouldn't figure me for a cowgirl. I'm sure he's as surprised to see me enjoying a rodeo as I am to see him at one."

"What is this Vinson guy's connection to Pass Creek? I only saw him the one time."

"He owns Vinson Print, the small copy and print shop on main, next to the post office, that's managed by different people at different times. In fact he owns a whole line of Vinson Print shops from Pass Creek to Seattle, but our town had the first and it's the smallest. He's become quite successful, from what I hear. He travels a lot on business. You don't see him much around town."

Jake took another, longer look at Vinson, then at her. "I'm guessing that you and this Vinson know each other pretty well? That you are, or have been, more than friends?" He growled before she could answer, "Shoot! That's none of my business, so forget it. Don't answer if you don't want to."

She shrugged and smiled at him. Jake sounded almost jealous. "You're somewhat right. To go way back, Locke Vinson worked for my husband at the newspaper before Locke got his first print shop. After my husband died, Locke and I dated a few times. I was lonely and was still adjusting to life after Ethan. It didn't take long for me to realize that getting serious with Locke Vinson would be a mistake. That's all it amounted to."

"The way he's looking at you, he'd switch dates with me in a second."

She laughed. "Let's drop this subject and enjoy the rodeo. If you'd stop staring at him, Jake, he'd stop looking at us. He surely has his hands full with that gorgeous little redhead at his side."

"You've got her beat all to heck for looks, Celia, and I'm not joking."

"*Thank you*, even for the exaggeration. Now, tell me about this next event. Our program says it's— Good grief, more bull riding?"

"Yep." He chuckled. "Folks just can't get enough of watching a cowboy wreck in a match with an eighteen-hundred pound bull."

Celia settled in to watch this stuff that, at least in part, made Jake who he was. She did her best to put from mind the man who continued to watch her from down at the end of the arena.

"Want to stop for a little something to eat or drink?" Jake asked on the way home after the rodeo. She agreed, and they hauled into the dusty, graveled parking lot of a barn-like structure called The Last Dime Bar and Grill, a café known for its homey atmosphere and good food. It was crowded, but they were soon seated at a table for two. Jake ordered a beer and a hamburger, and she ordered iced tea and a salad. Their orders had barely been placed on the wood plank table in front of them when Locke Vinson and the red-haired girl entered the cafe.

"He following you or what?" Jake muttered, squirting catsup on his burger.

"It's a coincidence," she answered quietly, hoping she was right. It hadn't been easy to convince Locke once and for all that she wasn't interested in him, but that was ages ago. He probably didn't remember they went out a couple of times. She'd put it from her mind until something like today came up to remind her. She sipped her iced tea. "I'm sure this is where a lot of people stop on their way from the rodeo."

"He could have kept going, far as I'm concerned."

"Be nice. He's coming over here," Celia whispered. She mustered a smile as Locke stopped at their table, his arm looped around the dimpled red-head's waist.

"Hey there, Celia! You enjoy the rodeo?" His golden moustache curved with his grinning mouth. His eyes were intent on her face.

"Hello, Locke. Yes, I did. I'd like you to meet my friend,

Jake Flagg."

"Flagg? Caxton's brother?" His hand shot out for Jake's. "Think we probably met sometime before the meeting the other night. Or maybe not. You were off on the rodeo circuit for years, right? Nice to see you, and you especially, Celia." Almost as afterthought he said, "And this is pretty Patrice." He kissed the young woman's cheek, making her smile.

The waitress informed Locke and his date that she'd have a table ready for them in a couple of minutes. The rodeo was briefly discussed and Celia finally said, in an effort to be more cordial than she was feeling, "We haven't seen you around Pass Creek much lately, Locke. The printing business must be booming. Congratulations on your success."

Showing nice teeth in an overly-friendly smile, he shoved Jake's shoulder with a tan fist, "She misses me! How about that? I need to get back to Pass Creek more often." He looked at Celia for a long moment, eyes agleam, voice low and sexy, "Maybe we can take up where we left off, huh, Celia? What do you say? I'm ready."

The young woman at Locke's side stiffened, her soft smile wiped from her face.

Jake's jaw set. He looked from the girl named Patrice to Locke. He shook his head, his expression indicating he would like to slam a fist into Locke's nose for his lack of respect toward the girl.

Celia felt sorry for Patrice as well. Hoping to diffuse the moment, she said quickly, her voice light, "You're joking, of course. We've both moved on, Locke." This pretty young thing was probably new and not aware of his history. She'd learn soon enough.

The waitress arrived to show Locke and Patrice to a table, and Celia felt relieved. The feeling was short-lived when he motioned his date to follow the waitress while he stayed to talk.

"You folks got a lot going on in Pass Creek, I hear. Gable

House sold to some woman from out of town? Sorry about that, Celia. I always figured you and your group would end up with it. I was planning to make a contribution toward buying the place, but next thing I knew, it'd sold to somebody else."

Empty chatter, Celia thought to herself. Locke Vinson liked his toys too much. Expensive cars, a yacht on Lake Washington near his Seattle condo and lately, fancy buildings to house his print shops, to have anything left to help buy Gable House. "Yes, Gable House sold." She added, "I suppose you've heard about Otis Peek, too? That he was murdered?"

Locke Vinson's expression could have been painted on for all it changed. He nodded and thumped their table with a knuckle. "I did hear about that, poor old guy. In fact, that's why I'm back. Pete Erdman wanted to question me about the murder. Hell, I'm never around there, nor would I have any reason to do Peek in. We always got along well enough. But I guess the chief is questioning everybody who ever knew or did business with Peek. The old cuss had his enemies, but I wasn't one of them. How about you, Celia? Pete pin you to the wall, too?"

"We've talked, that's all. I'm confident Pete will find out who did it, soon."

Jake nodded to where red-haired Patrice sadly looked over her shoulder at them and the waitress waited impatiently. He said, "Sorry we can't talk longer, Locke. Sure been nice seeing you." His voice grated with irritation, and his grin was phony as could be.

Vinson stroked the back of Celia's hand and smiled at her before moving on.

"I don't think I like your friend much," Jake said when Vinson was out of hearing.

"He's not really my friend, just an acquaintance." While they ate, she told Jake about Locke Vinson, a moody person who at least in the past could have used an anger management course. "Locke was a good worker when he was employed at the paper by my husband, but Ethan finally had to fire him."

"Fire him? How come?"

"For one example, Locke found out that our delivery boy was tossing his papers behind a barn and going off to play instead of making deliveries. Locke struck him hard enough to knock the youngster to the ground with a bloodied nose and a loosened tooth. Which was terrible enough, but a second altercation followed when the boy's mother came to protest. The language Locke used and his overall behavior didn't sit at all well with Ethan. He fired him on the spot."

"Vinson was arrested for assault?"

"No, I'm sorry to say. Vinson could win medals for sweet-talking. In the end, he managed to placate the mother, and she refused to press charges. She believed her son had done wrong in not delivering the newspapers as he should've. Maybe Locke paid her. It's hard to say. There were other incidents. Locke would drink too much and get into arguments with others down at the bar. He knocked one fellow into a coma, broke another's arm."

"Good Lord."

She said with a shake of her head, "I don't know what I was thinking when I gave in and agreed to go out with him. I thought perhaps he'd changed. He did seem like a different person as he became more successful. It didn't take me long to come to my senses."

"Good thing you did. You deserve lots better than him."

She shrugged. "I don't know about that, but I was never convinced of his sincerity anyhow. He was awfully interested in the property that came to me when Ethan died. Although Locke bent over backwards to convince me that it was me, only me, that he wanted."

"That part could have been true, that he wanted you," Jake claimed.

She shook her head. "I don't think so, but it doesn't

matter. All that is ancient history." She studied Jake for a moment, thinking how different and wonderful he was compared to Locke Vinson. "Do you mind if I ask you, Jake, why you never married?" Sure, he'd been on the road a lot, but that couldn't be the whole answer. The man would be a catch for any woman.

He took time answering, and when he did speak, his voice was tight. "Actually, I was married once, when I was a senior in college."

"Really?" She sat back in surprise. "I didn't see anything in the papers about you getting married. At least, I didn't see a write up, and no one has mentioned it." She sat forward again, wanting to know more, but at that moment Locke Vinson and his date huffed by the table. The redhead's chin was high and her step determined as she looked to neither right nor left. Locke's moustache twitched in fury, and he barely nodded at Jake and Celia.

"Smart Patrice," Jake growled.

Celia nodded in agreement as they watched the couple leave. After a minute she reminded him, "You were saying you were married at one time?"

"The marriage didn't last long enough for anyone but us and the judge who married us to know about it." Jake's voice was flat and emotionless compared to the pain showing in his eyes. "We got married because she was pregnant. When she…miscarried a couple months later, that was the end of everything. Our marriage was over."

Celia touched his arm. "I'm so sorry, Jake."

"Thanks. It's okay." But he wasn't. He seemed to have real difficulty finding words. "The thing is I really loved her. I wanted our baby more than anything in the world." He cleared his throat. "To her, the loss of our little one was the best thing that could happen. A former boyfriend was waiting. Her actual words were 'saved by the bell.'"

"God, Jake, that is just awful." Aching in sympathy and shocked, she reached out to cover his hand with hers. "Clearly, that young woman wasn't right for you. I dislike her intensely, and I don't even know her."

He took a swallow of beer, looked away as he talked. "I had a hell of a time getting over what happened, if I ever did. For sure I never wanted to put myself in a position to be hit again with that kind of pain. It was better beating myself half to death in rodeo."

"Listen, Jake, one bad experience doesn't mean you couldn't have been happy with someone else. We have to take risks to find love with the right person."

"Don't get me wrong. There have been flings." He faced her with his jaw jutting stubbornly. "I'm just damned careful not to get too involved."

She wanted to break in, but he wouldn't allow it.

"It's okay. I doubt I'm cut out for marriage anyway. The way I see it, this true love stuff is a fantasy that two people talk themselves into. If they're smart enough and determined, they're able to plot the fantasy to fit their life. Sometimes it works. Judging by most of my friends in the past, the fantasy more often fizzles and dies. I don't need that."

Celia wanted to rail at him for what she considered pure nonsense. Surely he didn't really believe what he was saying. One second she wanted to slap him awake, the next she wanted to hold him, console him with hugs and kisses. She did neither. It wasn't her right to scold or preach to him.

Of course he didn't want to be hurt again, and she didn't blame him for that. But to call love a plotted fantasy was idiocy. What she had had with Ethan was incredible and in no way a fabrication. She could point out many Pass Creek couples bound by long and lasting love. Elderly couples as much in love and as happy together as the day they met.

Finally, she told him what she was thinking and added,

"One of these days, Jake, love is going to hit you square between the eyes. The right one for you simply hasn't come along. Maybe you'll recognize right away when it happens, or you won't until it gradually grows on you. But love is going to catch up with you someday, Jake Flagg, and I predict you'll be happier than you ever thought possible. That might sound Pollyanna to you, but it's a fact. Love is real."

He looked embarrassed. "Lord, but I got you stirred up with my sad story, didn't I? I'm sorry. Didn't mean to spill my guts."

"It's okay. I asked. And I am right about love, Jake. You can count on that."

By silent assent, they dropped the subject and Jake asked for their ticket.

What a rollercoaster of emotion the day had been! Celia was thinking as they headed home. Up, down, scary, sad. But she wouldn't trade it for anything. "I had a good time today, Jake," she told him as they neared Pass Creek.

"Me, too." He wore a serious expression as his hand covered hers on the seat between them in the rumbling pickup.

She allowed her fingers to curl with his. Whatever happened next, the two of them were okay. Or did his solemn expression mean he was about to run again?

Back at Landrey's Inn, Chief Erdman's police cruiser was just pulling away from the curb as they pulled in.

Chapter Twelve

"Do you want me to come in with you?" Jake wanted to know as he turned off the ignition. "Trouble of some kind must have brought Pete to your inn."

"That isn't necessary, but thanks. Like Locke Vinson said, Pete is talking to any number of people about Otis Peek's murder, asking questions that might help solve the crime. It's possible something new has come up, or there's someone he wants to ask me about."

"Wait!" Jake caught her arm as she moved to get out of the pickup. "Off the subject, but did this Vinson guy ever lose his temper with you? Was he ever rough with you like he was with the newspaper delivery boy? Did he ever behave with you like he did with the guys he beat up?"

Well this *was* a change of subject. And possibly the reason Jake had been so quiet on the way home? He was brooding about Locke Vinson? She smiled gently at him. "Quite the opposite. I received no end of gifts and attention."

After a moment's thought, she added, "He did become something of a stalker for a while after I let him know I didn't want to see him anymore. What he was doing wasn't actual abuse. He was just insistent for a time that I continue to see him. I made it abundantly clear that anything between us was truly over, and he gradually gave up. I'm not concerned about his being at the rodeo and our running into him today, Jake, if that's bothering you. His being there was pure accident, I'm sure."

"I hope you're right, Celia." Jake jumped from the pickup and came around to open her door. "But something about the guy just doesn't seem right to me. You take care, hon."

"I will." She planted a quick kiss on his jaw. His expression changed to a pleased, quiet grin. She smiled at him and hurried up the walk.

This evening, entering her living room was like slamming into a wall of tension, whereas the cream and mossy green decor and comfortable antique furniture normally offered peace. Tierney and Lilly were seated opposite one another on overstuffed chairs. Conversation halted and they turned to look at her, expressions anxious.

"What is it?" she asked them, trying to calm her mind's alarm meter. She tossed her new cowboy hat onto the sofa. "Why was the chief here? Did he want to see me? I saw him leaving as we drove up."

There was a long silence as Tierney and Lilly looked at each other, each waiting for the other to speak. Lilly finally admitted, "Chief Erdman talked with both of us, but he was here mostly to see me. He—he thinks Mac had something to do with Otis Peek's murder."

"Mac?" Celia's mouth dropped. She found the remark almost funny. "Your husband Mac?" she asked inanely. Mac was a good kid, maybe a little quiet, but so in love with his wife, a hard-worker trying to get a college degree to help them get somewhere with their lives. Not Mac. He couldn't be responsible for Peek's death. But better to investigate everybody thoroughly, she decided, as she sat down on the sofa, than to settle on one person as the killer and miss clues leading to the real murderer. Pete knew what he was doing.

Tierney got to her feet, her hand resting lightly on the midriff of her mango silk pantsuit. "I'll leave you two alone."

There was no reason why Tierney couldn't stay. Mac was

innocent; they could discuss this together. Celia studied her. "Are you all right, Tierney?"

She explained, "I tire easily, but I'm fine. I simply have some tasks in my room that I want to get on with."

Celia nodded and smiled. Tierney read a great deal, wrote letters, and now and then sketched, seated in the light from her window.

Heavy silence filled the living room after her departure. "Lilly, dear, tell me what happened. Why would the chief suspect Mac?"

Lilly's voice was strained with worry. "Mac didn't do it, Mrs. Landry. He'd never do that to anyone."

"I don't believe he would, either. What motive would he have, after all?"

Lilly heaved a sigh, "Well, about that… You know that Mac's mother, Louise, worked for Mr. Peek as his housekeeper?"

"Sure I remember. But what would that have to do with Pete's suspicions?"

"Mac never did like the way Otis Peek treated his mother. She worked long hours for poor pay, did everything that old man demanded. Otis Peek was never easy to work for, but after Mrs. Strand took sick, it got worse and Mac got really angry."

Starting to recall incidents Lilly was referring to, Celia sat forward with a frown, anxious for Lilly to continue.

The younger woman hugged an apricot and green floral toss pillow to her chest. There was a shine of tears in her eyes as she talked. "Mac's mother had cancer and no health insurance to cover medical costs. She couldn't afford insurance on a cleaning woman's pay and Otis never provided insurance for her. She put off for too long getting the expensive medical help she needed. Mac went to Otis and asked him to help with Louise's medical bills. The costs added up so quickly when she finally did see a doctor."

"They would. Medical bills can reach astronomical

heights."

Lilly hugged the pillow tighter and nodded. "Otis turned him down, saying he didn't have the kind of money the doctors and hospital were asking for. He could have at least made Mac a loan or given him some money outright, any amount, but he didn't offer. Mac hated him for that. He believed his mother would have lived if Otis had helped from the start. When she died, Mac went to give Otis a piece of his mind."

"I remember," Celia quietly told her, giving Lilly a chance to dry her tears. "That argument between Otis and young Mac came to blows didn't it?"

"Yes, it did." Lilly wiped her cheeks. "Otis called the police to come arrest Mac for assault. He told Chief Erdman that Mac intended to kill him, but he didn't intend to at all, Mrs. Landrey. Mac was just mad and hurting over how his mother was treated."

"There was a hearing and the charges were dropped," Celia filled in.

"My husband was innocent then, and he is now!" Lilly said in staunch defense of the man she loved. "I told Chief Erdman that today, but he's still going to talk to Mac, and he wanted to know where he could find him."

Celia remembered Pete asking her about Mac, but it had seemed so incidental, so off-hand and not important at the time.

Lilly said, her voice faded almost too low to hear, "It scares me to death that he thinks Mac could have done it. That after all this time he would actually kill Otis Peek—out of revenge, or—or whatever."

Celia remembered the buzz of conversation following the memorial service for Louise Strand. Most folks would have helped had they known the truth about her situation in time. None of them faulted Mac for being angry at Otis Peek. Not a few of them stated that the old man should still be made to pay. Because Louise was indigent, the hospital bills were paid by various charities. Not in time, however, to save her life.

"The chief is just being thorough, Lilly. He's talking to everyone who ever had the slightest disagreement with Otis Peek, or who might know something of interest pertaining to the case. I'm sure he'll learn soon enough that Mac is innocent. I personally can't see Mac committing murder, even against an ornery old man like Otis. My goodness, more than two years have passed since their earlier set-to! They haven't had any arguments since then, have they?"

Lilly's voice trembled, and she looked down at her hands. "I-I don't think so. There's been no fights that I know of. Mac disliked Mr. Peek so much, he hated having anything to do with him. He's innocent, Mrs. Landrey. I swear he is! I'm just so afraid they'll find a way to build a case against him anyway." She cleared her throat, placed the throw pillow aside and stood up. "I need to get home, if there's nothing more you need for me to do today, Mrs. Landrey. I want to be at our apartment when Mac gets off work. Fix him a nice dinner."

"You do that, honey. Go ahead and go. I'm sure Mac's innocence will be proven, and I'll vouch for his character." Celia got to her feet. "I'll do anything I can to help you. But you have to tell me everything, Lilly. You have, haven't you?" She took her hand.

Lilly hesitated a second too long, her face wiped clean of expression. "Everything, Mrs. Landrey. I've told you everything."

Celia decided to let it go for the time being. "If you think of anything else, you will tell Chief Erdman? Or if you like, you can tell me and I can have a talk with him."

If the young couple had done something not quite right with the law, it might be easier to talk with her first, and she could clear the matter with Pete. In any event, she had a very strong conviction that Lilly was hiding something. But not murder. Surely not that.

Peek's murder was very much on Celia's mind the next day. How she would like the whole matter solved and behind them all and life in Pass Creek returned to normal. Preferably before someone else met an untimely demise.

She placed a call to Pete Erdman. When the city clerk said he was terribly busy and couldn't talk unless it was an emergency, she replied that it wasn't but that she would like a chat when he had the time.

Talking with folks on her own wasn't really interfering in the investigation, she decided. If there was more to Mac's disagreement with Otis than Lilly was saying, Myrna Hall could tell her. The strawberry-haired waitress knew as much about Otis Peek's life as anyone. When Celia had finished her writing and household tasks for the day, she rang the Mellow Mushroom, and Myrna's husky voice answered.

"Myrna, I've been thinking about making a lemon cheesecake tomorrow and would love to share it if you have time. How about coming over for dessert and coffee after you get off work? I'd like to chat." Myrna sounded so happy when she agreed to come, Celia felt guilty that her motive in having her over wasn't exactly a social invitation. She decided then to have a group of women friends come over more often. Perhaps Vivian and Salliebeth, and she'd invite Myrna to join them. Tierney was already here.

They could play cards and watch some old Carole Lombard movies on DVD if they could find them. She was a hoot in those comedies set in the early thirties; was only thirty-three when she died in a plane crash. Poor Clark Gable. He was just devastated, according to accounts.

After cards and a movie, they could just talk, Celia decided. And maybe together they could unravel the mystery of Peek's murder.

Myrna arrived on the dot of seven-thirty the next evening. She'd changed from her uniform into a turquoise sheath dress and heels, and she wore extra makeup and her strawberry hair in an attractive knot on the top of her head.

"That's a gorgeous dress, Myrna. It's so pretty on you," Celia told her when she welcomed her inside. Residents of the inn had taken over the living room, watching television and putting together jigsaw puzzles, except for Tierney, who had retired to her room early. For privacy, Celia led Myrna into her study off the hall opposite the living room. She'd cleared a small table there and arranged it with cups and saucers, a carafe of coffee and their dessert.

Myrna looked around the room, nodding. "You got it nice here, Celia. I like that little boy there." She pointed at a bronze sculpture on a nearby pedestal table of a boy sitting cross-legged, reading a book.

"Reading Boy is my good luck charm," Celia said. "When I get stuck with something I'm writing, I talk it over with him, and he almost always helps me figure things out."

Myrna looked puzzled and Celia laughed. "Never mind. That wouldn't make sense to anyone but me or another writer."

"I needed to get some use from the dress." Myrna turned away from the statue and smoothed her skirt. "Bought it from a fancy Salem store." She took the chair Celia motioned her to. "Thought if Otis could see me really fixed up, it might put him in a marrying state of mind. I'd tried everything else."

Celia gave her a conspiratorial smile. "Well, you know how men are."

"I took him nice meals when he didn't feel good," Myrna continued, her expression asking for understanding. "Helped him pick out new colors, curtains and appliances when he wanted to fix up his kitchen over there to Gable House. I did everything a wife would do for him," she said candidly, looking Celia squarely in the eye. "I mean everything. But it did me no good. Like they say, why buy the cow if you can get the milk for free."

"Well if he didn't notice how nice you look in that dress,

he was blind," Celia told her emphatically, meaning it. "You were too good for him anyway, Myrna. Otis could be a scoundrel without half trying."

"Tell me about it. Some men was just born to be bachelors, I suppose, and some of them mean and selfish." Myrna took the cup of coffee Celia handed her. "There may be some good men out there, but I ain't found them. I'm three times divorced, you know. I thought my last husband was Mr. Right for sure. Then, a few years being married to him, I realized his first name was Always." She chuckled at her own joke.

She took a sip of coffee and continued, "I don't think Otis ever would've changed his mind, even if he'd lived. Still, it don't do no good"—she shook her head—"to talk bad of the dead. 'Sides that, I was fond of the old cuss, very fond in spite of his failings. I would've married him in a second if he'd of had me."

Her face looked drawn when she asked, "Did you hear, Celia, the chief thinks Otis was murdered? That it wasn't no accident killed him? That he didn't fall off the roof but was beat over the head?"

Celia had already decided to get straight to the point and tell Myrna she wanted to talk about Otis Peek this evening. Evidently Myrna guessed why she was there and didn't mind.

"I'd heard. Now we have an investigation under way, and I hope Pete finds whoever did it soon. Did you see anything suspicious at Gable House that evening, Myrna? Was anyone else around? Anyone leaving as you arrived?"

"All I saw was Otis dead on the ground in a pool of blood." She put her coffee aside. "I was so shook up, there could've been a dozen killers in the bushes and in the orchard and I wouldn't have seen them. I run over to Mrs. Kemp's house and we called the chief. Looked to all of us like Otis just fell off the roof, pure accident. He was there in his carpenter's apron, tools all around…"

"It seemed that way at first," Celia agreed. "Here you

are." She picked up one of her best Bavarian dessert dishes containing a thin slice of lemon cheesecake, a delicate fork on the side, and held it out to Myrna.

She waved it away. "No appetite. But thanks."

Celia hesitated. "We don't have to talk about Otis if it bothers you." She went to open the window, allowing the evening air and fragrance of flowers inside.

"I want to talk. I come here wanting to. Three slices of chocolate cake I ate at the Mushroom today is the reason I can't eat your cheesecake. Sorry, 'cause it looks real good." She took up her coffee again and held it out for freshening.

Celia laughed as she poured. "I don't blame you. The chocolate cake you serve there is food for the gods." She had missed dinner and tackled her own dessert hungrily, asking after a moment, "Do you have any ideas who might have had something against Otis serious enough they wanted him dead?"

"Talk down at the Mushroom is that young Mac Strand did it. Chief suspects him anyhow, if his questioning everybody about Mac means anything."

"My feeling is that Mac is innocent, but what do you think? Were there problems between the two that you know of, other than the altercation they had over Otis not helping with Mac's mother's hospital bills? Did Otis ever say anything to you about that?"

Myrna waved an arm. "All he said was that Mac was making false claims. All nonsense. He told me he was fond of the boy, but he couldn't have him coming around making trouble."

"Making what kind of trouble?" Celia pressed. "Did you ever personally witness Mac and Otis fighting? I thought all that ended with Mac hating Peek so much he refused to go near him."

"I never saw them argue about anything, but that don't mean it didn't happen. Maybe they fought from time to time about how Louise died." Myrna shook her strawberry curls. "And who would blame the boy? You'd a thought that after all the years Louise worked for Otis, he'd of helped with her hospital bills. I didn't think kindly of him for treating her that way. She was a friend of mine. Of course, when you look at it like that, he didn't treat me much better, did he?" Anger tinged with hurt flared in her expression.

Seeing it, Celia's scalp prickled, and she wondered if perhaps Myrna might had done Otis Peek in. Motive was there to a degree, and opportunity. Myrna had had an affair with Peek, had had wishful dreams of becoming his wife. She'd hoped to leave drudgery as a waitress behind and for the two of them to enjoy the rest of their autumn years together. Nothing Myrna did from sleeping with Otis, going to social affairs with him to looking after him, had induced him to marry her.

Could there have been a violent argument over the matter that ended in his death? Reluctantly and despite doubt, Celia mentally put Myrna on her list of suspects.

"I don't think Mac Strand killed Otis," Myrna was saying. "He'd have too much to lose, for one thing. He'd be sent to prison. He'd no longer have a life with young Lilly and them so much in love. Killing Otis wouldn't bring his mother back, either."

"True." Celia nodded, picking up a last few crumbs from her plate with her finger. "Sometimes people hold a grudge a long time and then snap." She quoted Pete Erdman almost verbatim. "Perfectly normal people who wouldn't hurt anyone otherwise." She gauged Myrna's reaction, but Myrna didn't take the bait. Her expression remained as pure as milk.

"Maybe Mac did it, but I can't see it myself."

"Not everyone in Pass Creek liked Otis," Celia plunged on, hoping to learn anything at all to end the ugly matter. "He did have disagreements with other folk. Did Otis ever tell you about any of those problems? Did anyone ever make strong threats against him that you know of?"

Myrna shook her head. "I can't think of any fuss with

somebody big enough for them to want to kill him. Oh, he fought with neighbors who let their dogs poop on his lawn." She smiled, looking inward at the memory. "He'd rant and rave and shovel it up and dump it back on their grass." After a pause, her brow puckered in thought, she said, "He was on the outs with some of our business folk. Them that wanted to tear down the old houses and other buildings, bring in big box stores and the like. He was strong on the notion Pass Creek ought to stay how it is, except for some nice quiet industry that'd give folks jobs."

"Yes, that was his opinion, and I shared it with him." Celia hesitated, remembering that Locke Vinson had said Pete Erdman wanted to question him. "Do you have knowledge of business dealings between Otis and Locke Vinson?"

"The man that owns that print shop on Main? Otis might have gone to him for a print job, fliers or forms of some kind or other. I never heard Otis talk about their business, though. I'd say if he had differences with Locke Vinson, it would have been over Vinson wanting Pass Creek to go modern, torn down and rebuilt new. Otis wouldn't have stood for that. If Otis loved anything, it was this town."

"For certain, he only wanted the best for Pass Creek."

"You'd know more about Locke Vinson than I would, Celia. You dated him for a while, as I remember. Some of us thought you two might marry, you all alone after Ethan died. A darned good-looking guy, too." A mild puzzled expression replaced her smile. "Next thing I knew, you stopped seeing one another."

"This was for the best. We weren't a match. But back to what we were discussing. It's so hard to know who might have had anything so severe against Otis as to want him dead. No one I can think of stands out as a prime suspect."

"Maybe it wasn't anybody local that killed him," Myrna offered after a moment, shrugging. "Could be it was just somebody passing through. What I read in the papers is that a lot of the time, meth addicts or plain thieves from somewhere else hit a town with the idea of stealing what they can. Somebody's identity, you know, from folks' important papers. Antiques, TVs and microwaves. Metal stuff to sell to junk yards. If one of them addicts tried to rob Otis, maybe he fought back and was killed. And the killer is long gone and won't never be found."

"I suppose it's possible, I've considered that myself. Still, I hope whoever did it doesn't go free. You would think that with the murder taking place in late afternoon or early evening while it was still light, someone surely saw something suspicious. It's odd that no one has come forth." Maybe they had, of course, and Pete was keeping details of evidence to himself. Or if they hadn't, maybe they would yet, if persuaded.

"Well, our little town can be pretty quiet at times," Myrna was saying, picking up her handbag, getting ready to leave. "It's possible that at the time it happened, nobody else was around to see nothing out of the ordinary. Things happen. Sometimes they're seen and sometimes not, sometimes reported to the police and sometimes not. Like the time Otis caught that shiftless Harry Shull trying to rob him."

"Wait a second." Celia held up a hand. "What are you talking about?"

Chapter Thirteen

Myrna sat down again. "Don't know why I didn't think of this a few minutes ago. Probably because it was Otis after somebody else, not somebody mad at him. You know who I'm talking about. Skinny no-good fella, scruffy dark hair and beard? Never saw a day's work he liked? Bums drinks off others down to the tavern when he can?"

"Yes, I know who Harry Shull is." Among the residents of most small towns there was a shady character or two. Harry Shull was Pass Creek's mischief maker: a sticky-fingered thief who was in and out of jail more times than anyone could count. When he was around, he lived in a dilapidated camp trailer near where the old town dump was once located.

There was a time Celia had felt sorry for him and how he lived, and she'd offered him yard work. It wasn't a half day before he'd quit and several tools from her garage had gone with him. They were never recovered. "I haven't seen Harry Shull around for a while. Is he back?"

"He was in the Mushroom just the other day, having a timber float." She explained, in case Celia didn't know, "We bring him water but he doesn't order anything. He takes the catsup bottle there on the table and dumps half of it into his glass and drinks it. Leaving, he takes himself a free toothpick. Timber float."

"When did Shull try to rob Otis?" Celia asked, bringing

Myrna back to the subject. "Tell me what happened, please."

"Sure! Otis come home after eating dinner downtown one rainy day last January. No, it was into February, now I think about it. There was Harry Shull sneaking out the back door with this Civil War gun that had belonged to Otis's great-grandfather. Otis was so proud of that keepsake. 'Colt Dragoon Revolver,' I think he said the gun was. He kept it in a special glass-front box over the fireplace in the parlor."

"What happened?"

"Well, Otis took after Shull with a baseball bat, yelling what he'd do when he caught him and if he lived from that, he'd have him arrested. Shull dropped the box with the gun in it and kited out of there."

"Was this reported?"

"Oh, yeah. Otis told Pete Erdman what happened, wanted Shull arrested for attempted robbery. The chief questioned Shull but it never come to much, since he didn't get away with stealing the weapon and denied he even tried to. Otis was pretty put out over that."

"He would be, for sure. And I'm positive Pete was disappointed not to have enough evidence to arrest Shull."

Myrna nodded. "He advised Otis to put the gun where it wouldn't tempt thieves. Otis liked having it at home where he could enjoy looking at it, but he took it to the bank and had it put in a safety deposit box."

"Good plan." After a moment's silence, Celia asked, "Has Pete talked to you about Otis's murder, Myrna?"

She nodded. "He come to me right off as soon as he knew it wasn't no accident and me being close to Otis, his sort-of girlfriend." Her eyes filmed with tears at that thought; she brushed them away and continued, "I told him everything we been talking about. Of course he mostly asks questions. Doesn't really say who *he* thinks killed Otis."

"That's how Pete does his job," Celia agreed wryly,

wishing she could get out of Pete exactly what was going on. "I just hope he finds the culprit soon. Pass Creek doesn't need a criminal running loose, if it's someone local and still here."

After Myrna left, Celia's mind went back over their conversation, looking for a clue that might mean something. She couldn't help feeling guilty that she considered the other woman, whom she actually liked, a suspect in the crime.

Myrna's description of her shock at finding Otis Peek's body, her expressed fondness for him and regret at his passing, were all pretty convincing. Nor did Myrna seem the criminal type. But wouldn't anyone lie through her teeth rather than be found guilty? And point the finger at someone else? An outsider or a smalltime thug like Harry Shull?

Pete Erdman caught up with Celia in his blue and white police cruiser as she headed home following her walking tour the next day. She waited and watched him pull over to the curb and climb from the car. He struggled to keep a straight face as he took in her cowgirl get-up. "You wanted to talk to me, Celia?"

Chin high in her lovely grey Stetson, her fringed grey leather skirt—fifty dollars from the antique store and worn by a former Pendleton Roundup rodeo queen—and boots, she led the way to the bench in front of Rosa Jean's Beauty Shop on Main, motioning him to follow her. They sat down and she told him about her conversation with Myrna.

Hoping she wasn't throwing suspicion wrongly, she asked, "Do you think Myrna might've gotten angry enough at Otis for his treatment of her to kill him?"

Pete stretched his uniformed legs out in front of him, his shoe sidestepping a wad of pink bubblegum on the sidewalk. A couple across the street waved at him and Celia before they entered the old theatre building that had recently been converted into a well-stocked bookstore. Finally, he shook his head as he faced her. "I considered the possibility, but I have my doubts Myrna was the one."

"You don't really believe young Mac Strand killed him, do you? He seems standoffish and angry at the world at times, but I think that's really shyness. And maybe a little distrust. Despite the fact life hasn't always been kind to Mac; he's a hard worker, always polite when I've had him to the house to work for me. He's set goals for himself and Lilly that are positive, good things."

When Lilly had come to work this morning, she'd said that the chief had had a discussion with Mac, seemed satisfied with his answers, but warned him the investigation was ongoing and not to leave town. "You don't honestly think it was Mac, do you?"

"I really can't say."

Celia was exasperated at Pete's reticence, but held to the subject like a bulldog with a bone. "What about Locke Vinson? He might have had dealings with Otis that went sour. Or there could have been a violent argument between them over the changes Locke wants to make here in Pass Creek."

He didn't reply, so she went right on down her personal list of suspects. "Have you considered Harry Shull, that conniving thief that gives Pass Creek so many headaches? Could he have committed the murder during an act of robbery?"

"Darn it, Celia," Pete replied with a wry grin, "you should know that I can't tell you police business. All I can say is I'm doing everything I can to solve Otis's murder. These things take time. Not only do I want to find out who killed him, I want enough air-tight evidence so that the murderer won't get off on some trumped up technicality when it gets to court."

In other words, any one of the people she mentioned could have done the deed, Celia thought to herself. Or someone not on her list might have committed the crime. Pete could already be fairly sure who the murderer was, but without proper evidence he couldn't yet make an arrest. Of course she understood.

"I'm sorry, Pete, I don't mean to push at you. It's just that

Pass Creek has problems enough without murder to deal with. I want our town to be the peaceful little village it used to be. I'd like Gable House to be free and clear of all the troubles surrounding it so it can remain an unfettered part of my walking tour. Whatever is bothering Tierney Jones, I want so much for her to change her mind and let Gable House stand, to allow us to have tea and cookies there, show the inside the way we used to!"

Pete might have been listening, or he might have had something else on his mind; it was hard to tell. She continued, "The only thing at present keeping Tierney from going ahead with her plan of destruction seems to be her fragile health. I'm so afraid that once she's stronger, which could be any time, the first thing she'll do is demolish Gable House."

She took a deep breath, "When Tierney Jones visited Peek that first time she came here, did she have some terrible thing against him, do you think? She doesn't seem like a killer, but there she is, in my house, and one never knows…"

Pete said, with infinite patience, "I don't think she would have stayed around in Pass Creek if she was the one who killed him."

"Well, there is the old saying that a good place to hide is in plain sight."

"If I thought you or your tenants were in danger from the lady, or if I had evidence that I should take her in, I'd have done something about her before now. The investigation is moving along. I just ask that you be patient and not worry."

"All right, Pete." She gave in. Clearly their being close friends wasn't going to budge him from police protocol. "But I have to say that many a catastrophe has been diverted or solved because a woman had the good sense to be worried. You know? Joan of Arc. Harriet Tubman. Jane Adams. Carrie Nation—well, maybe she went a little far taking a hatchet to Kansas saloons, but she had the right idea about wanting drunken men to stay home and take care of their families. I could give you chapter and verse if there was time," she finished grumpily, "but I can see that you're anxious to get back to your job."

He laughed and helped her to her feet. "It's good to see you, Celia. I always enjoy it. And you *are* helpful when you let me know what you've heard or seen. Just let me do the hard work, okay? This whole situation could get dangerous."

She settled her broad-brimmed Stetson more tightly on her head. "I do want to say that our citizens appreciate your work Pete, very much. If we can just get this town on its feet the way we want, we'll see that you get a deputy again so you're not on duty around the clock."

"I'm on call twenty-four-seven, but that doesn't mean I don't get to bed to sleep or have time to eat and time with my family, Celia. Besides, I can call in extra police presence from Mackay County when it's needed."

"I hope you're using them now."

"They're on the job, too." He grinned wryly and shook his head at her.

"Then we should have all the answers soon." Celia returned his smile. "Tell Thea and the children hello for me." She waved as his cruiser pulled away from the curb, then set off again for home.

A few folks waved and complimented her costume, made a joke about "where was her horse?" or yelled, "Yeehaw!" She smiled and waved back, but her mind was too occupied with a new plan to stop and chat.

Back at the inn, she mulled the idea of investigating Harry Shull. If she could eliminate even one or two people from her list of suspects in the murder, it would help matters. Finding evidence they were guilty would be even better, although exactly what she should look for to do that, she wasn't sure. Should she drive to Shull's place, or walk?

Considering the price of gas these days, though Jolly gave the best deal he could, she settled on walking. She happily exchanged her cowgirl outfit for blue walking shorts and shirt and comfortable athletic shoes. It would be only a walk of three miles or so, anyway, and the same back. She could use the exercise. Carrying a trowel and burlap bag, leaving Lilly to finish cleaning and Mac mowing the lawn, she set off.

She was perspiring by the time she reached the area of the old dump south of town and at the end of a long graveled road. The few rocky acres were overgrown with weeds and scrub brush and divided by a shallow gulch. For years now, Pass Creek's trash had been picked up from homes and trucked to a landfill at the other end of the county.

Not everyone paid for garbage service, however, and if no one was looking, they'd dump their trash at the old site. Volunteers periodically cleaned the place up, chiefly because they didn't like the smelly, unsightly mess, but also because it was hoped the spot would eventually attract a buyer seeking an industrial site.

A sewer-like odor drifted from the gulch where some fool had dumped pickup loads of garbage that had yet to be cleaned up. Standing there looking around, Celia could think of more pleasant places to be right now: her own beautiful backyard for one. Under her plum tree with something nice and cold to drink. Her mouth set grimly, and she did her best to ignore the bad smells.

Finding what she was looking for, she settled herself on the ground next to a patch of dazzling yellow California poppies. Her yard would be even nicer with a few wildflowers growing by her creek. With her trowel, she stabbed at the hard ground around the clump in an attempt to dig them free.

Other than the occasional trill of a bird, the place was eerily quiet. Or maybe it was her nerves making it seem that way. Every now and then her glance stole to Harry Shull's battered hulk of a trailer a few yards to her right. He'd inherited his small, junk-filled lot from his grandfather, one of Pass Creek's earlier outlaws. The tools Harry had stolen from her would have been sold long since, of course, but that wasn't what she was here for. *Surveillance;* that's what it was called on television. Hoping to see something important that would set her poor town free from the horror overshadowing it.

Finally, she freed the California poppies from the hard, dry ground. She sat back to rest a moment, wiping her brow with her arm, her eyes furtively on Shull's place. There was no sign of movement, no evidence of him being at home. She was foolish to be here, she supposed.

Trying to focus on a patch of pale lavender foxglove, she dug furiously, thinking how convenient it would be if suspects could be dug out in the same way plants could. One by one, until the guilty one was proven and the rest could go free.

Her gaze returned time and again to Harry Shull's trailer. If he was home, there was no sign of it. Finally, she stood up, her heart thumping hard in her chest. It wasn't the heat that stifled her breathing now.

She pulled off her rings and put them in a secure pocket of her shorts. If Shull was at home, she could tell him she lost her ring while digging and if he'd help find it, she would give him a cash reward. Maybe get him to talking, ask a few questions. In a roundabout way, find out where he was and what he was doing the evening Otis Peek was murdered.

Leaving her plants in a pile, she entered Shull's yard. Goosebumps prickled her flesh as she took the worn dirt path through piles of junk toward his shacky trailer. Rotted rags spilled out of dirty cardboard cartons, old tires lay in heaps. There were rusted auto body parts, a stove tipped on its side, moldy men's shoes—she shuddered and tried not to see any more. By the time she'd reached the grungy door of his trailer, she'd almost changed her mind. Wanted to grab her things and run for home.

A sleuth worth her salt, of course couldn't do that. She

fought her fear and knocked on the door. *Nothing.* She pounded on the door again and again, then moved to the side of the trailer and tried to see through the fair-sized but grimy window. The window was blocked from inside by stacks of *stuff.* Exactly what kind of stuff, she wasn't sure.

Returning to the door, she knocked and waited. Again she knocked loudly enough to wake the dead, a thought that sent a shiver along her spine. Nothing happened. Ignoring personal recrimination that she was trespassing, she tried the door. It was solidly locked. She circled the trailer, found another window at the back, but it was too high to see through without something to stand on. She found an old chair without a back, and moved it below the window.

The glass here wasn't quite as grimy. By standing on her tiptoes and straining her eyes she could make out some of what was inside, and she swallowed a gasp. Maybe this was what she'd unconsciously known she would find; hoped to find. "I'm looking at reason enough to put you in jail, in the *cooler,* Harry Shull," she whispered to herself jubilantly. At the same time he paid for this lesser crime, it could be determined if he was Otis Peek's killer as well.

She counted two new-looking microwaves and three computers. There were power tools, stacked television sets, rifles, handguns, and a jewelry box on top of that. The small room was filled almost to the ceiling. However long Harry Shull had been out of jail this time, he'd been very busy. If the chief had been here, and she was sure he had been, he wouldn't have missed seeing all this stuff.

Did Shull have an excuse for possessing these things, or was the contraband recently moved in and soon to be moved out? She felt positive it was the latter. She had to let Pete know about this, and quickly. What was she thinking, leaving her cell phone at home? She'd give anything to have it handy to use right now.

Still, she'd discovered a stash of merchandise that was no

doubt stolen, and if so, it would be solid evidence to put Shull behind bars for safekeeping until it could be determined if he was not only a thief but a murderer.

Keeping low, exhilarated with triumph, she rushed back to where she'd left her plants and tools. She had kneeled to gather her things when the rumble of a vehicle brought her head up. A battered white van was coming fast up the gravel road, dust coiled in its wake. Harry Shull, and he'd seen her. Her insides turned queasy with fear. She debated whether to run, but there was no reason to. She wasn't on his property. As far as he knew, she was out here minding her own business. If he said anything to her, she'd bluff it out. She left her plants on the ground, proof of why she was there.

With more courage than she was feeling, she smiled and waved when he pulled to a stop in his yard. He jumped out and came over. "What the hell you doin' here?"

She motioned at the wilting wildflowers in their clumps of dirt at her feet and answered casually, "You can see. I'm establishing a wildflower garden in my backyard and came out for these."

"The hell you did." He took a threatening step forward. "I've been to your place, remember, Mrs. Landrey. You got plenty of posies and even if you wanted more, you wouldn't come here for 'em."

"I remember, Harry." She resisted an urge to run like fire was at her heels and stood her ground. "I also recall that some valuable tools disappeared from my place the same time you quit that job for me."

Suspicion flared in his eyes and she instantly regretted bringing up his thievery. He reached out and took her arm in a hard grip. "You been over to my place, haven't you? Snooping around?"

Cold chills traveled her spine. Her throat was dry as she demanded to know, "Why in heaven's name would I do that? I wouldn't be looking for the tools you stole from me. You would have sold them ages ago. Right?"

"Shut your damn mouth." He lifted a hand as though to strike her. "Something has got you to come out here, and nobody but a fool would believe it was to get these damn weeds." He gave a kick and the poppies and foxglove went flying.

"I dug those wildflowers to take home!" Celia tried to wrest her arm from his grip. His answer was to wrench her arm painfully, causing her to cry out. His dirty gray shirt reeked of sweat, worsened by the warmth of the afternoon. She was about to vomit. Suddenly, she was furious to the bone. "Damn it, let me go! I've done nothing to you!"

He slapped her then, so hard her head snapped. Her cheek burned from pain, and she stared at him in outrage. Lifting her other hand, she threatened him with her trowel. "Take your hands off me, you idiot!"

"Not till I teach you a lesson." He ripped the trowel from her hand, leaving her fingers stinging, and threw it as far as he could. "You ain't talkin' to nobody about anything you saw today. Nothin' about me, hear? I can make you sorry as hell if you do. You understand me?" He shook her so hard her teeth rattled, and it was impossible to answer him. She saw his fist draw back and she choked on a sob, tried to jerk away, but he held her tight and the blow landed like a hammer at the side of her head. "Teach you!" His voice seemed to come from a great distance as he struck her again and again. Her knees crumpled and consciousness shattered to nothing.

Chapter Fourteen

Consciousness came in a gradual, foggy haze. Celia felt ill, and her head rocketed with pain. Where on earth was she? Nothing felt right. It was hard to see with this scratchy stuff over her eyes and clinging to her mouth. Why couldn't she get enough air? She tried to move, to sit up, and her head spun dizzily. Why in the name of God were her hands tied tightly and painfully behind her back?

She lay in confusion, trying to get her bearings, to think clearly. Knowledge of her predicament grew. Whatever it was that made it hard to see and scratched her jaw raw with pain was a—bag that had been pulled down over her face and shoulders. What bag? Who did this? Her mind struggled for answers. *The burlap bag she'd brought for her plants.* That was it! Thank God the weave of the burlap was loose, or she'd be dead of suffocation. Harry Shull–Harry Shull–Harry Shull had done this to her.

She tried to quell her climbing panic. She again attempted to sit up, to get to her feet, with a stronger effort this time, but the more she struggled, the deeper she was pulled into some kind of slime. *Garbage.* He'd tied her up while she was unconscious, pulled her own burlap bag down over her head, and thrown her in the gulch with the garbage. She began to scream, a sound muffled to her own ears. It hurt to scream, and if she did, would the noise bring Harry Shull or someone to rescue her?

Celia began to cry from fright, anger, and feelings of utter confusion. How long had she been unconscious? It seemed an eternity since she'd left home to come out here. Was she missed by now and were friends out looking for her? Why must it be so hard to think? She lay quietly, examining her position as closely as she could. It finally dawned on her that her legs were free. She had to climb out of this terrible place. She moved to stand up, but her legs drove deeper into muck which already felt waist high.

Slowly she struggled one leg after the other, inch by inch, by feel, through the stinking garbage and up the side of the gulch, falling from time to time without the use of her hands to catch herself. It might have been minutes, but seemed to take hours. Trembling, panting with effort, her head reeling, she finally reached solid ground. She lay there a minute, trying to set aside the pain in her face and head from Shull's blows, the ache in her wrists and arms from being tied.

Which way? She didn't want to go anywhere near Shull's trailer; had to somehow keep out of his sight. She caught some of the burlap in her teeth and began to bite and tear. With an opening in the sack, she'd be able to better see where she was going. She'd like to find her trowel again, or a rock or piece of glass, something to cut the bindings on her wrists. With her teeth, she ripped and tore at the burlap, sobbing in frustration as she yanked her aching head this way and that to tear her face free.

At that moment she realized the sack was not tied to her, that if she lay on her back and wiggled downward enough and the bag stayed in place, caught on the rocky ground, she'd be free of it. She twisted and wiggled and used her heels to pull her body out of the bag. Panting, she rolled onto her stomach, raised her head slightly and took in her surroundings.

The road was *that* way, ahead. Shull's trailer was *over there*. There was no sign of his battered white van. She looked at the sky and in disbelief noted that the sun was in the east and early-morning high. But how could that be? Stunned, she realized that she had been blacked out for hours, or dulled and sleeping, semi-conscious with pain, half-buried in garbage all night.

She soon gave up a search for her trowel or anything else to cut her wrists free, and she staggered at a run from shrub to rock to hillock until she reached the main road. Tears of relief and humiliation ran down her face as she stumbled toward town and home, reeking of garbage, her neck too sore to turn and look for sign of Harry Shull coming after her.

～～～

"I was trying to help," Celia said, alternately holding an ice bag to her swollen, half-closed eye and then her right temple. She felt a lot better after a bath, clean pajamas and robe, hot tea and being home again after hours at the hospital being examined. Fortunately she had no skull or facial fractures or a cervical injury. Her concussion should progressively resolve, according to her doctor, but she was to take it easy for the next ten days.

The difficulty now was trying to explain her situation to Jake, pacing back and forth in front of where she sat on the sofa in her living room, his expression thunderous; and Pete, observing her tight-lipped from the other side of the room, notepad in hand after taking her statement. He put it down and picked up his cup of coffee.

"I'd just talked to you, Celia, and asked you to be patient and let me do my job," Pete told her. "You had no business going out there to Shull's place."

She wanted to argue that she was there for wildflowers, but that story wasn't going to wash with a cop any more than it had with a scum like Shull. "I'm sorry. I really am."

Jake was next to rake her over the coals. She winced at his shout. "That man could have killed you! Why in God's name did you put yourself in a position to get into that kind of trouble? Nobody knew where you were. Lilly told us you'd gone to dig up wildflowers, but she wasn't sure where. We checked out by the old dump site, found your trowel and some wilted flowers you'd dug. I talked to Harry Shull, but he said when he got home, you weren't around. He hadn't seen you."

"Did you look in the garbage?"

"Hell, yes, I looked in the garbage. I didn't see you. How was I to know that a burlap bag with garbage piled around was you?"

"I'm everlastingly grateful you came along and drove me back to town, Jake. I'm sorry about the mess in your pickup, all the stink and garbage, but I'll clean it for you."

"Forget the pickup. I left it at the station for a needed tune-up, and Jolly is taking care of the mess at the same time."

"Oh, good. Then I'll pay the bill."

"Dammit, don't try to smooth things over, Celia! I'd been looking all night, nearly out of my mind." His fingers plowed his hair; his voice was gravelly with emotion. "Everybody in town was looking for you."

"And even then," Pete said, shaking his head, "Harry Shull got away. Packed up the loot you claim you saw in his trailer, probably in that old van of his."

While she was being cared for at the hospital, Pete and Jake had gone to Shull's place and found it empty. Not a stick of anything she'd said she'd seen was still there. That part she hated most of all. With proof of his stealing, they could have caught him and taken him in.

Pete got to his feet, returned his empty coffee cup to her kitchen, and came back to the living room. "I'll put out a bulletin on Shull and charge him with your assault and kidnapping if we find him. He's not going to like it that you've accused him, Celia, and that you told us about the stolen stuff. You need to be extremely careful in case he comes back. He's not the smartest crook in the world, and he's stupid enough to try and kill you next time, to get even."

Jake cursed and threw his hands in the air. "All we need. You'll lie low, Celia," he ordered, his voice trembling, "not only to recover from the concussion, but so that this freak can't get back at you!"

"I don't think he'll try. I really don't. I think he's all big bluff and not very smart, like you said, Pete. I'm sure he thought that after the way he threatened me, even if I didn't smother to death in that garbage, I'd be too scared to talk, to point a finger at him."

"You can't be sure he's all bluff," Jake argued.

"We'll get him," Pete assured. "I just wish you hadn't flushed that sorry bird before I was ready, Celia. He pulled a slick one, keeping you out of the way and silent while he stowed his loot in his van and got out of there. He could be headed for California by now, or north to Canada." He gave a brief nod, his face stern with disappointment. "I'll be seeing you two." He headed for her front door.

She called after him, saying for the umpteenth time, "I'm sorry, Pete. I'll be careful to steer clear of your investigation and not cause any more problems." At the moment, she'd never meant anything more sincerely. What she wanted was to crawl into bed and sleep until all the troubles her town faced were gone. Wake up to some kind of miracle that everything was fine and nobody was mad at her anymore.

Jake seemed to read her mind. "You look awful, Celia. I'll put you to bed."

"I can manage." She stood up, staggered.

"No, you can't." He scooped her into his arms with a gentleness that seeped into her bones. "Which way is your room?"

She pointed with a sore arm. On the way down the hall, he whispered, his breath soft on her cheek, "If I lost you, Celia, it would kill me."

Or did she just imagine that's what he said?

Celia came gradually awake the next morning, surprised to see Salliebeth seated in the dim corner of the bedroom. She remembered groggily that Jake had sat in the same chair all night. At least twice he'd awakened her from sleep to make sure she hadn't lost consciousness again from her concussion. Arguing with him that she was fine and he should go home got her nowhere.

"Salliebeth," Celia said, clearing her throat. She took in her good friend's concerned expression, the determined set of her mouth. "Let me guess. Jake sent you here to be my bodyguard or something?" She scooted up to a sitting position, and plumped her pillows behind her shoulders. Her mouth tasted grungy and she was hardly prepared for company, not even that of a good friend, I'm-here-to-save-your-life variety.

"Yup, he asked, but I would have anyway." Salliebeth came over and gave her a hug. "Kiddo." She clicked her tongue. "You should see the side of your face. I swear that it's every color of the rainbow. That creep Shull should be taken out and shot, if they can find him."

"They'll find him—I hope." Celia reached up to gingerly touch her face and winced from the pain. She eased her blanket aside and sat on the edge of the bed yawning and stretching.

Salliebeth, back in her chair and watching, winced each time Celia did, causing Celia to chuckle. "I'm fine, really, Salliebeth. I don't need a nurse or a bodyguard, if that's what Jake's thinking."

"You went through a really dangerous ordeal."

"Okay, it was. But now I'm here and safe and it isn't as though I'm alone in this house, for heaven's sake. I have guests staying upstairs." She rolled her eyes in that direction. "Plus Lilly coming and going to help out. I haven't had symptoms indicating anything serious." In exasperation, she listed for Salliebeth, "No vomiting or dizziness, I'm not confused, there's no ringing in my ears."

She gave the latter a moment's thought and added wryly, "No ringing except for echoes of Jake's yelling at me. He was really angry that I got caught out there at the dumpsite by Harry Shull. So was Pete, although he didn't rail at me as hard as Jake did."

"You took a big chance going out there and snooping, my friend." Salliebeth brought her chair closer to Celia's bed. "The whole town was scared stiff for you when you went missing. They feared the worst: that Pass Creek had a serial killer on its hands and you would turn out to be the murderer's second victim."

"But they were wrong about me, and I'm fine," Celia reminded Salliebeth for the umpteenth time, weary of the subject.

"It's not over for everybody else. You might as well get used to folks coming by and checking on you for the next few days. Jake's given the orders, but of course people would have come anyway. In fact, since I arrived this morning, three people have come by. I shooed them away to let you sleep. Two casseroles and a cherry pie are put away in your kitchen."

"Good grief." Celia laughed. "I'm not dying, and this is nobody's funeral."

"Like I said. You're important to this town, and people care about you. On top of that, from the signs, Jake has come to realize he's in love with you." She continued before Celia could protest, "Knowing you were missing, and later seeing you hurt from that demon Shull's hands just about did him in. Jake's feelings toward you are in no way casual, honey-pie, and it shows all over him."

Celia's face warmed. Her hands smoothed her tousled mop as a smile teased around her mouth. She met Salliebeth's twinkling-eyed gaze with her own, and admitting finally, "He carried me to bed last night. Tucked me in, then he sat there in that same chair, waking me two or three times to make sure I was okay. It might have been my imagination, but earlier I thought he whispered something to the effect that it would kill him if I came to harm. Something like that. I was very tired and my brain was rattled. Maybe I dreamed he said it."

"And I'll bet my swanky new red high heels from Nordstrom you didn't dream it."

They laughed and Celia changed the subject, thinking she might drown in new-blooming happiness if she thought about Jake. She didn't want to lose her good sense altogether. "Catch me up on the talk around town the last day or two about Peek's murder. What are you hearing? Anyone coming up with new evidence, do you suppose? Pete won't tell me anything other than to stay out of it."

"Good advice, kiddo, and you have the bruises to prove it." Salliebeth sighed and waved a hand. "The usual suppositions continue to grow, all of them you know about. Old Mrs. Kemp is saying now she believes she saw a man in the backyard with Otis not long before the time he was killed. There's folks convinced that young Mac Strand hated Otis enough to kill him."

"Mrs. Kemp saw someone? She's not mentioned that before. But if she did, I don't think it was Mac, even though he had as good a reason as anyone."

"I'm with you. I don't see a sweet guy like Mac as a coldblooded killer. But people aren't always what they seem, either. Or something drives them to step out of the personality we think we know so well." Salliebeth hesitated, and said with a shake of her head, "Remember Ted Bundy? People closest to him believed that he was a nice guy. He was personable, charming—and a serial killer."

"Is anyone mentioning Locke Vinson as a possibility in the Peek crime?" Celia asked, thinking Salliebeth's description of Bundy could fit Locke to a degree.

"Sure are. A faction of business owners is ready to put money on a bet that Locke Vinson was the one killed him. They keep in mind the serious tangle he had with Otis concerning Pass Creek's future. I personally have no firm guesses. It could have been anyone. Maybe Shull's the killer. He did his best to silence you."

Celia noted that Salliebeth had left out Tierney as a suspect. Of course, she herself had all but eliminated Tierney in that regard, strange though the woman could be otherwise. The chief didn't believe Tierney was the murderer, and that added to Celia's confidence that Tierney was likely innocent. But who knew anything for sure?

"If you hear anything of interest about the case, let me in on it please, Salliebeth? I can't ask Pete questions. He and Jake have practically threatened to keep me under lock and key. This is all supposed to be none of my business, but that's a silly notion. Everyone in town wants to know who committed the murder. They want to feel safe and have the entire matter solved. I'm no different."

"It's your detecting that bothers them, Celia," Salliebeth chided. "And I agree that could get very dangerous. Look at your close call this past weekend." She held up a hand when Celia would have interrupted. "I know how you feel about the good of this town, and that's really all you're after. But you need to leave finding the killer to the experts. Now, is there anything I can get for you? Do for you?"

"I'm fine," Celia said, deciding to let the subject drop. She had stuck her neck out by going to the dumpsite and spying around Shull's trailer. It'd be a while before she'd do anything that risky again. She could have ended up dead, like everyone said.

Celia smiled, stood up, smoothed her pajamas into place, and hugged Salliebeth. "Go on to work. I'm going to take a shower, get dressed and have some breakfast. I'll take it easy today if that pleases everyone. Maybe get a little writing done. If I need anything, I'll put out a call loud and clear. Okay?"

True to Salliebeth's prediction, Celia was visited by a steady stream of callers during the next few days. Jolly came, looking unusually worried and bringing her a gift of two Almond

Joys and three snack-size bags of Doritos from his service station's vending machine.

"Come in, Jolly, and thank you so much for the treats."

"Well," he said, removing his baseball cap and taking a chair, "it's the least I could do. What I'd really like is to get my hands on that no-good snake beat you up like that. Durn his hide, anyhow. He ain't been nothin' but trouble from the day he was born, way I hear it."

"Have you had trouble from him?"

"Sure. Me and pretty near everybody else in Pass Creek! I stepped into the restroom at my service station for just a minute one time. When I come out, there was Harry Shull, rushing around fast as he could move, throwing brand new tires I'd just stocked into his van."

"Good grief! What did you do?"

"Grabbed him by the collar an' I ask what the blazes he thought he was doin'. Said he was intending to buy them." Jolly snorted and shook his head. "He went digging into his pockets an' claimed he forgot to bring his money after all. Durn liar. I made him unload them tires and said I'd make him sorry for the day he was born if he ever tried anything like that again."

"No more trouble with him after that?"

Jolly chuckled in derision. "He kept on with little stuff. He'd steal cigarettes or a soda pop when I was busy with a customer. Then he'd act innocent and vanish before I could grab his carcass and search his pockets. He's no good, that one. I wouldn't put it past him to be the one killed old Otis Peek."

"You think so?"

"Sure I do."

She nodded. "Well, I hope we'll all know the truth about who killed Otis soon."

"Yep, and see whoever did the dirty deed pay for it, too." Jolly put his hat back on. "Gotta get back to the station, Celia. Now you take care of yourself and don't go putting yourself in danger again like you did going out to Shull's place."

"I won't. I plan to take care." Jake and Pete would have her head otherwise

Chapter Fifteen

Celia's refrigerator was filled to overflowing with gifts of food. She offered some of it to her guests at the inn. A lot she sent home with Lilly to feed young Mac—Lilly claimed he was always hungry. Flowers filled practically every vase she owned. Mrs. Kemp brought her a beefsteak to put on her swollen eye and cheek but she declined. Mrs. Kemp huffed, "Well then, I'll have it for dinner."

With an offer of iced tea and a plate of peanut butter cookies, Celia was able to keep her around a bit longer. They sat by the parlor window, Celia holding Freebie on her lap and stroking his silky fur.

"Mrs. Kemp, dear, I know I've asked this more than once, but would you tell me again what you saw the day Otis Peek was murdered? Was there some little thing happening next door that seemed odd? You know, out of the ordinary?"

"Like I already told you and the chief, I saw Otis on the roof for just a minute. I told him to get his fool self down, and then I went inside to watch Oprah. Earlier in the afternoon I'd seen a woman leaving his house. When I remembered about that, I told the chief. According to him, both a' you thought that was Tierney Jones who we found out later was visiting Otis that day. I couldn't see that well who it was. At the time I just figured it was Myrna. She comes and goes to his house a lot, or she did before he was killed. For all I knew it was one of the women from the Heritage Club wanting to ask him something."

Celia nodded. "You saw a man over there that day, too, right? Salliebeth told me a couple of days ago that you thought you saw man there not too long before the time they say Otis died." Mrs. Kemp wasn't the most reliable witness, but who knew when she might actually have her facts straight?

"I did." Mrs. Kemp tottered over, picked Freebie up from Celia's lap and, cuddling him, went back to her chair. "I took him to be the roofer Otis hired and let go, like I already told everybody. Do you think he killed Otis? There was some arm waving, but I can't imagine a fella being that mad over not getting work that he'd kill somebody. Do you?"

At the rise in her voice, Freebie leaped from her lap and bounded toward the kitchen.

"Not really." Celia didn't want to put ideas into Mrs. Kemp's head by describing Harry Shull specifically—or Mac or Locke Vinson, for that matter. "You're positive it was a man having the discussion, possibly a strong argument, with Otis?"

"If I told you once, I told you ten times, Celia. I didn't get a real good look at whoever it was. Coulda been a man, or a woman, or a full-grown ring-tailed monkey, for all I know. The way you and the chief keep peppering me with questions, you make it sound like it was my business to go over there and wrassle the murdering rascal to the ground and prevent the killing! Well, I ain't up to that."

"Oh, no, of course you're not." Celia reached to pat Mrs. Kemp's hand to calm her. "I didn't mean to upset you. Enjoy your tea and cookies, and we won't discuss this anymore."

～～

Everyone wanted to hear about her ordeal at the dump, each detail of her tangle with Harry Shull and her time sunk in the garbage. About the latter, being out of it most of the time, she could only relate the smell, her fright and struggle as she regained consciousness.

More than one person thought they'd spotted Shull back in the area only to find on checking that it was someone else. The horror stories of what he could do to her should he show up again were never-ending, to the point they'd become privately laughable when not frightening her to her core.

Jake came often, sampling the cookies and pies that came her way, only to whip out again when their conversation approached anything too personal. At first she was disappointed, but then decided that neither of them was ready for more than what was occurring between them right now. They were falling in love. She had no doubt of that, but she wouldn't force Jake to recognize and accept his feelings until he was prepared to do so on his own.

It was impossible to hide her surprise when, three days after the Shull incident, she opened the door to Locke Vinson. Tanned, handsome, he looked as sharp as ever in an apricot silk shirt and off-white Dockers. His blue eyes took her in from head to toe and returned to her face.

Faked or real, his face expressed concern, and he cursed softly. "I hope to hell they put Harry Shull away till he rots, Celia. He's a damn thieving maniac, killing Otis in a robbery and then attacking you. If this town had a decent police force, he'd be behind bars for life. Not around to hurt you."

Taken aback, for a full minute she considered Locke's words, his flat-out remark that *Shull killed Otis*. How would he know that? Or was he just spouting a guess?

As much as she disliked his putting down Pete and would like to argue the matter, or better yet, just close the door in his face, Locke's statement had her curiosity humming. "Why are you here? Is there something I can do for you?"

His white teeth showed in a sudden, leering grin. "Oh, sweetheart, you have no idea what replies I could give you to that question."

She was about to change her mind and shut the door on

him when his demeanor altered, and he grew serious again. "Actually, I'm here to make you a business proposition to get you out of this Otis Peek mess."

Celia hesitated, frowning, trying to decide what to do. She wasn't in any "mess." She simply wanted the Peek murder case solved. Even if she was deeply troubled over the matter, that was no business of Locke Vinson's. On the other hand, this could be an opportunity to uncover something important.

She hadn't gone to Locke to learn if he had a connection to the murder. He'd come to her. So she was blameless in that regard, and neither Pete nor Jake could object. She stood back. "Come in. May I get you something to drink? Iced tea, a soda?"

"Ice water will do. I'm trying to stay healthy." He patted the beginnings of a beer belly.

When he followed her into the kitchen instead of staying in the living room, she shrugged and plunked the glass of water down in front of him on the kitchen table. "I'm pretty busy today, Locke. What's on your mind?" She sat across from him.

Although sunshine spilled warmly into the room from the kitchen window, she felt chilled. She rubbed her arms, debating if she'd made a mistake, allowing this man in her house.

He eyed her over the top of his glass and said expansively, "You're too good for this town, Celia, and always have been." He took a drink and wiped his mouth on the back of his hand. "It's beneath you, putting up with constant small-town squabbles, and now a murder and your attempted murder." He leaned toward her and frowned. "You need to kiss goodbye to this place, honey, while you can, and I'll help."

"Is this a warning? You don't hear me complaining. Please get to the point."

"You wouldn't complain, Celia. I know you, probably better than you have any idea. You're too gracious, too considerate of other people and this little burg to complain, but down deep, you must hate it. I've been thinking a lot about that, about you, especially since that day I saw you at the rodeo." He finished with a broad smile. "Spend some time with me, and I could show you a whole different life you'd love. I guarantee it." He reached across the table and smothered her hand with his.

She pulled her hand away, feeling irritated to her core. What made him think he could sweet-talk her into giving him whatever it was he was after? "To begin with, I don't hate Pass Creek. This town and my friends here mean everything to me. I want nothing else." As calmly as she could manage, she told him, "Harry Shull will pay for his little stunt, burying me in the garbage and threatening my life. Of that I have no doubt. If he's Otis Peek's killer as well, he'll be caught and prosecuted to the letter of the law."

Vinson scoffed, "You can't count on that. Killers run loose all the time. Some never pay for their crimes. You know that."

"And many *are* caught and given a life sentence in prison. I'm really curious, Locke. Why are you so sure that Harry Shull is the one who killed Otis Peek?"

He tapped the table with a knuckle, ready with the information. "Otis himself told me that he had an antique weapon that Shull tried to steal more than once. Evidently Shull had a shady customer who was prepared to pay as much as twenty thousand dollars for Peek's Civil War revolver. Shull tried one more time to get that gun, the way I see it, and he and Otis fought. A brick took care of Otis, and Shull got a gun worth a small fortune to a collector who'd want it too much to care where it came from."

Celia shook her head. "Your theory is way off, Locke. Sorry. Otis's valuable revolver was placed under security at the bank, right after the first time Shull tried to take it." According to Myrna, the gun and other valuables Otis had in the bank's vault were sent to his next of kin after he was killed.

Before Jake could put Gable House on the market, a

thorough inspection of the house's contents was made by both Pete Erdman and Otis's lawyer. Myrna, who had pretty thorough knowledge of the place, was there, too. According to inventory, nothing valuable was out of place or missing.

"So the gun was out of reach. That doesn't mean Shull wasn't trying to rob old Otis for whatever he could get. He killed him in the process, even if that wasn't part of his original plan!"

That was one possibility that had already occurred to her. "You told Pete your theory?" she asked.

"Of course I did. He reacted pretty much the same way you are, choosing to ignore important facts when they're right there plain as day. He said he would continue to check out Shull's connection to Peek, but you could tell he was already dismissing it. He was more interested in shelling out money to his wife and kids, who stopped into his office before going for ice cream, than my trying to help."

Celia seized the chance to defend her friend. "Pete is a good cop. Maybe things don't move along as fast as we'd all like on this case, but that's because he's meticulous at his job, taking time to do things right." She threw in for good measure and the fun of it, "He's a great husband and father as well."

"To hell with it."

She hid a smile at his displeasure and spoke calmly. "I hope you don't mind my asking, Locke, but where were you that evening Peek got bashed?"

For an instant he looked surprised, then affronted, that she would question him. He laughed. "Sweetheart, I have a watertight alibi for the day Otis Peek went to the big hereafter." He snorted. "As if I could have had anything to do with the murder. But, yeah, I was with one of my store employees at an early happy hour at the Vault Martini in downtown Portland. Your wonderful police officer wasted a lot of time checking out my story."

"I don't think his investigating folks' alibis, yours or

anybody else's, is a waste of time. That's his job."

"Why would you think I'd off the old guy, anyway?" Vinson asked, his forehead wrinkled in curiosity.

"It is common knowledge the two of you had a fighting difference of opinion about this town and what you wanted to do with it that he was very much against."

"Sure we did, although I didn't kill him. Otis was stodgy in his thinking, had no vision for this town's future at all. He couldn't see that Pass Creek has no chance as it is to survive. I have plans, big plans, and they include a nice proposition for you."

She squelched an urge to roll her eyes and laugh. Instead, she allowed him to continue, tapping her fingernails on the table's shiny surface.

"I want to buy this property, Celia. Give you an opportunity to retire while you're still young enough to enjoy yourself. I'll give you a better than fair price. You can move to the city. Go on cruises, see Europe—with me, I'd hope, but there's no need for you to stick it out here, fighting never-ending battles to breathe life into this dying town."

She was so incensed by his offer, which couldn't be more remote from what she truly cared about, that it was hard to find words to answer him.

He seized on her hesitation and continued, his voice smooth as cream, "I'm not about to rush you. I know you'll want to think about this. In the long run you'll see the sense of my offer, and you'll be glad to take me up on it. Name your price, honey, and I'll do my damnedest to meet it." Before she could get out what she wanted to say to him, he added, "As long as I'm in town, I'd be delighted if you'd have dinner with me tonight. If you like, we can talk this over further."

"I don't like, I'm not moving from Pass Creek, and your offer holds no appeal for me whatsoever. I have other dinner plans." She stood. "I'll see you to the door."

He bristled, anger flushing his face. "Don't toss this chance away, Celia. Change is on the way to Pass Creek, whether you like it or not. You people want an industry or two to move in to provide more employment and increase the tax base. Well, that's not going to happen until a lot of these old structures are torn down and the town brought into this century!"

"Nonsense. New and old can blend perfectly well." She added, "Whether we're speaking of buildings, businesses or people."

He stood up, his arms out in appeal. "I'm making this offer from the goodness of my heart, knowing that this is what Ethan would want for you. He was one of my best friends. I'm doing this for him as well as for you."

Her mouth dropped open. "Oh, Locke, you're a fool." Now it truly was hard not to laugh. "Please go. My husband was never a close friend of yours. He did you favors as he would have anyone. He was a great guy. You paid him back while you were in his employ by beating up his paper delivery boy and bullying the boy's mother. Do you want to hear more? I can discredit you to the ground without half trying."

This whole thing was giving her a headache, and she motioned him toward the door. "Suffice it to say you were never in the same league as my husband, and you never will be. Now go."

For an instant, it appeared he might strike her—his anger proving that she was right and had hit a nerve. He recovered and flashed a sulky smile. He caught her elbow forcefully in his palm, holding her. "You'll be making a mistake, Celia, a big mistake, if you don't take me up on my offer to help you out of this dangerous quagmire."

She refused to show fear, but wrenched her arm from his hand and retorted icily, "That sounds awfully like the threat Harry Shull made to me. Maybe I should mention the fact to Chief Erdman. Now you'd better go, or I'll call him right now."

He hesitated, clearly wanting to argue, and she held her breath.

Finally, with a bitter scowl at her, he turned away, his heels smacking sharply across her porch and down the steps.

Celia sighed in relief, her forehead against the closed door's cool panel. What a creep! She needed to get the bad taste of his visit from her mouth, she decided, and headed for the wine cupboard.

Chapter Sixteen

Carrying a bag of walnuts in one hand and her wineglass of white Zin in the other, Celia found a lawn chair down in her backyard near the creek. Sipping her wine, she tossed nuts to the gray squirrels who came chattering close enough to get them. She thought about Vinson's ridiculous offer to buy her land; his possible connection to Otis's death despite his insistence otherwise.

Locke had had a thing for her; he'd made that clear for some time. She'd made it equally clear she wasn't interested. He'd made it no secret, either, that he'd like to have her property for his big plans, whether she came with it or not. Fortunately, the majority of Pass Creek residents didn't agree with his vision to change everything. Otis Peek hadn't liked his ideas particularly, as Locke himself had mentioned.

How legitimate was Locke's excuse that he was having drinks with store personnel in Portland the evening Otis was killed? An employee, or more than one, might readily lie for him. Why was he so ready to pin the crime on Harry Shull if it wasn't a cover-up for himself? Or was Locke correct when he claimed that Harry Shull killed Otis in a failed attempt to rob him? Certainly, it was possible. And where was Shull these days?

She told a squirrel that had come very close, standing on its hindquarters and chirping, "I don't intend to get in the way of Pete's investigation, Squirrely, but I have to have answers, or I'm going to go crazy."

Two or three more squirrels came to join the first. She shook the bag of walnuts out on the top of a stump and said, "There guys, go nuts." She sat back to enjoy her wine and forget Locke Vinson for a while if possible.

Celia was glad when the daily visits from folks around town finally tapered off, although she'd welcomed the opportunity to learn what she could from anyone about Otis's murder. Unfortunately, she learned little that was new. Pete assured her that he had checked out Locke Vinson's alibi that he was sixty miles away, having drinks in Portland with a couple of employees, the day Otis was killed. Did he believe what he was told? Pete kept the answer to himself.

Stolen goods Harry Shull had sold to pawn shops and junk dealers were turning up and were being traced to their owners. His place was being watched for his return. It was believed that Shull had no other place to hold contraband until he could move it. He was still, in Pete's book, the world's stupidest crook, and his capture was imminent.

Pete refused to say anything at all about Mac, but Lilly had grown subdued and anxious and finally admitted when Celia pressed, that "Pete was hammering at Mac" for evidence he killed Otis. Both Myrna Hall and Tierney Jones seemed to have faded as suspects in most minds, if they ever were believed to be guilty.

The fourth or fifth day after her ordeal at Shull's hands, Celia was at work in her study just before dinner time, sorting notes for her local history project. Her head came up to listen as fire sirens began to wail from the main part of town. She walked out to her inn's front porch and scanned the town. Two of her guests, Maggie and Jim Houston, were seated there in the porch swing. Celia commented to them, "I don't see smoke anywhere."

Maggie came to stand beside Celia. She said, "Probably just a small kitchen fire from someone fixing dinner and already put out."

"It would seem so," Celia agreed, "thank goodness."

"Provides a little excitement, though," Jim threw in, coming to join them. "Speaking of dinner, honey-babe"—he put his arm around his wife—"want to walk downtown and find a chicken-fried steak?"

The Houstons joined hands and took off walking after telling Celia to have a nice evening, and she echoed the wish to them.

Mrs. Kemp stopped in a short while later to tell Celia the blaze happened at the Pass Creek Bar and Grill, was out now and didn't amount to much.

Carrying a tray with glasses of iced tea, Celia slowly led Mrs. Kemp, coming along with her cane, to the backyard. She nodded at the lawn chairs and small table placed under her ornamental plum tree, springtime blossoms long since spent and replaced by burgundy leaves. The neighbor's pack of wiener dogs came rushing to yap around their ankles. Celia put the tray on the table and chased them toward home. She returned to her chair out of breath and puffing. "No one was hurt in the fire then? No serious damage?"

"Fire department got there and put it out in two shakes of a lamb's tail." Mrs. Kemp heaved a sigh, dropped into a chair, and accepted the glass of iced tea Celia handed her. "When I left, everybody was back inside the restaurant to their dinners and drinking." She took the slice of lemon from the rim of the glass and licked it.

"A kitchen fire from grease, I suppose? Those can get out of control and do real damage at times. I had a small fire like that in my kitchen, years ago, making deep-fried donuts for Halloween handouts."

"Wasn't no kitchen fire. It was set a-purpose."

"Not really!" Celia looked at her closely. "They know that so soon? Was someone seen setting the fire? Were they caught?"

The dogs returned, and she ran after them, heaving her sandals uselessly in their direction. She came back, slipped her sandals back on, took a long drink of her tea, and sat down again. "Darn those dogs! I tell the neighbor to keep them penned, and he turns a deaf ear. I call the county dog control people and they say they don't have time or the staff to do anything about the situation. Let's try again: you were telling me about the fire."

"Nobody saw who started it. But Rosa Jean from the beauty shop says she saw somebody, she thinks a man or a big boy, stepping lively down the alley not long before she heard the sirens."

While Celia itched for more information, Mrs. Kemp took her time nearly draining her glass.

She licked her thin wrinkled lips and shook her head. "No way Rosa Jean could know if the fellow hurrying along the alley had been up to no good or if it was him did it, so she paid him little mind. How it was found, the bartender, he went out back to throw away some trash, and there was fire blazing up from oil-soaked rags piled a-purpose against the restaurant."

"Dear God!" Celia exclaimed in disbelief. "It's lucky the firemen got there in time. Someone could have been seriously hurt. Joe could have been put out of business."

"Well, everybody was doing their part. A woman customer called the fire department while the bartender took a water hose to the blaze. Everybody came out back to watch and help if they could. Fire was about out by the time the fire truck got there. Whoever set it got clean away, though, or so everybody was saying."

"Well, I hope whoever did it is found out and caught soon. It was probably a teenager pulling a prank and not realizing the seriousness of what they were doing. You know how they are, throwing firecrackers around just to scare people and totally ignoring the fact that they could start a fire in the dry grass and end up burning down half the town."

As Mrs. Kemp was leaving a short time later, she turned back, leaning on her cane. "I near forgot the other thing I come here for. I been worried about your walking tours, Celia, you down from the beating. You want me to take them over for you? I could, if it was just downtown and not a lot of wandering off on side streets."

"Thanks, but I'm well recovered from my concussion, and I'll be taking up the walks again myself tomorrow. I rescheduled requests from this past week and nobody had a problem with that. I really appreciate your asking, though." She added, to appease the elderly woman, "I'm sure you could tell stories more exciting than mine."

Mrs. Kemp called back from across the yard, "I hope you stick to the facts, Celia." Her pruny little face settled into a scolding frown. "And not just tell *stories*."

"I tell facts, I promise. And I'm sure you'll agree that the truth is more interesting anyway, than anything I could make up."

"Stick to that, Celia Landrey, and you'll do all right."

Toward dawn of that same night, Celia woke with a sick feeling of dread. At first she believed the growing wail of sirens and blasting horns was part of a nightmare borne of worry earlier in the evening. When she realized the cacophony was real and only blocks away, she grabbed a robe and ran out to her front porch. Farther downtown, in the area of the bookstore or possibly Viv's antique store, billows of smoke lifted into the dawning sky. Panic knotted inside her. All those buildings, close together—the town could burn.

Before she could make a move or decide what to do, she smelled smoke closer at hand and heard the crackling sound of fire. Gripped with concern, she raced off the porch in her bare feet and rounding the corner of her inn saw orange flames climbing up the outside wall below the window of her study.

She flew back inside and shouted for her guests by name,

three couples and Tierney, telling them that the inn was on fire. Grabbing the mobile phone from her study, she punched in the numbers for the fire department. "Fire at Landrey Inn on Second Street!" she shouted the moment she got a response. "Hurry!"

Shoving the phone in her robe pocket, Celia grabbed the fire extinguisher from its holder by the back door and hurried back through the house.

Her lodgers streamed down the stairs in their nightclothes, carrying whatever they could quickly grab: purse, wallet, a fistful of jewelry, an armful of clothing, an overnight bag. She quickly accounted for all of them, four women guests and three men. She herded them ahead of her out the door and onto the porch, Freebie padding along fast after her. "Scoot," she said, "way out in the yard, Freebie!" With relief, she saw one of women guests sweep the cat up into her arms.

"We didn't hear the smoke alarm," one man shouted at her.

Celia shoved the fire extinguisher at him, and shouted back, "Fire is around on the south side of the house. Use this!" She'd explain later that the fire outdoors would not set off the alarms that she'd had installed in every room.

Clearing the house, she motioned the others farther into the yard. She repeated to the dispatcher whose voice crackled on her mobile phone, "Yes, Landrey Inn, end of Second Street, Pass Creek. I know that there's another fire. The fire truck you sent earlier stopped downtown. I can't hear its siren anymore, so that's where it is, about three blocks from here. Send another engine to Landrey's Inn, the dead end of Second Street," she repeated. "Oh, my God, please tell them to hurry."

With more than one fire in town, the Pass Creek station would likely call on other nearby small-town fire departments to come help.

Fighting the panic about to overtake her mentally and physically, Celia saw that her tenant was spraying white powder in a sweeping motion from the extinguisher at the base of the fire climbing the south wall of her inn. But would there be enough of the powder? The fire was eating into the wood siding and spreading upward toward the roof. A breeze was sending sparks and ashes into the air.

She ran for the hose and faucet at the side of the house and began spraying water on first one patch of sparks and then another. How could flames move so quickly and so terribly? Her inn could burn to the ground if the fire department didn't get here soon. If the fire in town and hers got out of hand, all of Pass Creek could burn to the ground. Was that somebody's intention? If so, they had to be either insane or unutterably evil.

She darted a glance over her shoulder at the other fire, the smoke and the flames lighting up the early morning sky. Was it Flagg Realty that was burning, and was Jake there, trying to stop it? Was Gable House on fire? From the corner of her eye, Celia saw Tierney Jones standing off to the side with the huddle of inn guests and looking in the same direction. Tears were streaming down Tierney's face.

Until that second, Celia hadn't realized her own tears were flowing, from the smoke in her eyes, from pain in her heart, all a-mix. She sniffled and wiped her nose.

Jake suddenly appeared at her side and drew her into a tight hug. She could feel his heart pounding hard from his run. "You're okay?" he asked.

"Yes. What about you? Is your place all right? That other big fire in town…?"

"Is under control, and I came to help here. You're sure you're okay?" His eyes looking down at her with concern were red from smoke irritation.

"I'm fine, and my guests all got out okay." She didn't admit her fear, but told him, "I'm furious, though, with whoever the horrible person is who is doing this."

"Me, too." He gave her one last squeeze and let her go.

"We'll get it stopped. Take care of yourself. Wait over there."

Celia stood centered in the chaos of her yard where Jake had pointed. He led a group of neighbors, who pitched in with extinguishers and hoses attached to a variety of faucets located on her property. Heart pounding, she stared in disbelief at flames licking at the side of her house. As soon as one blaze was put out, another flared. In a period of time that seemed like hours but was only minutes, a fire engine arrived, and with siren screaming and horn blaring, pulled to a fast stop at the curb. At sight of the pumper-tank, Celia's panic eased into hope.

Coughing from the smoke, she and her guests hurried farther out of the way as the fire crew took over. Well-schooled volunteer firefighters moved with speedy efficiency as they uncoiled fat snaking hose to shoot water onto the flames that had now overtaken a portion of the roof. Thank God for these small-town firemen, she thought, with a long shaky sigh.

Flames were reduced to a few red licks here and there when the Mackay County Deputy Fire Marshal, a tall, dark fellow in professional uniform, arrived. He introduced himself as Reid McLeod and said that their police chief had contacted him, and he was there to investigate the fire.

"I'd like to ask you some questions, Ms. Landrey," McLeod said, leading her off to the side. "You're the one who called in the fire?"

"I am."

"I'd like your description of what happened, what alerted you to the fire and if you saw or heard anything unusual."

She explained that it was close to dawn when she'd heard fire sirens and had gotten out of bed. She didn't discover her own fire until she went outside to look for the other. "From my porch I smelled smoke close by, and I heard a soft crackling sound. I ran into the yard and I saw that my own house was on fire."

"Did you see anything suspicious, like someone in the vicinity who might have been leaving your yard? With three fires happening in one night, arson is a pretty sure bet."

"I didn't see anyone, but then I was mostly concentrating on the fire itself, which was small to begin with but getting worse by the second."

"Who was the first one to fight the fire with an extinguisher or hose? Would that be you?"

"No. That would be Mr. Rider, one of my guests here at the inn." She pointed out the lanky, gray-haired fellow still in his red-striped pajamas, the empty extinguisher hanging from his hand. The fire marshal called him over.

"Mr. Rider, I commend you for controlling the fire to the extent you were able. Unfortunately, a fire extinguisher sometimes isn't enough, but without your intervention, the fire could have gotten completely out of hand, the inn burned to the ground and the town threatened."

Rider nodded. "Sure had me scared for a while there. I could imagine the whole place going up if we couldn't get that fire out." His face, grimy with ash, broke into a relieved grin.

"Did you notice anything unusual about the fire?" McLeod asked. "Something that might tell us how it started?"

"Sure can. I smelled what I thought was gasoline. And there were these splash marks going up the wall, you know, darker than the rest of the light yellow siding. It was set on purpose, hard as it is to believe someone would do a thing like that."

The hard cold facts hit Celia like a blow, despite what she'd already suspected. That someone would deliberately set fire to her dwelling, her home and business, endanger not only her but innocent guests in the process, was beyond understanding. But it had happened.

When Rider had no more to offer, the fire marshal thanked him and moved on to question other inn guests and then bystanders who'd come to watch the fire. While she watched, Celia saw one of the firemen hand the fire marshal something.

On shaky legs she came closer and saw that it was a half-burned book of paper matches with enough of the Pass Creek Bar & Grill logo still on it to be recognizable.

Arson. Gasoline splashed on the wall of her inn and lit with matches from one of the town's most popular restaurants—who in the name of heaven would do such a thing? Despite the warmth of the coming morning, and that left over from the fire, it frightened her to death to know that somebody possessed such hatred, such resentment—whatever it was that had caused them to do this.

The smoke wasn't so dense downtown now. The fire was dying down and, God willing, close to being out. She sagged wearily to the ground and pulled a wandering Freebie onto her lap. Hugging the cat, burying her face in his fur, she prayed no one had been hurt and no lives had been lost, and that this terrible night would never, ever, be repeated.

Chapter Seventeen

The rest of the day was long and complicated. Firemen had remained on hand until there was every certainty her fire was out and wouldn't rekindle. Jake, Pete, and the fire marshal, McLeod, came and went from the scene of her fire to the others in town and back again, with more questions. They searched the grounds and charred walls of her house for the tiniest clue. Unfortunately, much evidence had been destroyed by the fire itself or lost in the immense amount of water used to put the fire out.

Once Celia and her guests were allowed back inside the inn, and she'd had an opportunity to clean up and put on jeans and shirt, a flurry of busy-ness overwhelmed her. Her heart sank, yet she understood when every last one of her guests, except for Tierney Jones, wanted to be checked out as soon as they could get their things together.

Too much was happening in Pass Creek of a dangerous nature for them to want to stay longer. She could hardly blame them. With weary resignation she saw them out, first collecting information as to where they could be reached in the future. McLeod wanted to know their contact details, should he need to question them further.

When the last of them were gone that evening, Celia turned to Jake, who had come over to check on her. From him she had learned that the bookstore in the old theatre building on Main had burned to the ground, hundreds of valuable books going up in smoke, the owners getting there too late to halt the fire.

Viv's Antiques, located in the old hotel building next to the bookstore, and Flagg Realty on the other side, suffered serious damage before the fire was brought under control. Luckily, her friend Viv and a son visiting for the week were awakened to the fire by Viv's cat, yowling and prowling the apartment above the store. Even so, they'd suffered burns on their hands trying to put the fire out before the fire department took over.

Obviously, the successions of fires on the same night were not accidents and had been deliberately lit.

Carrying that dreadful knowledge all day and wondering *what next?,* gave Celia a chill that wouldn't go away. Come evening, she sat on the sofa wrapped in a blanket, Jake holding her hand. "Why would anyone do this? Why, Jake? Is it kids, fooling around for the thrill of it? Was this done out of hate for the town, for me, by someone like Harry Shull? Who would intentionally set fire to businesses housed in these wonderful old buildings?" Tears blurred in her eyes.

She thought of Locke Vinson, who felt the town was useless as it stood. Plus he was angry at her for not cozying to his plans for her, for rejecting everything he stood for. He'd dislike her thoroughly for that and not give up trying to get her to sell out. But would he sneak around town setting fires as part of his persuasion? Perhaps, as far-fetched as it sounded, he would. She voiced those thoughts aloud to Jake.

"Could be anyone," he said, "and for crazy reasons we can't begin to guess at." He sighed and shook his head. "Rumors were going around during the fire that the bookstore owners, Andy Juster and his wife, had been having a tough time financially and might have set fire to their place to collect insurance. I doubt that's true. It sure as hell doesn't answer why the other fires were set—at the Bar and Grill, at Gable House and your place."

She jerked forward, "Gable House?"

"Wait a second. Don't get yourself more upset." He put his arm around her and drew her close to his side. "A fire was set at Gable House. It was probably the first in line after the Bar and Grill, and yours was last, following the bookstore. But the Gable House fire blew itself out before any damage was done. Pete has county deputies all over town in case the firebug returns. If he does—or she does—they'll be nabbed."

Celia was thoughtful for a moment, a river of shock running through her as a possibility registered. "Is Tierney Jones responsible after all? Maybe this thing with her health, being almost constantly under the weather, has been an act! Jake, do you think it was Tierney hurrying down the alley after the fire at the Bar and Grill? Could she have slipped out of her room later and started a fire at Gable House? Did she rush from there to start the fire here at Landrey Inn?"

Before he could answer, she continued, "Everything was such a blur after I found the fire, but I'm sure she came downstairs in her night clothes with the others. She cried, looking at the fire in the direction of Gable House. Till this minute, I thought she was here all the time. I didn't suspect her for a second." She sighed. "I don't know. I find it so difficult to believe she could commit murder and set fires."

"I think I'd have to hear her say she did it and show me proof to believe it myself."

"The whole thing is insane, and so scary. Wonderful buildings ruined or damaged, businesses hurt, my paying guests gone and likely to never come back, Otis murdered. And whoever is responsible is still free to keep up the terrorizing. For what reason, and who are they? Will the whole town be destroyed before we know the answer?" She fought tears that threatened.

He took her face in his hands and kissed her. "Hey there,

you've been a pit bull, going after facts to get to the bottom of what's happening in Pass Creek. Don't give up hope now." He told her softly, "We'll get the bad guys."

"I've tried everything I can think of to learn what's going on and why Otis was killed, and now with the fires, and I still can't figure it out. I'm not giving up, but I admit I hardly know which way to turn anymore or what to think." She reached to pull his arm about her tighter.

"Not that I'd want the firebug to try one more time," Jake told her, "but catching the culprit *in the act* would help solve the crime. Most evidence gets destroyed as the fire burns."

"Never. It can't ever happen again," she sat up quickly to say.

He drew her back. "No, of course not, but everybody in town will be keeping watch and for damn sure they'd be caught if they try again."

Maybe it was because she went to sleep in his arms there on the sofa that she felt much better the next morning. After getting dressed, she walked outside into bright sunshine, her spirits dipping as she took in the fire damage to the house and the strong odor of burned wood. Later, she sat on the step of her back porch, her mind mapping plans for repairs as soon as possible. She'd brought her cell phone outside with her and after a minute or two, made a call to Mac Strand, Lilly's young husband. He agreed to help her get started.

Glancing up, she yelped, "Darn you dogs, now you've caught a poor squirrel!" Down near the creek, two dachshunds, one tan, the other black and white, were engaged in a ferocious tug of war. Quickly tucking her cell back in her shirt pocket, she ran hard at them, waving her arms and screaming, "Put the poor thing down! Stop it you damnable animals!" As she reached them, the dachshunds quit and yelped their way toward home. When she saw what they'd dropped, she discovered it wasn't a squirrel they'd been ripping apart. She started to pick up the scrap of gray fabric, but closer examination stopped her. Blood rushed to her head and her heart pounded. She took out her cell and with shaking fingers punched in the number for the police station.

"I haven't touched it," she said a moment later, "and no, I don't know where it's been, Pete. Maybe the dogs had it at their place for a plaything, but you need to get over here."

The chief arrived moments later and kneeled beside Celia to look at the partially burned scrap of gray. He lifted it with a gloved hand and put in a plastic zip bag. "You think this is part of a shirt Harry Shull wore?" he looked over at her to ask.

"I'm positive." How could she forget what he'd had on the day he beat her up and left her in the garbage? "In fact, he wore that shirt most of the time. If he had another shirt, he seldom changed. Cleanliness didn't appear to be his forte."

"Yeah." The chief nodded. He stood up, helping her to her feet at the same time. "He did wear a gray shirt a lot. This could be his, we'll find out." He mused aloud, "In the process of setting the fire to your place, his shirt must have caught on fire. He got off down here to your creek, where he tore off his shirt and cooled his burns. This is pretty solid evidence to go with the broken bottle we found earlier."

"Broken bottle?" she asked as she rubbed her nose.

"Yesterday after the fire, the fire chief and I found a broken bottle with traces of gasoline down in the rocks here along your creek. If this was Shull, and I'm fairly certain that it was, along with a lack of good sense, he was in too much pain to hide the evidence of what he'd done."

"Looks like it was the front of his shirt that caught fire," Celia said. "He may have pretty bad burns on his chest. He's probably gone to some kind of clinic or hospital to be treated. You can track him down that way."

Pete looked at her and spoke dryly, "Believe it or not, Celia, I was thinking the same thing. Part of my job."

She grinned and touched his arm. "I know."

Later in the morning, wearing old jeans and shirt, gloves, and a scarf tied over her hair, she worked with young Mac, solemn in his work, tearing loose charred siding and tossing it into a dumpster, raking ashes into a pile and adding them to the rest.

Carpenters and handymen were at a premium because they were in town doing repairs at the other fire sites and on regular building jobs, but the construction crew she'd hired was due to show up later today or tomorrow. Jake would have a fit if he knew she was doing this hard, dirty work, but what he hadn't found out yet wouldn't hurt him.

More than once as they toiled, she tried to engage Mac in conversation, but other than telling her how much he appreciated that she gave him and Lilly work, he had little to say. About the fires he stated that, "Whoever did it ought to be put away in the cooler for a good long stretch."

The chief had warned her not to mention the broken bottle and burned shirt that had likely belonged to Harry Shull. So she kept quiet on the matter, but felt good that a widespread search for Harry Shull was underway that very moment.

When she brought up the subject of Otis Peek's murder, Mac shook his head. He claimed he didn't know anything about that and dove deeper into his work, scrambling up the ladder and ferociously ripping away burned roofing.

"Watch out!" she had to tell him twice, as debris he hurled to the ground barely missed her.

"I'm sorry, Mrs. Landrey." He looked truly chagrined. "If you want to go inside, I can do this job myself."

"No. With both of us working we'll get more done."

Celia waved at Pete Erdman when, an hour or so later, his police car pulled up out in front of the inn. She said casually to Mac crouched on the roof, "Wonder what's brought the chief here?" She told herself silently that, God willing, he was here to let her know Shull had been found and taken into custody.

"He's here for me," Mac stated flatly as he looked down at her, his handsome young face set like stone.

"You're not the firebug."

"No, and I didn't kill old Otis, either."

She nodded. "The chief can't think you're a criminal."

"Yeah, he can. One way or another, the way he's been after me, he'll make me one, whether I am or not."

Mac hurried down the ladder and started toward the house.

Pete yelled after him, "Don't try to run, Mac. You'll only make things harder for yourself." He slammed his car door. As Mac turned, he told him, "I'm here to take you in on probable cause for the murder of Otis Peek."

Celia watched, head spinning, her heart heading for her shoes that the situation had come to this. She couldn't help praying that Pete was wrong, wrong, wrong, to accuse her young friend.

"I figured that's what you came for," Mac declared, controlled fury in his eyes. "I just wanted to see my wife. I wasn't running." He held his hands behind his back so Pete could handcuff his wrists.

"Just get in the car," Pete ordered him.

Mac did as he was told, saying over his shoulder to Celia, "I was going to the house to get Lilly so she'll know what's happening. Will you tell her?"

"I'll get her, and we'll come to the station. We'll get to the bottom of this, Mac, don't worry."

She said under her breath to the chief, "Why now, Pete? Why are you taking him in? That boy is no murderer."

"I'm sorry, Celia, but I have plenty of cause to believe he may be. For one thing, I found footprints in the dust on the linoleum kitchen floor at Gable House after you were knocked down that night out back of the place. The tracks hadn't been in the house earlier, and they are Mac's."

"How can you be so sure?" she demanded. Of course he'd have ways to tell. Maybe it was a foolish question to ask, but she wanted so much for him to be mistaken about Mac.

"Not that I have to tell you, Celia, but I noticed something peculiar on the sole of his right shoe, the same athletic shoes he's worn anytime I questioned him. There's a jagged little gouge just before the heel in the sole of his right one. The imprint of that shoe was on the floor."

"But how could he? Why would he...?" Hands on her hips, she paced in frustration and concern.

Pete told her, "There was no sign of a break-in at Gable House, so I figure he has a key that his mother, Otis's housekeeper, once used."

"Well, so maybe he has a key and he was there. That's hardly evidence he killed Otis."

"There's more. I finally tracked down the roofer Otis hired. He says when he got to the house and discussed terms with Otis, the old man changed his mind at the cost and said he'd do the work himself. The roofer got in his truck, but after giving it some thought, he decided to lower his price. When he came around the house to make Otis the new offer, a young man had shown up from the back way. He was arguing fiercely with Otis Peek, saying, 'I could kill you for this!'

"At the time, he figured the young man had lost his temper and was spouting off, but no more than that. The roofer decided not to interrupt, that he'd call Otis later and tell him he would come down in his price, and he left. The description he gave of the young man fighting with Otis fit Mac perfectly. Time of Otis's death was within the next half hour—give or take a few minutes."

Celia felt sick. She stopped pacing as her mind scrambled to find other answers. "Okay, I know Mac and Otis had some heavy arguments from time to time, but I still don't think Mac is capable of committing murder. Maybe the roofer did it?"

"No motive. I'd like to think that Mac's not the killer, either, Celia. But the boy is hiding something, and I don't think it's only that Peek wouldn't help with Mac's mother's medical bills. Although that's reason enough to hate the old guy's guts. I probably would, too."

Celia nodded fervent agreement.

Pete reiterated, "I have a witness who has all but identified Mac being on the scene close to the time of the murder. We found Mac's footprints in the house a few days later, indicating he came back. Why he was in the house as well as out back is anybody's guess, but I figure he returned to find the brick he used as a weapon. You and Jake scared him off before he could retrieve it, and I found it the next day."

"Darn it, Pete, it had been a couple weeks since Otis's fall—his death, I mean. If it was Mac who killed him, wouldn't he have tried to find the brick earlier than that night?"

"Maybe he did and was unsuccessful. Coming too often would draw attention. He'll have to answer why he was in the house and the yard. We're wasting time here, Celia. I have to take him in."

"All right." She started to ask about Shull but Pete, reading her mind, waved her to silence. She stood back, shaking her head, her eyes on Mac in the back seat of the car. "I don't believe any of this," she whispered to herself. She watched Pete climb behind the wheel of the police car. As the blue and white cruiser pulled away from the curb with Mac in the back seat, Lilly, who must have seen what was happening from a window, came screaming from the house.

"Don't take him! Don't arrest Mac! He didn't do anything. He's innocent. He didn't kill Mr. Peek, and he knows nothing about the tea."

Celia, catching a struggling Lilly in her arms, stopped her from running after the chief's car. "It'll be all right, Lilly." She forced herself to be calm and firm. "Mac said to tell you what was happening. He's cooperating with the chief, and I'm sure we can clear this up."

Lilly pulled away and sank to the ground, sobbing, "Mac wouldn't hurt a soul. He hasn't done anything that'd cause the chief to arrest him. That was me who made the tea."

Celia dropped beside her and took the distraught girl into her arms. "Calm down, sweetheart. I believe Mac's innocent, and somehow we'll prove it. We need to go to the station now and hope the chief will let us talk to Mac. For sure he's going to need a lawyer."

Something else Lilly said just registered. She thought about it a moment, and asked, "What's this about *tea*? What on earth are you talking about?" *Tea*. It was difficult enough to grasp the fact that Pete had enough evidence to arrest Mac without this mysterious comment out of thin air about *tea*.

Lilly was sobbing so hard, she couldn't speak.

"All right," Celia said, giving her a squeeze and then getting to her feet, "let me get cleaned up and make a call to a lawyer friend of mine in Adkins. On the way to the station, you're going to tell me everything!"

At the house, she phoned her attorney friend, Randolph Westin. He said he would meet her at the Pass Creek police station in half an hour, forty-five minutes at the latest. She washed quickly and changed clothes, but the odor of ashes seemed to permeate her flesh.

Driving to the station minutes later with Lilly beside her, Celia said, "Okay, what's this about tea? What were you talking about? What *tea*?"

As she listened, Celia looked at the girl in dismay. "You're going to have to repeat this, Lilly," she exclaimed, "because it has to be the nuttiest thing I've ever heard of, and I can't believe it! You've been giving Tierney Jones some kind of tea that made her sick? Made her go to the bathroom? A diet tea, you say, and she was unaware that's what it was?"

"I only gave her this Chinese diet tea a few times." Lilly sniffled. "I'd heard about AloSen one time when I was visiting Mac on campus. A couple of girls were talking about it in the restroom. AloSen is perfectly safe if you follow directions. But if you drink too much or let it steep too long, it can make you sick. You know, vomiting, diarrhea, like that." She wiped her eyes on the backs of her hands.

"Oh, dear heaven, Lilly! Tell me, please, why you would do such a terrible, foolish, thing?"

Lilly's teary face held the most earnest expression. "For you, Mrs. Landrey. I did it to save Gable House for you. So it would always be there for your tours, for the town—it being the nicest thing we've got in Pass Creek. I was only trying to slow Mrs. Jones down, you know. Keep her just unwell enough to stop her from going ahead with what she wanted to do. Once the sale closed and the house was truly hers, she could blow it up with dynamite the very next day, was how I saw it. She had to be stopped. No one else was doing anything to stop her. The tea was the only thing I could think of that might work but not do real harm, so I did it."

"Oh, but you shouldn't have, Lilly. You might have done grave harm to her health."

"I guessed that later. After that time she went to the hospital, I was scared to give her very much of the tea. And I tried to stop."

"*Tried* to stop? You kept making it for her? For goodness sake, why?"

"She liked it, Mrs. Landrey! It tastes like licorice. You know, from anise seed? I'm not sure much of the flavor comes from the senna or aloe, buckthorn and other plants in it that cause you to—you know—go to the bathroom, have lots of bowel movements. After the first time, I was careful not to steep the tea too long, and I tried not to give her that kind of tea too often."

"Dear heaven, I wish I was only dreaming what you're telling me. Do you realize that to do a person bodily harm is a crime? You could go to jail for years. You might still, if Tierney feels you caused her serious injury and she wants to bring charges."

Lilly was hesitant. "I don't think she will. We talked, and I told her what I'd done and why. She was pretty mad at me for a while, and then she decided to let it go. She said there was trouble enough going around and she wasn't really hurt. Of course, she'd kill me if I ever tried to do anything like that again."

"When did you have this conversation?" Celia demanded to know.

"Yesterday. After the fire. Mrs. Jones was really upset that the Gable House might have burned. She was glad that it didn't, really glad, so it didn't make sense she would've set the fire. I thought right then that she might have changed her mind about getting rid of Gable House."

"Has she changed her mind?"

"I'm pretty sure she has. Mrs. Jones told me that as soon as you have time, Mrs. Landrey, she wants a long talk. She has a lot to say to you."

Celia welcomed the news but felt torn in two directions. Staring ahead and trying to concentrate on her driving, she said, "Well, whatever that is, it will have to wait until after we see into Mac's situation." She looked across at Lilly and asked, "Do you know if there are other reasons Mac hated Otis Peek besides the fact Otis didn't help with his mother's medical bills?"

Chapter Eighteen

To Celia's chagrin, for several minutes as they drove toward the police station where they'd hopefully clear up the matter of Mac's arrest, Lilly remained silent. Finally, the young woman spoke. "Mac has told me some stuff, but he doesn't want me to talk about it to anyone else."

Celia reached down to clutch Lilly's hand, telling her, "If Mac is innocent and we're going to save him from prison, you and he will have to tell everything you know, and tell the truth, whatever that is." She waited a bit, staring straight ahead along the street, trying to swallow her irritation. It was clear Lilly was going to ignore this very important moment when she should confide in her. How was she supposed to help the kids if they wouldn't talk?

Sighing deeply, Celia said, "I was able to reach my lawyer friend on the phone before we left. Randolph Westin is a very good lawyer, and he's going to meet us at the station. He'll do his best to help you and Mac, but you must cooperate and tell him the facts."

Westin, a tall, bony man in his fifties who looked somewhat like Gregory Peck, arrived a half hour after Celia and Lilly got there. A half-hour spent mostly in worried silence, staring at the pea-green walls and though the window at an occasional passing car.

Celia rose from her chair to shake the attorney's hand.

"Hello, Randolph. Thank you for coming. This is Lilly Strand"—she turned toward her—"Mac Strand's wife."

Randolph smiled pleasantly, and in turn took Lilly's hand and held it gently. "We'll do everything we can for your husband. Keep in mind that you have a very good friend here in Mrs. Landrey."

Lilly looked at her feet, then at the attorney and said quietly, "I know."

Celia informed him, "Pete Erdman, our chief of police, has just stepped out of the office for a minute. He'll be right back. He informed Mac of his rights upon arresting him, told him that he could remain silent, and that's what he's done. Now that we have you here, I hope to heaven he'll tell you the facts about this whole tangled business."

She had no more than gotten the words out when Pete returned and the two men talked for a few minutes. Afterward, Westin turned to Celia and Lilly. "If it's agreeable with Mac, I'd like to talk to him alone, and then I'd like to ask you and Lilly some questions."

"Certainly," Celia answered.

"Okay," Lilly said nervously, biting her lip as she watched Pete lead Westin through a door into the back of the station where the jail cells were located.

Minutes later, Celia went over to Pete's desk to quietly ask about Shull. "Half the police force in the valley is on the case," he muttered, "so leave it be, Celia."

She leaned over to say in his face, "You could thank me. I found what you needed to clinch it, you know."

"Thanks. Tell the dogs thanks, too. Now go sit down." He tried to look grim, but there was a smile in his eyes.

A dozen hours seemed to pass while Celia and Lilly drank horrible black coffee from Styrofoam cups, and waited. In actuality, a little over an hour passed before Randolph Westin, wearing a worn, frustrated expression, returned to where Celia and Lilly waited.

Celia jumped to her feet, and Lilly did likewise.

"I got him talking, but it wasn't easy." Westin sat down and motioned them to take a chair on either side. "This kid doesn't really trust anybody."

Tell me something new, Celia thought. "Does he have an alibi?" she asked. "What's his story?" She rushed on, "Do you believe he's innocent, Randolph?"

He gave her arm an affectionate pat, a reminder that she had dated him, a widower, a few times after Ethan died. The romance didn't take, but they were good friends.

"I believe he's innocent, yes. Proving that as fact is something else again. Mac has a big problem he's kept to himself for far too long."

Celia said with relief, "I'm glad you believe in his innocence. Whatever this other thing is, let's please straighten it out." Her arm circled Lilly, who nodded and at the same time chewed her lip nervously.

Westin explained, "Mac tells me Otis Peek loaned Mrs. Strand, Mac's mother, some money a few years before she contracted cancer and passed on. She borrowed two thousand dollars from Mr. Peek to use as a down payment on a house. Collateral was a Civil War weapon, a valuable dragoon revolver, which Mac's mother inherited from her great-grandfather."

Celia drew in a sharp breath, stunned at this switch in the facts as she'd heard them. But when she looked at Lilly, there was no surprise in her expression, only hope mixed with concern. Why hadn't the youngsters said anything about this before? Was this the same antique gun that Otis claimed was handed down from *his* ancestor? Had he lied? Or was Mac lying? She motioned for the attorney to continue.

"Mrs. Strand was trying to make payments on the loan, but she died before she could completely pay off Mr. Peek and get her ancestor's gun back. She wanted it for Mac, as both a keepsake and insurance toward his future. To collectors, the gun would be worth more than ten times what Mr. Peek loaned her." He hesitated, then continued on a note of sadness, "Moreover, as Mac says, the money his mother was cheated out of might have saved her life. If Mr. Peek had turned loose of it as he should have."

"Good grief." What he was telling her corroborated Locke Vinson's statement that the gun's value could be upwards of $20,000. And it should have been Mac's and his mother's— either the money or the gun. What Peek did only made matters look worse for Mac, providing strong motive for the murder.

"As he explained it to me, Mac tried to make small payments whenever he could. Peek refused the payments, insisting he bought the gun fairly from Mac's mother for $1,700."

"Dear heaven, that's grossly unfair. Is there some way it can be proven the gun was only on loan as collateral? That it originally belonged to her and should be Mac's?"

"That's the hard part. Mac says there is a signed paper giving details of the loan, as well as papers recording the authenticity of the gun and how it came to be bequeathed to Mrs. Strand."

"Then that proves it!"

"Unfortunately, Mr. Peek held on to those papers 'to keep them safe,' he said. Over time, he gave one excuse after another for not providing them to Mac. No matter how much Mac insisted, Mr. Peek wouldn't allow him to have them, or even to have copies. Several days after Mr. Peek was murdered, Mac returned to Peek's house hoping to find the gun and the papers. He had a key his mother once used to get into the house to do the cleaning. Mack didn't find what he was looking for. He feels badly about shoving you that night in the dark, Celia. He says he didn't know until later that it was you. He knew he wasn't supposed to be there so hasn't said anything about it until I dragged it out of him today."

Celia nodded slowly, glad for the explanation. "We have to find those papers! And I think I know where we can find the gun. From what I understand, the gun and other valuables were placed in a safety deposit box in the bank. The contents were sent to Otis's heirs, a distant cousin and his wife."

"If we're fortunate, everything was kept together in the safety deposit box, gun and papers," Randolph Westin told them. "We'll sure find out. Do you have an address for Peek's heirs?"

"Not yet, but I'll get one!" Celia answered.

"Can Mac leave jail? Can we take him home today?" Lilly spoke up, breaking her long silence. Although she had listened carefully to the attorney, her deep frown had begun to ease only in the last couple of minutes.

"Not just yet. All we have is Mac's word as to what happened and his innocence. Until we have proof otherwise, it could be said that Mac murdered Mr. Peek trying to force the issue of the gun and the papers."

"Poor Mac." Celia rubbed her jaw and sighed in frustration.

"Or," Randolph Westin said, "it might be argued that the gun story is cock and bull and has nothing to do with the homicide. I'll do all I can for Mac, but for now that's where matters stand. The police chief wants him here."

After leaving the station, Lilly said repeatedly, "Mac's telling the truth, Mrs. L. He's telling the truth about the gun. It belonged to him and his mother. It's the truth."

"I believe you, but it appears that proving it will be difficult."

Celia dropped Lilly off at the couple's small green-shuttered house where earlier Mac had lived with his mother. The house Louise Strand borrowed money from Otis to buy. "Wait a second, Lilly." She let down the car window and called her back. "Why didn't Mac tell Pete about Otis's dishonesty early on and ask for help getting the gun back?"

Lilly turned around, youthful shoulders sagging. She clutched the glass of the open window and said quietly, her eyes meeting Celia's, "Like your lawyer friend said, Mac didn't have the proof he needed that the gun was his and his mother's. Mr. Peek had those papers. And who would believe Mrs. Strand, poor as they were, ever had anything that valuable in the first place? She never talked to anybody about the gun but Mr. Peek, for fear it would get stolen. She was always careful to keep it put away, safe, till she used it for collateral on our house." She licked her lips. "Besides all that, Mac is a guy who thinks he can handle stuff himself. Kind of like his mother."

"I see." Celia smiled and patted Lilly's hand on the window. "Take care, honey, and try not to worry. We'll do everything possible to get Mac out of this mess. I'll stay in touch, and you call me if you have anything important to tell either me or Mac's lawyer, okay?"

Her next stop was at the bank to see if they might have a list of contents that had been in Otis's safety deposit box at the time of his death. As expected, she was told that would be private information if they had it, which they didn't.

Otis Peek's lawyer would have been in charge, the one who notified Peek's relatives of his death. He also would have seen that the heirs received whatever money Otis had in the bank, plus valuables in the safety deposit box. Otis's home, Gable House, was of course sold according to these same folks' wishes.

At Flagg realty, Celia learned that Jake was out showing a property. She told Salliebeth of Mac's arrest and the reasons she needed the name and address of Otis Peek's relatives who inherited Gable House. Digging into the records of the sale, Salliebeth found that information and as well, the name of the attorney who'd handled Peek's affairs.

Celia hugged her. "Thanks so much. I'm giving this information to Randolph Westin, Mac's lawyer, right now.

Excuse me a sec." She called the attorney on her cell and recited the couple's name and how they could be reached at their home in Palm Springs, California.

Afterward, she explained to Salliebeth, "Mac's attorney will contact Otis's heirs, and if he can't reach them, possibly he can find out what's what from Otis's lawyer. I hope to heaven the gun, the loan papers and the other documents were all together in the safety deposit box and that Otis's relatives will still have them. These folks have to realize that the gun is crucial to Mac's case. Might actually *belong* to Mac, depending how one views the matter."

"What's next?" Salliebeth sat forward at the desk, excitement shining in her eyes.

"Next is a long chat with Tierney Jones! It appears she's finally going to open up about a few things. At least I hope so."

"Gosh, I'd love to be there, but I have to hold down the office."

"I'll tell you everything later."

At the inn, Celia and Tierney sat in the parlor, on the opposite side of the house from where the outside wall burned. Nevertheless, there was a faint smoky smell that no amount of lilac air freshener could eliminate entirely.

"I can't tell you how sorry I am, Tierney, that someone in my employ would pull such a stunt as Lilly did, serving you the diet tea. It was a foolish, dangerous thing to do."

Tierney nodded. "Yes, but fortunately the tea didn't do me any terrible harm."

"But the stuff might have. I've heard those diet teas aren't really safe to use. Will you press charges? Even temporarily, Lilly was causing you bodily harm."

Tierney shook her head. "That young one has enough trouble on her plate, particularly now with what you've told me. That's a heavy situation, her husband being accused of murdering Otis Peck."

"Well, he's innocent until proven otherwise. In my heart of hearts, I don't believe Mac did it. But who can know for sure until the investigation is complete? In any event, I'm just very, very sorry for what Lilly did to you on my behalf. If I'd guessed for a minute…"

"In a way, I suppose it was my own fault," Tierney broke in, a shadow of guilt crossing her face. "Coming here and expressing outright that I wanted to get rid of Gable House—without a thought to anything but my own wishes."

"Do you still intend to demolish it?" *Please, please don't,* Celia thought.

"No. In the time I've been here, I've come to see how important Gable House is to Pass Creek. I've grown fond of the people I've met and come to know, you in particular, Celia. First and foremost I wanted this talk to tell you that."

"Thank you." Celia remembered how bitterly Tierney had viewed Gable House throughout much of her stay in Pass Creek but insisted on staying mum as to her reasons why. "Do you mind telling me now what bothered you so about the house?"

"That's my other reason for wanting this conversation. I want you to know." She sighed, and made a small motion with her hand. "It's a simple story, and complicated at the same time. I'm not sure anyone else can understand my feelings, my obsession, to do away with the place."

"I'll certainly try."

"I know you will, and I'm sorry I've kept my reasons private for so long." Her shoulders lifted in resolution, she clasped her hands in her lap, and her voice was calm but sad. "You see, years ago when we lived in Pass Creek, my mother's dream was to own Gable House. My father's chief ambition was to buy it for her. More than anything else in the world, my father wanted to give my mother that house."

Celia's eyebrows rose in surprise, in question, and Tierney continued, "After Peek's Mill closed, my father, along with other men, couldn't find work. Many went on welfare to get by until work could be found. My father's pride was broken when welfare became necessary for our family. He saw himself as a failure, and he began drinking heavily. He was driving drunk to my high school graduation when all three of them, my parents and little brother, were killed in the accident."

"I'm so sorry," Celia whispered. "So very, very sorry."

Tierney cleared her throat. "Thank you." She took a tissue from her pocket and blotted her tears. "I always thought I'd like to come back here to Pass Creek and buy the house my mother loved, in her memory. But then when I got here in May, I began to feel differently. It was like day became night. All at once I was absorbed by the conviction that *this town* was to blame for my family's deaths."

Her voice shook as she continued. "The whole situation, the mill closing, no jobs to be had, able-bodied men forced to go on welfare—that was this town's fault. A crazy way of thinking, but at the time it made such sense. Pass Creek had no right to Gable House. If my mother couldn't have it, why should anyone else? There was nothing stopping me from buying it and tearing it down. I had the money to buy the house and then get rid of it if I wanted. It would be for them, for my Mom and Dad and little brother.

"When I came to Pass Creek, I was still grieving my husband's death—which had hit me harder than I could ever make anyone else understand. Being here revived memories of what happened to my family. That old terrible hurt returned. I was more depressed than I've ever been before in my life."

"Understandably so," Celia said softly, her head feeling like a filling balloon with all Tierney was telling her. "I'm really sorry for what happened to you. I realize that sometimes the pain of one's feelings causes them to act, to think, much differently than they might otherwise." *Pain.*

"I'm glad you can see how it was. I suppose I was too

deeply depressed to recognize what I surely know—that hurting others does nothing to resolve your own hurt and would more than likely compound it. Gable House will stand."

Celia blinked back her own tears, took a deep breath and smiling, went to hug her. "Bless you for changing your mind. In your situation, I might have felt as you did. You were very young when you lost your entire family. I can only imagine such pain, but I understand how a loss like that would affect a person's entire life."

"It does. But much of my life has been truly wonderful, and from now on I intend to focus on that."

Celia nodded, smiling.

They returned to the subject of Mac's arrest. Celia explained about the valuable antique gun that belonged to his mother, and the details of how Otis Peek had literally stolen the gun from the Strands.

"The attorney I've hired for Mac will be contacting Otis's relatives to learn if they have the gun. It's a good guess that the gun was among the contents of the safety deposit box that was sent on to them, separate from whatever money was in the bank and so forth. There were documents, both a handwritten loan deal and others that signified the gun's authenticity and how it came to be bequeathed to Mac's mother. The papers might have been with the gun, but I doubt they were."

"How is that?"

"Otis was blatantly dishonest about that antique gun. I believe he would keep those documents at home, close to his person, hidden."

"Unless he destroyed them," Tierney said.

"God forbid he did that! We have to find those papers if they still exist."

"You'd like to search Gable House for them?" Tierney guessed correctly.

"Yes, I would. If the papers are there and I can find them,

it would most surely prove Mac's telling the truth, at least the part of his story about ownership of the valuable gun. In any event, I think it would help prove his innocence."

Tierney stood up. "I'll get the key. I'd like to go with you. Maybe I can help in the search, but it's also time I had a good look inside the wonderful old place myself."

Eureka! Celia thought, doing a little hip-wiggling dance when Tierney was out of sight.

Chapter Nineteen

It felt creepy to Celia, entering Gable House for the first time since Otis's death—musty smelling and cold, but the feeling soon fled. The fusty Victorian furnishings, floral wallpaper in soft wisteria blue and sage green, she flat out loved. Give her such charm and richness any day. Those who preferred shiny and new were welcome to it.

"What do you think?" she asked, watching Tierney.

Tierney moved farther into the room, nodding, looking about with a quiet, delighted smile. No animosity now. In fact, Tierney Jones looked comfortable, at home. Celia could imagine her as a movie star in this room with its gilt-framed paintings and mirrors, the lush, bittersweet-red mohair sofas and fat, barrel-back chairs, the thick Persian carpet. Maybe co-starring with Clark Gable himself, if not for the age difference and him being dead.

"Beautiful, if a bit overdone," Tierney finally answered, hesitating in her stride before the tall ornate fireplace at the far end of the room, "and in need of dusting." She traced a finger along the deeply carved oak mantel. Nodded toward the mirror in the over mantel.

Celia had already noted the heavy film of dust on the mahogany tables scattered about the room. There was the usual clutter, too, that one would expect in an elderly bachelor's home, Otis's pipe and a spill of tobacco on an end table; house slippers, one at odds with the other, under a chair. Five or six books piled any old way on the floor. Otis himself was gone forever to wherever curmudgeons go. Who did kill him, if not Mac? Today was another step toward finding that out, providing luck was with them.

"Otis didn't have a regular housekeeper since Mac's mother worked for him. Hence the dust and clutter," she said. "Plus the house has been locked tight since he fell—was killed."

"It wouldn't take much to make this house truly special again," Tierney mused, circling the room.

Celia smiled agreement. "Many of the furnishings go back to the 1800s when the house was built. More were added when the widow, Hannah Blake, ran Gable House as a hotel. Otis Peek enjoyed antiques, too, and didn't get rid of anything. He did add a few modern touches in the kitchen, but otherwise left the house alone. Well," she said, turning toward the fireplace, "time to begin the search. Can't just stand around appreciating forever."

"What in the world are you doing?" Tierney's eyebrow shot up as Celia began to rap her knuckles here and there on the fireplace's carved ornamentation.

"A *thonk* sound instead of a solid *thunk* would indicate a hollow place behind the woodwork, a hidey-hole of some sort. I've seen it in movies many times," she explained.

"And are you hearing a hollow, hidey-hole sound, then?" Tierney asked with a teasing smile.

"Nope, but there's nothing lost in trying."

While Celia continued to knock at the wood with her knuckles and listen, climbing on a chair to reach the higher places, Tierney went to a marble-topped table at the end of the sofa and opened a drawer. "Nothing here but old junky papers," she said, rifling through them. "Why do people keep this stuff?"

"What junky papers?" Celia asked, hopping off the chair, satisfied that the fireplace had no secret hiding places.

"Well..." Tierney, tossed papers to the floor. "Old voting

pamphlets, for one thing. Outdated catalogues, old grocery store flyers, free sheets of return address labels—so many of those Otis Peek would have to have lived to be a hundred and ten to use them all... Oops, that was a bad slip." She threw up her hands. "I'm going to the kitchen and see if I can find trash bags. Might as well collect the useless stuff as we go and throw it out."

Celia hurried over and shook the catalogue pages and unfolded the grocery fliers, just to make sure nothing was inside them. While Tierney was in the kitchen, she went to each painting around the walls and looked behind them. In a mansion like this, in movies, there was invariably some kind of safe installed behind a painting.

Not here, though. She moved on, completing a search of other tables in the room, including a tall curio cabinet, finding interesting odds and ends, among them a blue glass boot holding a lot of very old pennies, a little souvenir railroad mug, three or four ancient and empty liquor decanters, a pair of Rhett Butler and Scarlet O'Hara figurines, which Celia instantly fell in love with. She moved aside a trio of porcelain cats, a Bavarian chocolate set, and the skull of a medium sized animal with what looked like fool's gold for eyes. Good grief! None of the objects, which might or might not be valuable, hid what she hoped to find.

Her heart picked up a beat when she entered Otis's office a few minutes later. Her glance swept a secretary desk with slanted lid, bookcase above, and four deep drawers below. Under the bay window sat a pine chest. She smiled to herself. Plenty of places in this room to keep private papers away from the eyes of others.

She went through the books first, pulling them out and looking between and behind them, and shaking the pages. In quiet desperation she searched the writing compartments over the desk, finding all sorts of paper stuffed in square nooks—bills, photos, business cards, note paper. An antique ink well, magnifying glass, and the usual pens, pencils, and rubber bands. She slapped her hand on the desktop in frustration, causing scattered paper clips to dance.

She desperately wished the legal papers connected to the antique gun would suddenly materialize and settle matters. If such papers actually existed, Celia reminded herself. She prayed Mac was telling the truth and this wasn't a wild goose chase.

She stooped. In the lower drawers of the secretary desk were an assortment of unused envelopes, a dictionary, and more than one atlas. Where did the man keep his important papers, for heaven's sake? She closed the last drawer and turned to the pine chest. It was locked. Who would have the keys? Tierney, of course. It was her house now. She hurried through the house to find her.

Back in the office in high excitement, they tried each of the smaller furniture keys until one finally worked. In the top drawer of the pine chest was a money box containing eighty dollars in bills plus a few coins. There were old bank statements, copies of contracts for purchases Otis had made for kitchen appliances, a few old letters. Income tax records, lots of plain *stuff.*

Celia threaded through the whole mess a second time without success. Deflated, she sat on the floor, her face in her hands.

"We're not finished," Tierney encouraged. "I'm heading back to the kitchen and pantry to look."

"Okay." Celia sighed and got back to her feet. "I'll get the dining room."

She pawed through a sideboard, finding table linens, most yellowed with age, silverware, a pair of silver vases, pairs of cut-glass and silver candlesticks. She looked in the vases for papers, but they were empty. Other cabinets in the dining room held nothing but china—so old and beautiful she hardly dared touch it—and crystal.

For a long time, they continued to methodically search. With lack of results, disappointment continued to climb. While Tierney tackled floor to ceiling shelves and drawers in the kitchen, Celia was in Otis's bedroom, going through chests of drawers, a dresser, and nightstands. Cartons, shoe boxes, and wooden keepsake boxes in the closet were searched to see what was in them.

A lot of what they found was tossed into the trash bags they dragged along with them.

"It's getting late," Celia said finally in the kitchen. She leaned against a cupboard and spoke to Tierney, who was sifting through boxes and baskets in the connecting pantry. "There is no way we can finish this today. There are still other bedrooms we haven't set foot in yet, and the attic. And then the garage and tool sheds outside." She brushed her hair back from her face and stretched her aching back. She felt grubby, in need of a shower.

"Look at this. I think I've found something," Tierney said.

Tierney held a Thrifty Market announcement of a huge canned goods sale in one hand and a much smaller piece of paper in the other.

"An old newspaper? So what?" Celia asked, feeling cranky and tired to the bone.

"Not the ad! This!" Tierney let the newspaper fall to the floor and held up the small, single sheet of paper. "It isn't what we were looking for but—wow! This handwritten letter was tucked in a stack of old grocery flyers and newspapers on the pantry shelf over there, like somebody was just tidying up and shoved a bunch of stuff there to get it out of the way."

"Okay, so what is it, anyhow?" Celia sagged to the floor, her elbows propped on her knees. She looked up at her friend.

Tierney's eyes twinkled in astonishment as she sank to the floor beside her. "It looks to me like Otis Peek was thinking of turning Gable House over to your Heritage Club."

"No! You've got to be kidding!" Celia grabbed the sheet

of paper Tierney held toward her. "Dear heaven, can you believe this?" she whispered, then read aloud:

"*To members of the Pass Creek Heritage Club,*

I haven't discussed this yet with my attorney, but it is my intention to leave Gable House to the Heritage Club on my passing. The town has always supported me in the endeavors I chose, befriended me when I wasn't always the most agreeable of fellows. This is my way of giving back. In the meantime, I would like to stipulate that this agreement shall include the help of members of the club in keeping up Gable House from this time on according to my needs, for the remainder of my life. There are roofing repairs to be made, the orchard needs pruning. I can't continue to keep mowing the lawns, raking leaves, and taking care of the flower beds on my own. If the group is in agreement with my plan, I will see to it that the provision for awarding Gable House to the town is included in my will.

Respectfully,
Otis Peek

Celia, trembling from shock, scooted to lean back against the wall. "The old bugger! He was going to do this to make up to the town for his being such a scoundrel?" Her mind raced. "What happened? Did he change his mind? Maybe he was killed before he could tell this to his attorney. This was not in his will for sure or we, the Heritage Club, would have heard about it." She babbled on in tortured excitement, "No date on the letter. Was he just musing? Only considering? I'd give my soul to know what this means…"

Tierney put a calming hand on her shoulder. "It's unfair the house went to his heirs, who really had no interest in it, then sold it to me before his plan could be legalized—if that was his serious intention. I'm sorry, Celia. We'll talk to a lawyer and see how this letter affects the situation and what can be done about it."

Celia patted Tierney's hand on her shoulder and shook her

head. "I don't blame you for any of this. You couldn't have known his wishes any more than I did. Honestly, I don't know what to think. It's just too puzzling. Is it possible someone knew of Otis's wishes to pass this place on to the Heritage Club, to the town, and killed him to put a stop to it? But then"—she shook her head—"what would that achieve? Our club would lose out, but Peek's relatives would still inherit. How could that help the killer? Truly, this drives me crazy."

"You'll figure it out somehow, Celia. Let's leave all this until tomorrow."

"Okay." She staggered to her feet. "At the moment I'm too tired to think."

Once at home again, Celia found a wizened little monkey of a man rocking in a chair on the inn's front porch, waiting for her. Her first tenant since the fire, he signed her register in a shaky scrawl: John Wayne Stewart. When he was a "young sprout," he told her as she showed him the Edna Ferber room that would be his for his stay, he was a stunt man in Clark Gable's later movies. He'd come to Pass Creek to see and get pictures of the town where Clark lived and worked when he was a "sprout."

The rattle of John Wayne Stewart's false teeth gave Celia's weary nerves fits as he told a long story of his stunt days, and she patiently listened. He showed her his tiny Flip video camera, "No bigger than a soda cracker" that his wife had given him for Christmas. "I have a whole collection of Clark Gable memorabilia," he told her. "Now I'm going to walk the ground he walked hereabouts and get me some pictures."

"You'll have a good time here in Pass Creek, I promise," she finally told him, laying a hand on his wrist. "I know you won't mind if I excuse myself. I've had quite a long day."

"Me, too," he said. "Going to turn in early so I'm in great shape for tomorrow." He looked so excited, she couldn't help but love him.

"Yes, you do that. The bathroom is right there next to your

room. There are plenty of towels, and if you need anything else, let me know." She hurried from the room, wondering how much time she'd have to show him around. Maybe she could send him off on his own and he'd be happy.

She bathed, changed into comfortable jeans and loose shirt. She sat at the kitchen table with her uneaten sandwich in front of her and stared into space, thinking. Would Locke Vinson kill for his goals? Moody, obstinate and self-serving, he wanted Pass Creek revitalized as much as anyone, but for his own gain and according to his plans. In a rage, in midst of an argument and to talk Peek out of his intentions to award Gable House to their town's Heritage Club, she thought he just might kill him. A chill traveled her spine.

The telephone rang, making her jump. Her throat was dry when she answered it. "Yes, Randolph. What do you have for me?" She listened, her hopes sinking the longer her attorney friend spoke, letting her know that he'd been able to contact both Otis Peek's lawyer and Peek's relatives in Palm Springs. There had been no antique gun, no papers legal or otherwise referring to such a weapon, in the safety deposit box.

Which could mean Mac was lying, but she still hoped not. She thanked Randolph and told him that they were searching Gable House but so far hadn't found papers or gun there, either. "We're not finished looking, though," she said. After another minute or two discussing how bad this latest news was for Mac's case, they said goodbye and she hung up the phone.

The phone rang again just seconds later and it was Jake. "I'm coming right over," he told her, "so stay put. I have some news."

While she waited for Jake, she considered how Otis's letter expressing his intent to bequeath Gable House to her group would affect Mac's case, if at all. Were the two matters connected in a bad way? In any way at all? She couldn't see how, and her gut told her that they were not.

She hoped her gut was right.

"A kiss for good news?" Jake asked when she let him in. "Deal?" He reached for her.

"Bribery like that will get you everywhere," she said, returning his kiss.

They sat on the sofa, Jake's arm around her shoulders, Freebie stretched out asleep across Jake's foot. "What do you have for me?" Celia asked. "Something about Mac? Heaven knows he needs good news."

"Sorry, honey, this is not about Mac." He leaned to kiss her cheek. "I came to tell you that Shull's movements have been traced to a medical clinic in Salem. They have record of treating a man of Shull's description for bad burns to his upper body. Yeah," he said in answer to the question he saw she was about to ask, "I was talking to Pete at the Bar and Grill just a few minutes ago. He told me about the bottle and shirt, and he said I could tell you the latest. They haven't found Shull yet but they are hot on his trail and it should happen any time."

"Good!" She shook her head and laced her fingers through Jake's. "I don't understand it, though. The foolish man could have burned himself to death in the process of ruining the town. I hope they get out of him why he did such an awful thing."

Did Locke Vinson have a part in the scheme? Had he hired Shull to set the fires? Because, her mind raced in thought, if the town was leveled by fire, Locke could buy the land cheap and proceed with his plans that had him so obsessed: the big resort he wanted, upscale hotel, golf courses, discount mall.

She shared her ideas with Jake. "Maybe Harry Shull wasn't alone in what he did. He could have been hired by someone with bigger stakes in the town. Something more than just dislike of me and wanting to strike back."

"You're thinking it was Locke Vinson?"

"Yes." She gave her reasons, expanding with details.

"It's possible," Jake said. "We need to run this by Pete,

although what we're thinking may have already occurred to him and he's on it. If Locke wanted to be rid of the town but not appear to have any part of its destruction, why wouldn't he hire Harry Shull to commit the crime for him? He could step in later, the big guy willing to rebuild Pass Creek. Wonder what he paid Shull. Wonder what he promised."

Celia shrugged. She lifted their entwined hands and absentmindedly kissed Jake's fingers. "Maybe we can find out. Or, like you say, maybe Pete and the county officers working with him, already know if Vinson was involved or not."

"In any regard, Shull, when they catch him, will be a long time cooling his heels in prison for his thievery, for assaulting you and setting the fires."

"And for Otis's murder?"

"Pete thinks that's about the only thing Harry Shull didn't do." A frown furrowed Jake's brow. "I know you don't like to hear it, Celia, but from what I get from Pete, he feels Mac is his most likely suspect." After a few minutes, he added under his breath, "I'd still like to personally knock the soup out of Shull for what he did to you. You could have died, smothered to death in that garbage."

"Speaking of smothering," she murmured softly and buried her face in his neck. She nuzzled him with her nose. Her lips planted tiny pecks above his collar.

"Smother away." He chuckled, pulling her closer and returning her kisses.

"Double darn it," Celia said finally, drawing herself from his arms. "I suppose I ought to call Pete right now tonight and tell him my ideas about Locke Vinson."

Jake sagged back into the sofa with a ragged growl. "Double dammit, I guess so."

With a sigh of regret, she went to her study where she called Pete at home—interrupting dinner with his wife and kids—and told him her belief that Locke Vinson could have hired Shull to burn the town and that he possibly killed Otis, too. She also told him she was searching Gable House for the papers, and possibly the gun, that would help Mac.

She headed back to the couch and the delicious interlude that had been taking place there.

"What did Pete have to say?" Jake asked. He caught her waist and pulled her down beside him.

"Pete thanked me for the information. He asked if I had proof pointing to Vinson as the killer. I don't, so he reminded me that hearsay is not of a lot of help, which of course I knew already. He told me to be careful. He said he's on track with the case and for me to remember that it's his job, not mine, to determine Otis Peek's killer and whether or not Shull acted alone in setting the fires." She made a face and shrugged. "I tried."

"But you'll take his advice and stay out of it?"

"I'll be careful." She gave him a noisy kiss on the chin. "Now, where were we?"

Chapter Twenty

Late the next day, Celia dropped into an overstuffed chair in the Gable House parlor and moaned, "Darn it! I was sure we'd find the papers here, and maybe the gun too, but there's not a crook or cranny we haven't searched. They aren't here, and I guess it was stupid to bother."

"Not stupid." Tierney said, taking another chair. She smiled at Celia and the other women in the room. "We gave it the old college try."

"I'm sure Mac is telling the truth," Celia told her friends with half-hearted confidence, "that the papers and the antique revolver exist. But I have no idea where to go from here."

News traveled fast in Pass Creek. Mrs. Kemp had hobbled over mid-morning out of curiosity and stayed to help look, although her actual accomplishments were questionable. Viv had dropped in, hoping to take on consignment any antiques Tierney might want to part with, and she pitched in. Myrna, who'd heard what was going on from customers, helped for a while and then left to come back with food and drinks from the Mellow Mushroom.

By the time Salliebeth arrived after getting off work from the realty office, the group was too tired for anything but the impromptu meal and conversation.

"Not stupid," Tierney repeated, "and in searching, you all have helped me clean out a mess that needed to go. That would have been a huge job for me alone."

"And those wonderful vintage dresses we found in the upstairs closet!" Celia perked up, remembering. "I'm so glad we discovered those, and thanks, Tierney, for offering them to me. They'll be perfect to wear when I lead my tours. I was running out of suitable finds at my Goodwill treasure trove."

Salliebeth said, "Who'd have thought that Otis, a confirmed bachelor, would keep women's old-fashioned dresses, probably hanging right where they were from when he got the place?"

"He knew they were nice things." Myrna spoke around a mouthful of sandwich. "But he should've loaned them to you to wear, Celia. Never even told you he had them just hanging there, serving no purpose at all. He was stingy that way. Never did make sense."

Celia shrugged. "I'm just tickled to get to wear them now, those that I can fit into, that is."

"I'm thrilled that you're going to open up Gable House again, Tierney," Salliebeth said, lifting her glass of Pepsi in salute. "Guests on the tours loved having tea here and seeing the bed where Gable slept."

Celia laughed. "Getting to see that bed was the highlight of their life, some visitors said." John Wayne Stewart had been in the house briefly and had taken endless videos of the bed and other rooms.

"Years ago, Gable House was part of a Candlelight Evening event," Viv put in. "Children were invited to decorate the community Christmas tree here in the side yard. The celebration got its name from the luminaries, candles in bags of sand, set up along the walks on the grounds. The lights were sponsored by community members who donated a dollar for each luminary, either in memory or in honor of a friend or a loved one."

"I remember that!" Mrs. Kemp declared from where she

sat nearly buried in an overstuffed chair. "Oh, that was so much fun. We had hot chocolate and cookies, horse drawn wagon rides, a bonfire." She giggled. "You know, I got my first kiss at a Christmas-time Candlelight Evening. Mrs. Jones," she addressed Tierney, "could we go back to having those fun times here again? Easter egg hunts, too, like we used to have here on the grounds?"

"That all sounds so nice," Myrna broke in quietly. "I wish I'd lived here then. Only thing I know about is the tea and cookies for Celia's tours of this place."

"No need to look so sad," Tierney said, reaching to Myrna in a nearby chair and squeezing her hand. "I remember Christmas and Easter celebrations here at Gable House from when I was a young girl. It's possible we can do those things again."

"I'm glad. I am." Myrna looked around the room with a sparkle of tears in her eyes. She appeared to be gathering courage for her next words. "But I won't be here for 'em 'cause I'm going back East to find my sister, maybe live with her again. But I gotta tell you, I'll miss you all so much."

Her announcement brought exclamations of surprise. She explained, "Things here in Pass Creek just haven't turned out very good for me." Her bright red lips trembled. "I thought maybe me and Otis could have a life together, traveling or enjoying each other's company not doing much of anything except fun stuff, you know? That didn't work out. I'm getting too old for that nonsense, anyhow. Too old for working so hard. My sister, she's single, too. We can take care of each other."

Without being too obvious, Celia studied Myrna thoughtfully. Leaving town? Was it only to be with her sister, or was there something more prompting this move? Goosebumps stood at attention all over Celia's body while inside, she began to feel sick. It was Myrna who'd told her that the chief advised Otis to put the valuable antique weapon safely in the bank. Myrna who'd said that's what Otis had done. Did Myrna know that he hadn't? Had she lied? Was she lying—Celia found it hard to breathe—when she described how she *found* Otis dead when the truth was that she'd killed him?

Except for Myrna, each woman as she came had pitched in wholeheartedly in the search. Myrna's efforts had been half-hearted at best before she went to bring the food.

Celia realized with sudden conviction that Myrna didn't put her all into the search because she knew the location of the gun, and it wasn't Gable House. All those lies!

The gathering, fortunately, ended in another few minutes. One or two at a time, the women, after hugs and goodbyes, departed for home or to do various tasks downtown. Tierney, engaged in a last bit of tidying up, told Celia she was stopping by the library before having dinner at the Mellow Mushroom.

"All right," Celia answered numbly, her mind abuzz with conviction that Myrna was Otis's killer, and that something had to be done about it before Myrna left town. She looked around. One moment Myrna was there; now she was gone. Celia flew out the door and hurried to catch up with her.

Myrna was halfway down the block, walking fast. She looked over her shoulder and when she saw Celia, she broke into a run. Celia, younger and faster, ran after her. "Wait, Myrna! Let's talk!" She ran hard, caught up, and grabbed Myrna by the arm. "Don't run away from this. It won't help," she panted. "It'll only make things worse."

For a minute, Myrna fought back, doing her best to get away. With all her strength, Celia held on. Finally, Myrna gave up and collapsed in Celia's arms, sobbing.

"Let's go to my house," Celia said softly, "and talk."

They sat on the sofa in the parlor. Weeping, Myrna said, "You're on to me, ain't you, Celia? You figured it out about Otis? That I did it? I killed him? I saw the look on your face right after I said I was leaving town. You don't mean to let me do that, do you?"

"No, I can't let you go. It would only make matters more

difficult for you in the long run." Celia swallowed through a dry throat. "Do you want to tell me your side of what took place?" She placed a box of tissues in Myrna's lap.

For a second Myrna sagged like she might faint before drawing herself up and mopping her eyes and nose. "Yes. It's eating me alive, and I know it's over."

"Go on, then." Celia held Myrna's hand as she told her story.

"I could see Otis was starting to change after being such an old rascal for years. He talked about owing the town for being good to him. I guessed maybe he intended to leave Gable House to your Heritage Club. I wouldn't have minded that. It was fair. But it seemed to me that if he could look kindly on anything, why not me?"

Celia squeezed her hand as her throat filled in sympathy.

Myrna wept afresh as she talked. "It was my break over at the restaurant that day. I slipped across the street to see him for a few minutes. One last time I tried to talk him into marrying me. We could be happy together. I knew it. I begged him. He was out back of the house, getting ready to go back up on the roof. But what I was telling him just went in one ear and out the other. He paid me no attention at all, other than to laugh. He went right on working. He bent over to pick up a tool, a scraper, to get some moss off the roof. While he was like that, without really thinking, I grabbed a brick that was there loose on the side wall." Her voice trembled. "And I slammed his head with it. I hit him real hard, Celia."

"Oh, Myrna..." She could imagine Myrna's hurt and the frustration behind the blow.

"What I'd done scared me to death. I threw that brick as far as I could. All of a sudden it seemed like the worst thing I'd ever had my hands on. I tried to help him, thought I'd call for an ambulance real quick, but he was dead."

The silence between them was thick with emotion before

Myrna continued. "I don't know, but it was like my brain stopped working. I went back to the Mushroom, doing my job like a robot. I thought sure someone would find him. Every second I expected to hear police sirens and see Pete coming to get me and take me to jail. But the rest of day was quiet. None of that happened."

In a choked voice Celia said, "I know how you must have felt."

"No, you probably don't, Celia. I threw up two or three times in the restroom while I waited to be arrested. I didn't mean to kill Otis, or even hurt him. But it all come down on me, you know, about how things went wrong all my durn life. Capping it off was him, treating me like I was nobody. I was a nothing and he didn't care."

"I'm so sorry for how he treated you, Myrna, truly."

She wiped her eyes. "When I got off work I went back across the street to see Otis. I was hoping for a miracle by then, praying I was wrong and he'd be alive and back in the house nursing his head and cussing me. But he was dead, laying right in the same spot, and so cold."

Silence weighed heavy in the room.

"What did you do?" Celia asked when she could.

"I sat there with him for a while. I know I should have been truthful and said that I was the one did it. But how could I? I loved him. How could I tell anybody I killed him? I made out I found him just that minute, and I started screaming and screaming. Mrs. Kemp came over and we called nine-one-one. You know the rest."

"I suppose I do. I wish Otis had been kinder, hadn't driven you to the brink. The only thing I haven't been able to figure out is what happened to the antique weapon, the Civil War revolver we've been looking for."

"It's at my house. The papers you're looking for are there, too."

"Otis never put the revolver and papers in the bank?"

"No." She shook her head. "Otis hid them in the bed springs of that bed Gable slept in. He told me no matter what happened, if he took sick or something else where he might be helpless, I was to not let nobody get that revolver that used to be his ancestor's. I didn't know that it wasn't really Otis's and never was. Anybody who heard the stories he told about the gun would believe it was his. I sure believed him."

"When you heard the revolver had belonged to Mac and his mother, why didn't you tell someone?"

"By then I was in deep, you know? I hoped, when the gun wasn't in the house and it turned out it wasn't in the bank, neither, people would believe an outsider killed Otis for the gun. He'd been looking into buyers, talking to them on the phone and so on. Any 'a them and people they talked to would know about the gun he owned, where he lived and all. One of them could have been the thief, the killer."

"The revolver is a valuable relic. Why didn't you...?"

"Why didn't I take it and run? Sell it somewhere and start over? I've asked myself that a lot and I figure that I'm just not that kind of person. I'm not a thief, and I don't go around killing people, neither. If I had it to do over, I sure wouldn't have hit Otis with that brick. I ruined my life for good in the second I did that."

With a deep sigh, Celia placed an arm around Myrna's shoulders and told her, "It's best you turn yourself in and tell the truth. You know that, don't you? If you still tried to leave to go to your sister and were caught trying to get away, that would only add to the charges that will be brought against you."

"I know I need to go to Pete and confess what happened." Myrna shook her head. "I'd have left before now to my sister's, but every time I was about to, I'd picture the cops coming for me. That would nearly kill my sister, seeing that happen to me." Her voice quivered. "This w-way maybe she won't e-ever have to know." She wiped her eyes. "Will you go with me, Celia, to talk to Pete?"

"Sure I will. What you did happened in a moment of pure anger, Myrna. You didn't plan to kill him. The courts will take that into consideration—we can hope they'll go easier on you since it wasn't a premeditated murder. I can see involuntary manslaughter as a possibility, and I'll certainly be a character witness for you. Folks in town love you, and every one of them knows what Otis was like. They'll support you, I'm sure."

"Thank you, Celia." Myrna heaved a deep sigh, "Yeah, it's the thing to do. Let's go to my place and get the antique gun." She added, "I hate it that that nice boy was being held in jail when he did nothing wrong. I been itching to tell the truth so he can be out of there. It's time."

Celia agreed, "Mac's been there too long. Let's go get him out."

Chapter Twenty-One

That evening, at John Wayne Stewart's invitation, Celia had dinner with him at the Mellow Mushroom. Remembering Myrna's work there, the many friendships the woman had made and how matters had ended made it difficult to enjoy the food. She did her best to show interest in the old fellow's constant chatter, stories of his time "in the movie business."

"Clark played the part of an aging cowboy in *The Misfits*," he was telling her, "but I don't think the ladies liked seeing him old. At the time, I was so lolly-gagged over Marilyn Monroe in *The Misfits*, I wasn't hardly myself. Nowadays," he said, chuckling, "I'd be more apt to feel that way over Thelma Ritter—she was in the movie, too."

Celia smiled and nodded. "I saw that movie, and I agree it wasn't fun seeing Clark Gable age." Her mind again skittered back to the day's events. Turning Myrna over to Pete was one of the hardest things she'd ever done. But nothing in the world could make her feel better than seeing Mac released to go home to Lilly. She smiled across the table at her dinner companion. "Shall we have dessert? Butterscotch pie, maybe?"

After finishing their pie, Celia walked back to the inn with Mr. Stewart. They said their goodnights and afterward, she sat in her study thinking for a long while. Otis Peek's killer had been discovered and was in custody. Mac had been allowed to go home. All they needed now was to find Shull—and the police were closing in on him—and learn for sure if Locke Vinson had hired Harry Shull to burn down the town. If he had, there was no way Locke should go free. He could try again, and next time he could succeed.

Celia couldn't sleep, stewing the matter over and over as she tossed and turned into the long hours of the night. *Proof, the chief said they needed. Hearsay wasn't worth a tinker's dam.* Okay, then, she told herself. We need to find proof. And she finally got an hour's sleep around dawn.

After a breakfast she could eat little of, Celia looked up the telephone number for Locke Vinson's company headquarters in Portland, some sixty miles north of Pass Creek.

It took two more hours before she could begin to fulfill her plan. Taking deep breaths for courage, she punched in the phone number. She asked if Vinson was there in the office and the secretary assured her that he was, for a while today anyway. While Celia waited for him to come on the line, she wondered if he would believe her.

"Celia?" he sounded wary.

"Yes, Locke, I need to talk to you." She made her voice calm and matter-of-fact. "When you were here before, I admit that I rushed to judgment when I should have given you a chance to spell out your proposition to buy my place."

"Oh?" his growl was ripe with suspicion.

"You're a very successful businessman." She played to his vanity. "And I admit I haven't given you the credit you deserve for that."

"Don't fool around with me, Celia," he snapped. "If you've got something to say, spit it out."

"All right. Okay. I know it's hard for you to trust me at this point, but things have changed a great deal around here. Someone I liked very much and thought well of has turned out to be a—a coldblooded killer." She explained about Myrna then continued, "The fires have been frightening. Even with all that,

I'd probably stick it out and never leave. You know how much I love this town. But the thing is…Jake has asked me to marry him." It was an enormous lie but worth telling to get what she wanted. "He wants me to move with him to his uncle's ranch in eastern Oregon. It would help if I had money from this place to help him over there."

She could hear his breath quicken on the other end of the line. But still he held off for another minute, probably as long as he was able. "You're ready to sell, then?"

"I thought we could talk about it, today maybe. Or come down some other time if you'd rather." She banked on his greed to choose the first option.

He seemed to measure once more everything she'd said to him. "Nobody makes an ass of me. You know that, don't you, Celia?"

"I know it very well." She controlled a shiver and spoke firmly, "You don't have to take my offer if it bothers you, Locke. I'd understand. Flagg Realty…Jake, could probably find a buyer for me. You know…" She hesitated, praying he'd take the bait. "I'm going to have him take care of the sale. That's probably best, anyhow. He's close. Bye, Locke…"

"Wait! I didn't say I wasn't interested. I am. I'll be down in about an hour."

"Oh, well, all right. Can't hurt to talk. See you then." An hour from Portland was all it would take, especially in his fancy Porsche. Even if he didn't really believe her, he was greedy enough to make sure she was being truthful or not about selling out. He'd come, and she had one hour to be ready.

Tierney was over at Gable House, sketching plans for furniture arrangements and other things she wanted to do there. In case the situation got out of hand with Locke, Celia didn't want anyone else at the inn other than police. Leaving her study, she found John Wayne Stewart shooting a video of Freebie in the parlor. This came as something of a surprise, because Freebie hadn't known Clark Gable.

"You know, Mr. Stewart," she told him as she took a chair, "there's going to be a lunch meeting of our Heritage Club at the Mellow Mushroom today, followed by bingo." Her hand stroked the chair's upholstered arm as she made every effort to be casual. "I can't go, but I know you'd enjoy it." She smiled and leaned forward, relaxed, elbows on her knees. "A fine meal is served, and it would be an opportunity for you to meet some of the older people in town who might have Clark Gable stories for you—about when he lived here in Pass Creek. They might even have other video suggestions for you to take—like where a girl he dated lived, on a farm out on Finney road."

"I don't know," he said, getting down on his bony knees for closer shots of Freebie. "I thought I'd stay in today and visit with you."

"Well, that would be nice, but I'm going to be busy. Women stuff, you know."

He nodded slowly, rising when Freebie took off at a run for the kitchen. "I'll think about it. Yup, might as well go. See what folks might have to tell me about Clark. He was a good man, you know. He and I used to tell jokes on the set. There was one time..."

Celia, on pins and needles, listened. Fortunately, this was a shorter story than some he'd told her. Finally John Wayne Stewart headed for the stairs and his room to "clean up and get fancy for the lunch."

She watched the clock until a half hour passed. She didn't have the nerve to face the chief in person—Pete was going to be furious—but he had to know the set up and be there. Bracing herself, she phoned the station and waited.

Even if Pete was out of the office, he could get back in a hurry from about anywhere in the mid-valley and bring county officers with him. Let him know too soon, and he'd ruin the plan. Order her not to get involved. But she was the one, she and her property, that would get Locke here. He was nobody's fool, but greed would propel him right into the trap she was setting for him. She was sure of it.

Celia listened in shock to the clerk who manned Pete's office in his absence. Goosebumps sprang on her skin and she began to quiver. "Portland! He went up there when?" *God no. He had to be* here. Her free hand went up to jab through her hair. "You have to get him back in town fast. This is urgent. Okay, yes, you're right. If he went up there about Harry Shull"—her voice trembled—"that's important, t-too. But please, get him back here to Pass Creek as soon as possible. To Landrey's Inn." After the clerk said she'd try to get Pete but would also try to find someone from the county police force to come if it was important, Celia thanked her and said that it was very important. She explained that Locke Vinson was on his way to see her and she was afraid of him.

Important? Life and death important, in all probability. What in heaven's name had she done? Suddenly, Celia wanted to run, to get as far away as possible from what she'd set in motion. But she couldn't. She had to stay and face Locke Vinson and trap him into admitting his part in trying to burn down her town. She had to stay. She was the one with the opportunity.

Celia went to run cold water and wash her face, but her hands were shaking so hard she gave it up. She took four aspirin for her tension headache and went to sit in her parlor and wait. She prayed that the chief had finished with his investigation in Portland and was well on his way back. Otherwise...

When she looked out the front window to see Locke's red Porsche rolling to a stop at her curb, she stood up, prepared herself to meet him at the door. At the same moment, Freebie meowed back at the kitchen door to be let out. Potty time. She welcomed the excuse to put off facing Locke a few seconds longer. Celia hurried to let the cat out into the backyard.

On her return, Celia noted the hall closet door open just a

sliver. Looking out at her was a watery blue eye. "John Wayne Stewart!" she hissed, "what are you doing in there? Come out right now. You have to leave, by the back door. Now."

He opened the door a sliver more. "No. I'm staying. I heard you talking on the phone. You sounded awful scared. I can help." His showed her his black video camera. "The way I figure, it's a man coming and you can't be by yourself. I'm here as your witness."

"I thought you'd left," she wailed softly. "Please come out of the closet and go by the back door. You have to go."

"No," he said again, and warned her, "You better get that front door before the darned fool pounds it in."

"Fine!" she snapped, "but don't move. Stay in there, for God's sake."

"Locke." She met him at the door. "Come on in." Her pulse pounded. She led the way, turning to him in the parlor and motioning him toward a stuffed chair. "May I offer you some coffee or wine?"

"Nothing stronger?" He was well-dressed as always, smelled of expensive men's cologne.

"I'm sorry."

"Forget it then." He sized her up, still suspicious, but he said, "I'm glad you're willing to discuss a deal for your place. You know I've wanted it for a long time, and I'll give you a good price."

Celia said creatively as she sat down, "I'll need the money. I think Jake's uncle's ranch is pretty run down. We'll want to bring it up to date, re-stock it, do all of that. What are your plans, exactly, for my place?" She did her best not to show her dislike of him, her mortal fear at what she was attempting.

She let him talk about his investors who were champing at the bit to turn Pass Creek into a resort town, starting with her property on Eden creek.

"I'm sorry, Celia, because I know how you feel." He

shook his head in an attempt to show compassion—which she knew he didn't have an ounce of. "But a lot of the old buildings will have to go."

"I'm glad I won't be here to see that," she told him sadly, playing his game. "This place has meant a lot to me, as anyone can tell you." She rose from the sofa. "You know, I think I do have some brandy, after all. Left over from making fruit cakes last Christmas. I know I need it. I'll get some glasses and pour us a tad to celebrate our deal."

A flash of gloating glittered in his eyes for a brief second, then he looked at her blandly. He stretched and took his time getting to his feet to follow her toward the dining room and kitchen.

When they approached the area of the closet, she stopped and faced him. "The fires that were started a while back would have helped a lot in leveling the old buildings, wouldn't you say?" He looked startled, but she continued, "I think somebody had evil intentions that failed to come off, unfortunately for them. Maybe you know who tried that stunt, Locke?"

He was alert, dangerous. His smile didn't make to his eyes, which were cold and hard. "If you're inferring I set those fires, you're wrong. I didn't do it."

She was tired pussyfooting around and besides, John Wayne Stewart was in perfect line with his video camera, the closet door barely cracked. "Those fires really bothered me, and I've thought a lot about them. I'm not saying you set them personally." She stood her ground when Vinson took a step toward her. "No, we know who did it. But Harry Shull wouldn't have tackled a big job like that alone, what with all the risk, and not unless he was paid a lot of money. That fact sort of points at you, Locke, and your obsession to redo Pass Creek your way."

"I don't know what the hell you're talking about!" His face blazed with rage.

"Sure you do. You hired Shull to fire the buildings, and

we both know it."

He lunged to grab her by the arm. "Where do you get off accusing me?" He twisted her arm. She bit her lip against the pain and tried to pull away. He yanked her back. "You tricked me, getting me here, but it's not going to change a thing. Yes, I wanted this town nothing but ashes. Wouldn't have been a loss. Shull set the fires, but the fool messed up the job."

"He'll confess to the authorities that you hired him. He'll save his own skin."

Vinson laughed at that. "Shull talk? No, sweet-face, Shull won't ever talk again. I saw to that."

Ice ran in Celia's veins as his meaning came clear. "You killed him? Or had him killed?" She wasn't surprised, but still she was shaken. She got a grip on her nerves and continued. "There is a big search on for Harry Shull, you know. They'll find what you did to him, and then they'll come after you. You'll go to prison for life for killing him and for your attempt to destroy Pass Creek." The look he gave her turned her knees to water, and despite her efforts to stay calm and collected, she began to shake. "Let go of me," she choked out, struggling hard to free herself.

He gripped her tighter and shook her violently, making her head snap. "Quit fighting me, Celia. I'm in charge here now. Yes, I killed Shull. He's a goner, the same way you're getting yours, darlin`, for tricking me into coming down here. But first you're going to sign over your property to me. I have record of your phone call in which you offered it to me. How about that?"

He tried to drag her toward the study while she fought back with every bit of strength she could muster. With an arm freed, she jabbed her fingers in his eyes. He caught her flailing arm and twisted it. She cried out, "Damn you! Let me go. You can't get away with this, Locke Vinson! The police are waiting for you outside."

"Nice try," he grunted. "I checked when I got here, and there's not a soul around. You're going for a ride in my car's trunk, and nobody'll ever know where to look for your body. You never should have tried tricking me, Celia. Your big mistake."

Celia fought for her life with her whole being, biting the hands that held her, jabbing her elbows into Vinson's ribs, slamming her heels back against his shins. In that same moment, the hall closet door burst open. John Wayne Stewart leaped out, the steel extension tube from her old vacuum system lifted and swinging, "*Hee-yah!*" He brought the pipe down on Vinson's head with a bone-cracking thud. In that same second, Vinson's grip loosened and Celia fell free.

Vinson, blood blossoming near his hairline, turned on the old man. The two of them hit the floor in a vicious struggle that quickly showed John Wayne Stewart losing. Celia dashed for her study, grabbed up Reading Boy, which had to weigh ten pounds or more. It was hard to lift over her head, but the moment Vinson half rose, his fist doubled to hit John Wayne Stewart's jaw, she brought the statue down hard. It was a glancing blow, but enough to lay Locke Vinson out flat, unconscious.

It seemed to Celia she'd barely caught her breath when Pete, Jake, and several officers poured through the door. "Book him!" She pointed at Locke Vinson unconscious on the floor. "He tried to burn us down, and he killed Harry Shull. My friend"—she nodded at Stewart sitting slumped nearby and shaking his head to clear it—"hid in the hall closet. He has proof. He got a full confession on his video camera."

Then she fell into Jake's arms, shaking like a leaf and too wobbly to stand.

Chapter Twenty-Two

Townspeople and tourists streamed in and out at the grand re-opening of Gable House. Through the open windows came the fragrance of summer roses and barbecue being prepared on the grounds. Mrs. Kemp had told Celia moments earlier that it was the "opennest" open house she'd ever been to. It was for Celia, too, and happily so.

She waited as Lilly and Mac weaved through the crowded parlor toward her after they had signed the guestbook on a table just inside the wide open front door. "How are you two?" She smiled at them.

"Just fine, Mrs. L," Lilly said, giving her a hug. "We're so happy that Mac's not in that awful jail cell anymore. We have his Civil War revolver back, and now we're here at this party. Things are pretty cool to say the least, and we have you to thank."

"No need for thanks. You were innocent, Mac, and I knew it all along."

He grinned. "I felt there for a while like I might be hanged. Then you came to the rescue." He snagged her into the circle of his arm and shyly hugged her.

Celia blinked away tears as she hugged him back. She grinned and kissed his cheek. "Just remember, son. From here on out you have to speak up when the going gets rough. There are some things in life we can't get through all by ourselves."

"Got it," he said. "Jail kind of reminded me of the same thing."

"There's plenty of food at the picnic tables out by the orchard. You two kids go on and enjoy yourselves." She waved them off, watched them wend their way through clusters of laughing and chatting folks in the direction of the back door.

Her kids were going to be just fine, she told herself, glowing with satisfaction. Over time they'd become like her own children. With luck she'd see them through Mac's college graduation, their careers, and the coming of babies.

"Celia," Pete Erdman said, suddenly appearing behind her and interrupting her reverie. "I'd like to talk to you for a minute if we can find a quiet spot."

"Sure. There are a few less people over in the corner by the fireplace. C'mon." She led the way and turned to face him. He'd already bawled her out thirty ways from Sunday for what she'd done. What was one more scolding?

"Like I've already told you, Celia, I could've had you arrested for interfering with police business. But as long as things worked out, I suppose I need to thank you."

"It didn't go exactly as I'd planned it to," she replied ruefully. "I intended that you and police backup from the county would be hidden around the place, to overhear Locke Vinson admit he was the real party behind the fires. It wasn't supposed to be a little old man hidden in the closet with a piece of vacuum pipe to settle the score." She nodded to where Mr. Stewart was regaling a group with a story about his friend, Clark.

"You both were damned lucky."

"I know, Pete. I really do. And I'm sorry if you feel I got in your way. The thing is I wasn't sure you agreed with my suspicions about Locke. It'd be hard for anyone to believe that someone intended to burn down an entire town building by building."

"I have to admit I thought your theory was pretty lame at

first." He sighed. "Unfortunately, you were right. We found Shull's body in an old abandoned building this side of Portland. He had had infection from the burns, but it was a bullet that killed him. The place is a few miles from Locke Vinson's print company. I was on my way back here when the call came that you expected Locke to show up at your place."

"Has he told you anything, other than what Mr. Stewart has on his video?"

He nodded. "Everything we need to send Locke Vinson up for years. We got it out of him that he paid Harry five thousand dollars to set the fires here in Pass Creek. According to the deal, Harry was to get another five grand when we were in ashes. I'm sure he would have burned the town to the ground the first time he tried if his shirt hadn't caught fire and badly burned him. Locke claims Harry Shull wanted the second five thousand in advance, before he tried again. Locke wasn't about to go for that, by then he felt Shull wasn't right for the job anyhow. He had to kill him, he told us, because of the botched job. Plus, Harry threatened to talk if he didn't get the money."

"Wow." Celia's mouth went dry, and it was a minute before she could speak further. Finally, she said, "Locke could never understand that we wanted to keep Pass Creek unique, that in the cookie-cutter glass and concrete world we're becoming, small towns like Pass Creek are too special to lose." She added, "I'm glad he's going to prison for hiring Shull, then killing him, but I feel sorry for Myrna."

"If it's any consolation, I figure she'll likely get a lighter sentence on a charge of manslaughter. Hers was an act of passion, not a planned killing."

Celia nodded. "If Otis Peek had treated the women in his life halfway decently, he'd be alive today and Myrna wouldn't be facing prison at all."

"What's the sad face about?" Jake asked, showing up at that moment and leaning down to kiss her cheek. "This is supposed to be a happy day." He shook hands with Pete who, after a brief chat, moved away to join Thea and the kids.

"It is a happy day!" Celia said, throwing her arms around Jake. "C'mon, my friend, I want to show you something." Upstairs a few moments later, they found themselves alone in the master bedroom. Most of the others had gone outside to eat barbecue.

"So this is it," Jake said, "the famous bed where Gable slept."

"This is it," she answered. "I know it looks like an ordinary old-fashioned walnut four-poster, but it's exciting to know that someone of Clark Gable's fame actually lay there in that bed."

He nodded slowly. "Yep, I'm impressed. And infinitely inspired." He swept her into his arms and kissed her. "In fact," he said, taking a break from their kissing, "I say we should think about getting married and get us a bed like this one."

"Excuse me? Does this mean you're not going anywhere? You're staying in Pass Creek?"

"I'm staying if you are." He grinned. "Yes, I'm kinda liking the real estate business, plus there is a little ranch outside town I'm thinking of buying." He grew serious. "All I need is *you* to complete what I hope for."

She was so touched by the honest emotion in his voice and the look on his face, she wasn't sure she could answer. "I second the motion, then," she finally got out. "We can think about it." She chuckled in protest as he pulled her onto the bed and kissed her soundly. She kissed him back, more than once, and after a minute they had somehow gotten close to the edge of the bed. They rolled off together, landing with a loud thump on the floor, where they roared with laughter.

A voice from downstairs called out, "What happened up there?"

A second voice Celia recognized as Tierney's asked from

the foot of the stair, "Is everything all right?"

They answered in unison, "Everything's fine. No problem." Together they smoothed the coverlet on the famous bed, and with their arms around each other's waist, went to join their friends in the finest little town anywhere. Just the way it was.